Into the Flames

Mitchell Mountain

To Paul, Joyce, John, and Patricia, old souls who kindled a youngster's dreams

ACKNOWLEDGMENTS

I would like to thank my good friend, Seth Adelsperger, for his continued support since this was nothing but ramblings on a page. As well as Gal Ron, who is always eager to share his thoughts as the story develops. Also, Ana Joldes, for making it better.

The Archipelago
Nabal
Illion
Papuro
Crystalline Mount
Lucia
Fifth Division
Danforth
Second Division
Seventh Division
Third Division
Lundur
First Division
Alstair
Lamenfell
Takata
Blade's Trench
Colkirk
Eighth Division
Sandur
Sixth Division
Fourth Division
White Horn
Bushgrove
Demon's Cavity
Southern Plains
Forked Tongue
Kelveux
Ville de Larmes
Skovgade
Frostbitten Peaks

1

Gwen's eyes fluttered open to the sound of distant shouts. The kitchen of Damian's old home resembled the remains of a battlefield. Anden sat beside her, hat tilted to the side, fast asleep. Wesley's torso sprawled out over a nearby table, one of his pistols loosely held in his grasp. Damian rested against the cabinets opposite her, clutching a mass of cloth covering his wound. The events of the rebels' vicious attack on the Militia headquarters raced through Gwen's mind in a blur. The floating fortress raining down fire from the sky, the mad dash to the underground bunkers as fighting between rebel troops and Militia soldiers broke out in the streets, and finding the three men before her lying helpless on the cobblestone, injured and near death. A terrible nightmare on any other day, but this time, it was real. She glanced at the bottle of whiskey sitting between her and Anden, but it was too early for that. Her body ached with pain as she rose to her feet to see the cause of the commotion outside. None of the men stirred in their slumber as she wobbled with sore legs toward a window and peered through the broken panes into the ruins of Danforth's once glorious plaza. The fires blazing throughout the night had finally died down, leaving trails of smoke drifting into the sky. The statue of Cain Bezok, who kept a keen eye over the square atop the wide fountain, lay crumbled on the ground along with debris from other surrounding buildings. The shouts grew louder and more distinct as a wave of blue uniforms marched down the main road from where the guildhall once stood. Leading the march were two Militia captains garbed in their blue padded jackets, Ben Green and Edward Quinn. Armed with their weapons and glowering looks on their faces, they headed straight for Damian's old house.

Gwen spun around, ignoring the stinging pain in her muscles. "Wake up," she said, trying her best not to yell but at least loud enough to wake her companions. "Wake up. We have a problem."

Anden groaned, wiping a hand over his face and rubbing his eyes. Frowning at her, he said, "What are you on about?"

Wesley awoke as well, his body stiff with pain as he pushed himself off the table and into the back of his chair. "Can't we just have five more minutes?"

Gwen pointed a panicked finger toward the window. "In about five minutes, we'll have Militia soldiers barging in through the front door."

Anden exploded to his feet, grimacing the entire way as he hurried to look out the window. "Shit. Not good." He turned to Wesley with fearful eyes. "It's Green. We need to go. Now."

Damian remained on the floor, his skin as pale as his hair. He lacked the strength to stand on his own two feet. Wesley and Anden flung Damian's arms over their shoulders in an attempt to carry him, but the weakness of their own bodies caused them all to collapse to the floor. Gwen tried to help as well, only to meet the same result.

"It's no use," said Anden. "Even if we could run, they'd easily catch us."

He was right. They might have stopped the bleeding, but Damian appeared to be on the brink of death. Anden and Wesley fared a little better, severely battered and bruised. With two Militia captains and a platoon of soldiers waiting for them outside, they stood no chance in a fight. Gwen's heart raced as she tried to think of something—anything—to get them out of their current predicament.

"Come on out, Damian," a voice rang out across the square. Ben Green rested his mace on his shoulder as he stood in the plaza square with soldiers at his back pointing rifles at the house. "Or should I address you by the same name everyone else does these days? The Burnt Coat. There's no need to turn this into a fight, but if you'd rather be killed by my hand than the executioner's, I'm willing to oblige."

"There has to be something we can do," said Gwen.

Anden looked at Wesley, then at Damian. Defeat was plain on

all their faces. Picking up the bottle of whiskey, he took a swig. "We're not going to do anything. You, on the other hand, need to tell them who you are. They'll make sure you get back to the capital."

"You can't be serious? If they find you with me, they'll have you killed."

"Our agreement was that we'd get you back to the capital, wasn't it?" he said in a bitter tone. "They can take you there—safely. What happens to us afterward doesn't matter."

"It matters to me," she said. "I'll tell them you helped me. That I would probably be dead if it wasn't for you."

"Gwen," said Wesley with a weary voice. "I'm afraid it won't work like that. Not for men like us."

She looked at him with glassy hazel eyes. "What about Liz? You're just going to abandon her on that vineyard?"

He diverted his gaze from hers. "She knew the risks I was taking."

Damian had yet to utter a word, but Gwen thought back on the story he told of killing his own men. The guilt he felt, unsure if he really had gone mad or acted in self-defense. She balled the tattered fabric of her dress into clenched fists. They might have accepted their fate, but she couldn't. Criminals or not, they proved to be good men and helped defend Danforth from the rebel attack. Surely that was worth something.

"If you won't come out willingly," Ben continued, "then we'll be forced to—"

"Look over there," said one of the soldiers. A chorus of guns being cocked and blades being drawn erupted.

"Hold!" shouted Edward Quinn.

Gwen, Anden, and Wesley hurried back to the window. The Militia soldiers turned their attention to the fallen statue of Cain Bezok, where a figure draped in a shabby poncho with a cone-shaped hat stood. The wide brim concealed much of his face except for a pointed beard protruding from his chin. The man's presence seemed to put all the soldiers on edge, including Ben and Edward.

"Who's that?" Gwen asked.

"That," said Anden with a smirk, "is none other than the Hand of Death."

Gwen's head snapped around in shock. For the longest time, she thought the Hand of Death was only a legend, a myth Militia soldiers shared to tease and frighten each other. The stories portrayed him as an ethereal being, a force of nature leaving fields of corpses in his wake. For him to be a real person standing between them and the Militia was surreal.

Ben Green stepped forward with a casual strut. "This is a historic day," he said with a wild glare. "The rebels defeated, the Burnt Coat sighted in the city, and now you appear at our very feet. It's almost too good to be true."

The Hand of Death's reply was firm, offering a warning. "I

advise you and your men to stand down, Green."

Ben scoffed. "We have over twenty men at our back. Along with Quinn and myself, I'd say that's enough to take you on."

"Perhaps. With both of you, you might be able to capture me." He gestured to the ruins of broken stone and houses burned to soot. "But what of your men and the remains of Danforth? Our battle would only reap more destruction and casualty. Can you truly afford more of such an outcome with no guarantee that you'll actually win?"

Ben gripped his mace tightly, scowling. His olive-green eyes burned with rage as he took another step forward. He was halted, however, by the shaft of Edward's lance pressing into his chest.

"What do you think you're doing?"

A calm expression gleamed through Edward's spectacles. "He's right. We can't afford to fight someone like him. Not here. Not now."

Ben shoved the lance from his body. "You're suggesting we let them go? We may never get another opportunity like this."

"Maybe not with the Burnt Coat and the Hand of Death in one place, no," Edward replied. "Although, the kingdom now knows for certain they're out there. We'll be sure to hunt them down, but for now, we need to rally our forces and rebuild. Many people in the city still need our help, as it seems the war with the rebels hasn't ended." The Militia captain turned to the other soldiers. "Forget about the Burnt Coat. Spread out through the city and help any survivors."

Lowering their weapons, the soldiers did as Edward commanded and hurried out of the plaza into the rest of the city. Ben continued to glare at the Hand of Death, who remained as still as the statue he stood on. "Only because it's you," he muttered before walking away.

Gwen watched the scene unfold in awe. Never before did she expect to see one man stand against two captains aided by a platoon of Militia soldiers and emerge victorious without even raising a sword.

"That's the second time that man has saved my life in this city," said Damian. Somehow, he managed to prop himself onto the counter. His breaths were shallow, and the massive gash in his side caused his body to falter. "We should take this chance to leave."

"You sure you'll be all right?" asked Wesley as he and Anden held him up.

"Yeah, let's just get out of here."

"Gwen, grab the whiskey," said Anden. "Not letting that go to waste."

Gwen grabbed the bottle and followed them out the back door. Limping through the desolate streets of Danforth's ashes, they blended in just fine with the other surviving citizens. People tended to the seriously injured bleeding out on the streets. Others dug through debris to find bodies crushed into a fleshy paste. Witnessing such dismal sights made Gwen more nauseous than the rotten stench of climbing down into the sewers. Still held aloft by Anden and Wesley, Damian guided them through the maze of tunnels, deeper and deeper, until arriving at the cavern in which they originally entered. Anden cursed as his sandaled feet once again submerged into the muck of sewage pooling at the tunnel's end. Crawling out of the cavern at the base of the mesa, the cobbled pile of scraps serving as their chariot awaited them, along with the Hand of Death leaning against its side with his arms folded. His cone-shaped hat turned to greet them.

"Good to see you remember your way through the sewers," he said in a jovial tone. Gwen was taken aback seeing him stand on level ground. Atop the statue in the plaza square, he seemed taller. Looking at him now, he appeared to be closer to her own height.

"You have an odd sense of timing," said Anden as he and Wesley settled Damian into the chariot's back seat. "Couldn't you have shown up a bit earlier when we were taking down that flying fortress?"

"I was busy with other matters," the Hand replied.

"I'm not complaining," said Wesley, giving the man a warm embrace and patting him on the back. "It's good you showed up when you did. Got us out of a tight spot."

"Couldn't leave you for dead, could I? Five years may have gone by, but we still look out for each other."

"Damn straight," said Anden, also embracing him.

Something felt odd to Gwen about watching them greet each other so casually. Moments ago, death seemed inevitable for them, and now, they bantered back and forth without a care in the world.

The Hand of Death rested an arm on the side of the chariot next to Damian. "You holding up? Looks like you took one hell of a beating."

"Lost quite a bit of blood," said Damian, "but I'll be fine after getting some more rest."

The Hand nodded before turning his attention to Gwen. Even from up close, all she could see from beneath the brim of his hat was his pointed beard. Stepping forward, he offered a bow. "It's a pleasure to officially make your acquaintance, Princess Guinevere."

Gwen returned his greeting with an awkward curtsy. She felt embarrassed introducing herself, wearing a ragged dress with frayed hair and covered in dirt and grime. "Likewise," was the only word she forced from her lips.

"I've visited the palace on a few occasions in the past," he said. "You commonly frequented the gardens, correct? Your face is not one to easily forget."

Unsure of how to respond, Gwen looked at Anden and Wesley.

"It must be more than a coincidence that you're here," said Anden.

"Not as much as you think," the Hand replied. "I was attending to some business in Illios when a strange sensation guided me here. Suddenly, the rebellion attacked. Imagine my surprise hearing whispers that the Burnt Coat was sighted somewhere in the city. Didn't take me long to find the old girl here, figuring you'd use the sewers as your escape. I assume this reunion has something to do with your unusual traveling companion."

Anden rolled his eyes, heaving a sigh. "It's a long story. One best shared over a drink and some food."

"I couldn't agree more." The Hand of Death paced alongside the chariot, running a hand over its metal surface. "She seems a bit banged up. There's an acquaintance of ours who probably wouldn't mind fixing her up in Laminfell. We could head there, and you can catch me up on what's brought you all together like this over a cold tankard of beer."

Gwen looked at Damian, who rested in the car, chest heaving with every breath and face growing paler still. "We should stop along the way," she said. "For Damian's sake. Laminfell is quite a journey, and his wound needs to be properly treated."

"Gwen's right," said Wesley, taking out a water sack and pouring some into the former Militia captain's mouth. "Damian's tough, but he looks just as bad as he did in Kelveux."

"Then we'll stop at one of the smaller towns along the way," said the Hand. "They're bound to have someone who can treat him." With a sharp whistle, he summoned a horse and mounted it.

Anden, Wesley, and Gwen hopped into the chariot and rode westward.

*

Laminfell, more commonly known as the Gate to the West, served as the only way to cross the Blade's Trench into the western plains without a ship. The bridge merging the two sides of the river was massive in scale, a marvel by any means, built even before the rule of King Edward. The red-tiled roofs covering mounds of cottages constructed along the slopes of the rolling hillsides came into view as they neared the bridge's end. Damian seemed to be faring better after being treated by a local doctor in a small town, hardly a day's journey from Danforth. His skin still lacked color, and every so often, Gwen would notice him wince with pain. The Hand of Death continued riding his horse beside them. While Damian was being treated, Anden and Wesley filled him in on the events since their encounter in the capital. Strangely enough, the mention of the cloaked figure in Nabal appeared to pique his curiosity.

Entering the city, Anden slowed the speed of the chariot. The roads of Laminfell were narrow, constructed over a series of man-made canals where small boats could also pass through. Many of them hauled cargo from the numerous ships making port on the southern end of town. They eventually rode up a hill on the outskirts where a small hut resided at the crest. Beside it was an open shack containing an assortment of unfamiliar smithing tools. The Hand of Death dismounted from his horse and knocked on the front door of the cottage. A hairy, barrel-chested man answered and swallowed him in a bone-crushing embrace.

"Mushi," he bellowed. "Emperor be praised, it's been too damn long."

"Good to see you too, Leon," said the Hand.

The man's dark eyes lit up upon seeing the rest of them climbing out from the chariot. "Well, isn't this quite the surprise? I never thought I'd see you lot all together like this again." His long arms tangled the other three men together into an awkward hug.

"You're not the only one," wheezed Anden.

"So, to what do I owe the honor?" Leon asked. His hands were thick and rough as he rubbed them together. All the hair from his bald head must have migrated to his chin, forming a bushy beard. The smell of smoke also seemed to follow him wherever he went.

"A favor," said the Hand. "Seems Anden has put the old girl through the wringer."

He studied the chariot with dismay. "What have you done to my baby?"

"Don't give me that," said Anden. "You know how tough she is."

Leon opened the front of the machine, shaking his head. "Aye, but you've really done a number on her. You even blew out one of the sparks. I can get her up and running better than ever, but it's going to take quite a bit of time."

"How long is quite a bit of time?" asked Wesley.

"About a month or so. Maybe more."

"A month?" said Gwen in shock.

"That might work out," said the Hand matter-of-factly, "but we have some things to discuss before you get started. Any good tavern recommendations?"

"The Shepherd's Pen is a personal favorite. No other place in the city cooks lamb as they do."

The Hand nodded. "Noted."

"I think I'll hang back here with Leon if that's alright," said Damian. "Not really feeling up to concealing my identity at the current moment. Especially with being covered in all this blood."

"I might be able to find you some fresh clothes," said Leon. "Besides, I'd like to catch up with at least one of you after all this time."

Damian followed Leon into his cottage as Anden, Gwen, Wesley, and the Hand of Death strode down the hill back toward the city.

Gwen scuttled closer to Wesley. "Who was that man?"

"Leon's an old friend," he said, "and a rare individual. He's the only man I know of who transferred his skills of smithing into those of a master engineer. One of the best if you ask me. He crafted the horseless chariot as well as all our weapons." Taking out one of his pistols, he twirled it around his finger in a display.

Gwen glanced at Anden sharing a conversation with the Hand of Death a few paces in front of them. Lowering her voice, she said,

"And did he call the Hand of Death 'Mushi?'"

Wesley chuckled. "That is his name. You don't think his own mother gave him such a title?"

She wasn't sure what to think anymore. Despite her travels throughout the eastern part of the continent, meeting hunters of the Core, encountering fleshlings, hunting down the Burnt Coat, and surviving the attack on Danforth, Gwen hardly believed anything could surprise her. Turns out she was wrong.

After traversing the city, they entered Shepherd's Pen and grabbed a table in the back corner of the tavern. The Hand of Death— or Mushi—remained hidden underneath his hat and poncho. Anden ordered them a round of beer, slamming down a few silver and copper coins. When the barmaid left, Mushi stroked his beard in a pensive manner. "Earlier, you mentioned something about a stranger in a cloak."

Wesley downed a few gulps of beer before responding. "Yeah, and whoever it was is no joke in a fight. Nearly killed me and kidnapped Gwen if Anden and that hunter hadn't shown up. Said something about not drawing too much attention."

Goose pimples covered Gwen's skin as she felt Mushi's gaze shift to her.

"Interesting," he said.

Anden narrowed his eyes beneath the brim of his bucket-shaped hat. "You know something, don't you?"

Mushi flung the front of his poncho over his shoulder and tugged at his tunic, revealing a web of scar tissue across his left shoulder and up his neck. "As it so happens, I also encountered one of these cloaked strangers. Luckily, I managed to escape." He covered himself back up and glanced over his shoulder to make sure no one was listening. "As mentioned before, I was attending to some business in Illios before heading to Danforth. Part of that business was attempting to discover what their motives might be. During my little run-in, I got the sense they were searching for something. A relic, possibly mentioned in the deciphering of the ancient text. Unfortunately, I ended up stumbling upon a strangeness in regard to a series of murders. The locals attest them to be a result of the city housing too many refugees, but I got the sense there was a more nefarious purpose behind the killings. One maybe involving more of these cloaked figures."

Gwen took a large swig from her tankard. If talk of these strange people was to continue, she needed something to take the edge off. "How many do you think there are?"

"I'm not sure, but as you've experienced yourselves, they're extremely dangerous. Which is why I want to discuss with you—"

"You can stop yourself there," said Anden. "No need to dance around the pond. Might as well jump right in. You want us to help you investigate these creeps just like in the old days."

"Yes. I think a need has arisen for the Gray Phoenix to make its return."

A toothy grin crept across Anden's face. "It should have never ended, to begin with. I'm in."

Mushi turned to Wesley, who fiddled with his tankard, staring into the sloshing liquid. "I'm not sure," said the sharpshooter. "While the nostalgia feels invigorating, we agreed to leave that life behind us. Five years have gone by, and I've started a new life—one I'm content in keeping."

"What about coming along to help the princess?" said Anden, leaning across the table. "You were willing to leave your life behind for that. Hell, you were even willing to accept death back in Danforth. Why is this any different?"

The look in Wesley's yellow eyes burned with scorn as hot as the sun. "Because that was repaying the debt for her help in freeing Sandur. This is asking me to ignore what's happened these past five years. The fact that I took up my family's legacy and found people whom I care for and who care for me. You may have done nothing for yourself from the time we all separated, but I have. So, excuse my hesitance to dive headfirst back into an abyss we were lucky to walk away from in the first place."

Mushi spoke in a sympathetic tone, defusing the situation. "No one is forcing you to accept. The choice is yours to make."

"Come on," said Anden. "I know it was crazy, and we nearly lost our lives, but you can't deny the exhilaration of fighting side-by-side with each other again."

Wesley lifted the tankard to his lips for another drink. "I'll think about it."

"Bringing the conversation back around to Anden's earlier point," Gwen added, "what about me? They're supposed to help me get back to the capital."

"I haven't forgotten," said Mushi. "In fact, quite the opposite. Having learned that these cloaked figures have an interest in you, I find it may be important to train you in using a sword for self-defense."

Anden spat out his beer, splattering it across the table. "You can't be serious? Look at her. Before this whole thing started, she'd never touched a sword. You can't expect to train her to defeat a foe that nearly killed Wesley in a short amount of time. It would take years."

"She doesn't need to best them. Just have a fundamental understanding should the need arise."

"I agree with Mushi on this," said Wesley. "No offense, Gwen, but back in Nabal, all you could do was helplessly offer yourself to them. If such dangerous people are hunting you for a mysterious reason, then it might be best for you to learn how to defend yourself. You're not surrounded by an army of Militia soldiers here. Just us."

Gwen thought about Victoria and her secret training sessions with Kaylin in the palace gardens. Her sister had more interest in combat and swords, while she enjoyed books and the continent's history. Touching the hilt of the blade at her hip, the face of the rebel soldier she had killed at Danforth flashed through her mind. "I'm not a warrior. I need to go home, back to the capital. If I need to learn how to wield a sword, there are plenty of people there who can teach me."

"Maybe," said Anden, "but how do you expect to get to the capital? Need I remind you none of us can get within a piss length of the wall without nabbing the attention of every Militia soldier there? We gave you the chance to part ways at Danforth, but you decided to stay."

"That's because I didn't want to leave you to die," she said, crossing her arms in defiance. "Not to mention I would've had to turn myself in to that despicable Captain Green whose men had me gagged and almost bound in chains."

Anden lifted his tankard in a mockery of a toast. "And who had to help you out of that predicament?" He took a swig. "Mushi could be right. Training you to fight might actually allow you to get back home. Give you a chance to survive should you run into some rogue Militia soldiers or fleshlings before crossing the wall."

"I'm not sure it's wise to take her to Illios, though," said Wesley. "If you claim one of those cloaked freaks is behind a series of murders there, we'd be bringing her right to them."

"Which is why I would take her west to train," said Mushi. "To a place no one would find her. During which time, the rest of you would investigate the strange events at Illios. By the time we'd return, I'd have her trained up to at least put up a fight before being captured. Also, all four of us would be there to protect her."

Wesley silently accepted Mushi's logic, while Anden lightly tapped his tankard against the table. They each turned their attention to Gwen, awaiting her response. She bit her lower lip, pondering. "If it provides a better opportunity for me to go home, I guess I don't have a choice."

"With that settled," said Mushi, "we should all get something to eat."

"Saints be damned," groaned Anden. "I'm starving."

*

The following morning, Leon procured them each a horse for their travels. Gwen saddled up beside Mushi, making sure her provisions were properly secured. Damian struggled to mount his horse, requiring some assistance from Anden. Some color returned to his face, but it was obvious he still suffered from a decent amount of pain. Wesley was the last to leave Leon's cottage. No answer had yet been provided regarding whether or not he would join them in their investigation. Saddling up, he gripped the reins tightly and bowed his head in reluctant defeat.

"Son of a bitch," he said. Jerking the reins, he steered the horse beside Damian and Anden. "If things were to go more to shit, and Liz found out I could've stopped it, I'd never hear the end of it." Taking out a piece of parchment, he handed it to Leon. "Mind sending this to my estate in Sandur?"

The hairy man snatched the paper from Wesley's grasp with a wide grin. "Easiest job you've assigned me thus far."

Mushi smiled, tipping his hat. "Safe travels, then. We'll meet you in Illios when we're ready."

Anden mirrored the gesture as Wesley and Damian nodded.

"May the winds bring good tidings," said Gwen. As they parted ways, she reared her horse down the road alongside the Hand of Death, heading west to Emperor knows where.

2

Blackwood's ass grew numb against the cold, hard stone of his chair. He was unsure how long he had been sitting, for no natural light penetrated the thick walls of the Tomb. The only indicator of his tenure in the dreary chamber was the pang of hunger rumbling in his stomach. The usual time for his lunch passed, which meant at least a few hours wasted away listening to all eight of the kingdom's ambassadors debate. His attention waxed and waned throughout their extensive conversation. The news of the rebels' assault on Danforth served as the focal point of discussion, and everyone felt the need to share their thoughts on the matter. All but the one whose perspective actually held any weight, Noreen Archer, who sat at the far side of the circle, arms crossed in a guarded manner. Her pale blue eyes remained frozen on the same spot of the room since she initially sat down, seeming even more disinterested in the conversation than Blackwood.

Rahm Krawczyk ostentatiously shot out from his chair, snatching Blackwood's attention. "Anyone who dares contend the idea of a full-scale retaliation against the rebellion might as well resign from their position." His bulbous chin shook as his lips flapped without pause. "They've dishonored the kingdom with treachery through a false treaty, sent an assassin to kill the king, and mounted a devastating attack on the headquarters of our military. I would also like to remind you all that this could have been avoided if the king had taken action when evidence of the treaty's falsehood came to his attention, but he requested we gather and debate instead. Now, Danforth stands in ruins because of it."

"The king did what he thought was best for the kingdom," said Mary Katherine. Even in such dismal lighting, her fierceness radiated with beauty. "Isn't that what you consistently preach should be done?"

"Best for the kingdom?" Rahm scoffed. "Ever since his daughter went missing, the old fool doesn't know what's best for his health."

Blackwood raised his voice. "Careful in how you speak, Krawczyk. While he may not be present, I will not allow you to speak ill of Peter in such a way."

Rahm glared at him, the light from the flaming pit between them reflecting in his spectacles.

"No need to get testy, Chancellor," said Natalie Parson, ambassador to Argust's fifth division. Her scarlet eyes burned into him as she flitted them in his direction. Despite being an old flame from years gone by, she always found ways to continue burning his wick until nothing remained. "Here in the Tomb, we are free to speak however we'd like on the kingdom and its ruler. Besides, Rahm has a point. The king brought about consequences we must now face."

Rahm collapsed into his chair, wearing a smug expression.

"You criticize the king as if he was supposed to know the rebels possessed a weapon capable of flattening a city," said Mary Katherine.

Natalie tilted her head in amusement like a cat stalking its prey. Her auburn hair cascaded over her shoulders as a playful smirk stretched across her lips. "I'm not criticizing the king on his lack of foresight. If someone had been able to foresee such a tragedy, the Lucius Ambulate should name them a prophet. The consequences lie from believing peace was ever a viable option with the rebels, to begin with."

Mary Katherine's nails scraped against the armrest of the chair, leaving faint chalky streaks across its surface. "If we had declined the treaty, we would have only proved the rebels right and given more reason for others to join their cause. At least now the rest of the continent sees them for the warmongering monsters they truly are."

"At the cost of losing a prized city like Danforth," chirped Rahm. "A symbol of the Militia's might. Sure, the people see the rebels for what they are, but they also see that we're powerless to defend against them. Unless we strike back."

"Have you forgotten about Gwen, Peter's eldest daughter? If the rebels have captured her, a devastating counterattack would certainly lead to her death."

Slik Weyman raised a ringed finger decorated in a sparkling gem. Due to his sloping, pointed nose, high cheekbones, and angular jaw, harsh shadows covered much of his face, but the jewelry he wore glowed in the fire's light. "I think it's fair to say the rebellion doesn't have the princess. If that were the case, they would openly use her as a deterrent against any measures we might take, yet no such threat has been made."

"I agree with Ambassador Weyman," boomed the ambassador of Argust's seventh division, James Lawson. The metal components of his prosthetic leg, lost during his service as a Militia captain, groaned as he straightened himself from hunching over his cane. Silver streaks penetrated his dark hair, presenting his age as the oldest member of Parliament. "While devastating, the attack on Danforth did end in failure, and the rebellion would no doubt have lost many men and resources as a cost. The princess would prove a strong asset for them to have in their possession, yet they remain quiet. Ambassador Krawczyk's assessment is also correct. For the time being, we look weak, and the longer we remain idle, the more time we allow the rebels to reassemble their forces."

"If their forces have not already disassembled," said the

ambassador seated next to Rahm. Petram Fletcher was a man who kept his garments as clean as his reputation. Not a single wrinkle creased his clothing as he sat with proper posture, back straight and chin held high. The tuft of hair on his head was neatly combed to one side. "Has there been any word about Reed Skokna being present at Danforth? If she fell along with their contraption, then the head of the snake has already been cleaved, and all that remains is a wriggling body waiting to die."

"According to reports from Captain Green and Captain Quinn," said Blackwood, "there was no sighting of Reed Skokna. Although, they managed to identify the bodies of Elliot Durham and Vargo Vasallo amid the wreckage."

"Let's not also forget that both the Hand of Death and the Burnt Coat were sighted at Danforth as well," added Alyssa Brookshire. Her bronze skin painted an elegant portrait against the dull gray color of the surrounding stone as she twirled a strand of her dark, raven locks. Out of all the ambassadors, she took the most liberty in wearing a formal wardrobe. Her short cape swathed behind her bare shoulders as her garment, which closely resembled a silk dress, outlined her feminine features. "A strange occurrence for such undesirable characters to be sighted at such a monumental event, especially after being ghosts for these past five years."

"Ghosts tend to bring bad omens," said Natalie. "It could be extremely dangerous if they've decided to join forces with the rebellion."

Lawson bowed his head in a pensive manner. "Unlikely. If the rebellion had the Gray Phoenix on their side, I doubt they would've surrendered so easily after the fall of their contraption. As hard as it may be to believe, it all might just be a coincidence."

Rahm slammed a meaty fist into the stone. "We're losing focus on the matter of discussion. Damn the Gray Phoenix for now. They can be dealt with later. The rebels must be dealt with utilizing a greater force than they showed us."

"How?" questioned Mary Katherine with a critical glare. "We don't know the location of their base of operations. You intend to level an entire city just to prove a point?"

"A city?" said Rahm. "I suggest we purge the entire southern plains of the rebels' presence. If we're lucky, we might happen across their base and rip them out root and stem."

"All you'll do is create more martyrs and kill innocent civilians."

"Innocent civilians have already been killed." Noreen Archer's first words turned everyone's heads in her direction. Her gaze remained fixed on the same singular point, not glancing at any one of them. "We gave them an olive branch, and they decided to burn it with fire."

"Their crimes against the kingdom must be punished," said Lawson. "Even if the methods may seem extreme."

Mary Katherine looked at Blackwood with desperation in her eyes for him to do something, anything. He cleared his throat.

"Ambassador Brookshire deserves a say in this. The land once resided under her jurisdiction."

Alyssa tossed her head back in disdain. "Let it burn. If the king is willing to give it away without my counsel, then it must not be worth much to the kingdom, to begin with."

Rahm turned to Blackwood. "I believe a vote is in order."

Blackwood breathed a heavy sigh. His time to fully take the stage finally arrived. "Parliament presents the action of launching a full-scale counterattack against the rebels by raiding the southern plains and purging their presence."

Each of the ambassadors' voices resounded off the chamber's walls as they stated their vote. All around the circle, nothing but the word "aye" echoed against the stone. Mary Katherine stood as the last one to speak, weighing the inevitability that her vote could not affect the outcome. Succumbing to the pressure, she uttered the same word as her peers. Blackwood couldn't hold it against her. There was no use fighting a losing battle, especially within this particular circle.

"It is unanimous," continued Blackwood. "Ambassador Brookshire, order Captain Freeman to mount an attack with infantry aided by Captain Ivarson and Captain Hardee." Brookshire stiffly nodded. "With the matter settled, I believe this conclave meeting is concluded."

"There is one more matter I feel is worth discussing," interjected Rahm. "While it may be tough for you to hear, Chancellor, the king is clearly unfit to rule over the kingdom due to his diminishing health.”

“I echo Ambassador Krawczyk’s concerns,” said Natalie. “In troubling times, the people need a vigorous leader, and the king’s age is catching up to him.”

“Guinevere is the rightful heir and, as previously mentioned, still missing,” said Mary Katherine in defiance.

“It’s been weeks since even a rumor of a sighting has surfaced,” said Rahm. “Besides, the king has another daughter. If it comes to it, she can take his place.”

Blackwood stroked his goatee. “True, but Victoria cannot take the throne while Peter draws breath unless he decrees it so.”

“Under normal circumstances, but these are unusual times. Parliament is gathered, and with our power, we can decree for her to take the throne. Therefore, I call for a vote.”

Blackwood’s brow furrowed in anger as he rose from his chair. His legs ached with stiffness, but he managed to stand tall over the gathered ambassadors. “The motion has been noted, but I believe we’ve discussed enough for one day. The matter regarding the king’s ability to rule will be shelved for a later date. As for now, we are dismissed.”

With Blackwood’s final words, the ambassadors climbed out from their stone seats and hurried to scale the winding staircase out of the Tomb. Mary Katherine flashed him a concerned look before making her exit. As Blackwood made his way toward the stairs, Rahm stopped him with a firm hand on his shoulder. "Delay as much as you like, but sooner or later, you'll have to come to terms with the end of the old man's reign."

"If it is to end, you won't be the cause of it." Blackwood pulled himself away from the ambassador's grasp and marched up the spiral staircase. Not far ahead of him trudged Noreen Archer, still wearing an absent expression. "Ambassador," he called after her, hurrying to catch up.

"Chancellor," she said without looking at him. "To what do I owe the unusual pleasure?"

"I wanted to ask how you were. When word reached the capital of the guildhall collapsing, I, as well as many others, thought you might be dead. Emperor be praised that is not the case."

"I'm not sure whether to be appreciative or surprised. Honestly, I didn't think you cared all that much." Each word contained an icy chill stabbing into Blackwood. The young ambassador always had an air of contempt swirling about her when interacting with other members of Parliament. It was clear she despised the game being played, but she played it well, regardless. Unlike Weyman, who played both sides for the largest sack of coin, Noreen was a wild card. No one ever knew which way she would vote, and no one could ever convince her one way or another. The only fact known was she would vote for what she believed the best course of action to be. Admirable, but in some circumstances, dangerous depending on which side of the circle one sat.

"It's my responsibility to care for all of the kingdom and its inhabitants," said Blackwood. "Which is why I offer my condolences for the tragedy you and everyone within Danforth faced. It should never have happened, and while I'm sure you rightfully retain a fair amount of anger, I hope you do not hold it against the king."

Her pale orbs stared at him from the corner of her eyes. "That's very kind. I'll be sure to write a letter telling the few remaining people that they can rebuild their lives on the foundation of your condolences. As for my anger, I'll hold it against whomever I deem fit for it."

"Condolences will not be the only thing I or the crown will offer. We shall aid in the effort to rebuild by offering a steady flow of coin. It's pertinent that our military headquarters regains the prestige it held as an impenetrable fortress."

They reached the top of the stairs, where Blackwood held the metal door open for her to cross. She turned to him with a speculative gaze. "The coin will prove much more helpful and, no doubt, is an extension of your responsibility to care for the kingdom's inhabitants."

"Well, I—" he paused, realizing it was a foolish endeavor to force a favor on the backs of those suffering in a time of need. "Of course."

"Then, on behalf of the people of Danforth, I offer thanks to the crown for its charity. Now, if you'll excuse me, Chancellor, such a long duration of discussion has left me famished. I would benefit greatly from a hot meal."

Blackwood offered her a stiff bow as she marched down the elegant halls of the palace. His gut growled with a desire for a meal as well, but he could hardly stomach the notion of eating in the same chamber as those he'd just spent hours listening to drone on about their qualms with the kingdom. He had his own problems to handle. The most pressing being a plan to stop Rahm from usurping Peter from the throne.

3

Rage simmered in Noreen's empty gut, and her conversation with the chancellor had left a sour taste in her mouth she wished to wash out with a glass of wine. The nerve of that man. Danforth lay in ruin, and he tried using it as a bartering chip to ensure she would not agree to usurp the king. The other ambassadors were no better. Sure, they all preached about the travesty befalling their illustrious military headquarters, but little discussion revolved around providing any actual support. Instead, they wished to expend resources, turning a part of the continent into a wasteland. The rebels would be dealt with for the most part, at least. The thunder of cannon fire still echoed in her ears, drowning out the fervent screams of those caught in the midst of the conflict. The expression on their desperate faces in the aftermath haunted her memories. Her people were suffering, yet here she was, pacing the extravagant halls and chambers of the royal palace leagues away, unable to help. She should have stayed, making the ambassadors believe she had died. All of them would probably be gracious for it while she actually got to do some good. Everyone would be happy. Unfortunately, that was not the case.

Many ambassadors who were also looking to fill their stomachs found their way into the Great Hall. Nobles and wealthy aristocrats curious to learn of the proceedings in the Tomb joined the ambassadors as servants brought them plates of hot food. Noreen proceeded down the rows of tables toward the kitchen entrance. The clamoring of the various cooks could be heard from outside and only grew louder once passing through the door. Each of them scrambled around the room to fulfill their daunting task of providing a luxurious meal for the elite members of society waiting to be fed. Not a soul stopped Noreen from entering the kitchen except for a large dog bounding up to her and barking wildly. It didn't jump or bite; instead, it just stared at the ambassador with a cocked head that said, "You shouldn't be here."

One of the cooks sprinted out from the madness. "Artemis, I just took you out not but five minutes ago." The ends of his mustache were twirled, and his ginger hair was pulled back into a ponytail. Upon seeing Noreen standing next to the hound, his slender frame went stiff as he hurtled his torso forward into a bow. "Ambassador Archer, please forgive my pet, Artemis. He gets excited when visitors arrive."

"It's no trouble," she said. "He seems like a sweetheart." She patted the dog's head as it plopped its furry hide onto the floor before her. Its tongue hung from its wide grin of a muzzle.

"To what do we owe the pleasure of your presence?" the cook asked, still bowing. "Was the food not to your liking?"

"I can't say as I haven't been able to try any yet. I was hoping to remedy that with this visit."

He looked up at her with a confused expression. "Of course, my lady. We will send it out with a servant right away."

"I'll wait here for it, actually," she said. "In the mood to get the meal myself at the moment."

The man stood back up, his ponytail flipping behind his head. "As you wish." His eyes narrowed as he turned to the hound. "Artemis, don't misbehave in front of the ambassador."

"I'll keep him in line," said Noreen with a soft smile.

The cook disappeared back into the chaos of the kitchen as Noreen patiently waited next to her new companion. The dog, Artemis, didn't take its dark brown eyes off her as it continued to pant and form a puddle of drool on the floor. Staring back, Noreen felt an odd sense of familiarity with how the hound's gaze measured her. Easy going, yet brimming with dangerous potential to unleash the slumbering beast within. It reminded her of an old friend, one she thought never to see again. Before her mind wandered further, the cook returned with a steaming plate of sliced beef, vegetables, and a baked potato. He presented the dish, pulling at his mustache and bowing slightly.

"I hope you find it satisfactory," he said.

Noreen carefully took it, the heat of the food touching her skin through the porcelain. "I'm sure I will. Thank you." As she turned to leave, she glanced over her shoulder at the hound. "Goodbye, Artemis. Be sure to stay out of trouble."

The dog watched her leave, giving a low, guttural bark. She nearly mistook it for the growling of her stomach as the smell of the food caused it to ache with hunger. With no desire for idle conversation, Noreen secluded herself at a far table on the opposite side of the Great Hall, where hardly anyone resided. Such a reclusive effort led to greater displeasure when Rahm Krawczyk lumbered over and sat across from her.

"Ambassador Archer," he said, setting down his plate, "would you mind sharing a word?"

Noreen glared at him through slitted eyes. "After all that talking you did in the Tomb, I'm surprised your voice hasn't gone hoarse to actually spare one."

Rahm cut into the meat on his plate, shoving a large piece down his gullet. "Our voice is that of the people. It must be strong and endure, just as they and the kingdom have for so many years."

Noreen tapped the blunt end of her fork against the broth-coated slice of beef. She wanted to eat, but the sight of Rahm stuffing his massive jowl while carrying on a conversation deterred her from doing the same. Not out of decency, but strictly from revulsion. "What is it you wish to speak to me about?"

"I wanted to share with you my joy to see that you did not meet a tragic end at Danforth, like so many rumors claimed following the attack," he said. "It would be a shame for Parliament to lose such a promising woman as yourself. The youngest ambassador to ever be elected in history who possesses a brilliant mind beyond her years. Indeed, a terrible tragedy it would have been." Rahm used compliments like cheese on a mousetrap. A sweet and delicious treat to distract someone from being blindsided by his true intentions. "Although, I couldn't help but notice you were uncharacteristically quiet throughout the entire meeting. You almost seemed absent-minded, if you don't mind me saying. Having witnessed the attack firsthand, many of us expected you to herald a large part of the discussion."

"You seemed so eager to herald it for me. I didn't want to impede in any way."

"I will say, however, that little line of yours at the end there was powerful. Hit everyone like a brick wall, including myself. It even got Ambassador Brown to bite her tongue, and that is no small feat." He continued to shovel food into his mouth while Noreen toyed with hers, untouched on the plate. "This retaliation of ours will catalyze the end of the rebellion. If Skokna met the same fate as Durham and Vargo, the Red Rebellion would have fragile leadership to rely on as we march across the southern plains. If only it had been done sooner, we could've avoided this mess with Danforth. I commend you for maintaining such a calm demeanor. If it happened in my division, I'd be furious."

"Who says I'm not?" asked Noreen, with a frostbitten chill to her words. "Just because I don't go around shouting until my face turns red doesn't mean I'm not angry with the situation."

Rahm swallowed the food he was chewing with an audible gulp and washed it down with wine from his goblet. "Justifiably so. Just remember, while the rebels were the ones who launched the attack, it was the king's inaction that opened the gates for them to do so."

"The king had nothing to do with Danforth's destruction. He didn't construct some flying machine that rained cannon fire from the sky. He didn't send troops to raid and kill our soldiers and citizens."

"Quite right. He didn't do any of those things. In fact, he didn't do anything at all. Even now, he doesn't do anything. He just rots away in bed."

"Mourning for his missing daughter," added Noreen.

"Who has been gone for weeks. He's the current ruler of Argust, and in troubling times such as these, people look to their king for guidance and strength. All we can offer is a frail, old man barely clinging to life, as he seems more focused on finding his daughter than taking care of the kingdom."

"As would any father. By crowning Victoria as queen, would you hold her at fault for doing the same as a sister?"

Rahm pressed his sausage of a finger hard into the wood of the table. "We both know the girl would be nothing but a symbol. A vibrant, young ruler for the people to applaud and cheer while we in Parliament continue to watch over the kingdom and make sure it flourishes. Rebuild it to be the fortress it once was before any faction or rebellion dared take up arms against it. You claim the king had no involvement in the ruin that befell Danforth. He was the one who used Blackwood to push us into making peace with the rebels. He believed this war could end with words when all our enemies sought was bloodshed, and you witnessed that firsthand. There have been many follies during his rule, but this towers over the rest. If we are to perform our duties to serve the people of the kingdom, the king must go. Even if we don't do it, nature will take its course, so why not accept the inevitable?"

Noreen glanced down at her uneaten food. While she would not verbalize it to bolster Rahm's ego, he had a point. Despite his intentions, Argust grew unsteady in the king's hands. As she knew all too well, Danforth was not the first city to burn under his rule. The news of Gwen's disappearance filled her heart with sorrow, but reality needed to be faced. If Parliament didn't remove the crown from Peter's head, then death would surely do it for them soon enough, and Victoria would inherit it, anyway.

Rahm set his utensils on his empty plate before picking it up. "Food for thought," he said in the absence of a response. "Please, pardon my disturbance."

Noreen waited until he reached the end of her table before

sticking her fork into the slice of beef. Cutting off a chunk, she placed it in her mouth. It was cold. Exhaling a defeated sigh, she continued to dig into the meal. She should have stayed in Danforth. At least there, she wouldn't have to worry about being involved in this game of politics where people tried to convince her to vote one way or another. She wouldn't have to enter verbal fencing matches with every person she interacted with. She wouldn't have to sit for long hours of the day listening to people prattle on, trying to present their interests as those of the kingdom. She wouldn't be disturbed from enjoying a hot meal. At least there, she could do some good.

4

Reed's eyes shot open, staring at the flames of an open fireplace. A quilted blanket spread neatly over her as she found herself lying on the floor of a shambled room. Splinters of wood, along with piles of bricks, cluttered her surroundings. The remaining furniture was overturned and strewn about. Shifting under the blanket, her foot hit something metallic. Reed glanced down to see her pair of sheathed daggers placed beside her. She reached to grab them, but her muscles stiffened with soreness, causing her to grunt in pain. This caught the attention of a stranger she failed to notice tinkering away at a table on the other end of the room.

"Easy now," he said, motioning with his hands. "Don't get up too quickly." At one point, he might have been a dashing man with a rigid jawline and voluptuous dark hair. Life, however, took its toll as his hairline thinned and jowl sagged, coated in a peppered stubble.

Crossing the room, he offered her a cup of water. Touching the cool liquid to her lips, Reed realized how parched she truly was and emptied it in one swig.

"Where am I?" she asked, feeling a bit lightheaded.

"Danforth," said the man. "Must've taken a nasty blow to the head to forget that. You've been out for quite a while."

The last thing Reed remembered was falling through the black clouds of smoke toward the fiery surface of the inferno engulfing the city using the airship's descent cable. Orange tendrils lashed into the air at her from the burning buildings as she careened past them and onto the hard surface of the cobblestone road. Her body went limp, and her vision grew dark. Judging from the ruined state of his home, the man spoke true. She was still in Danforth, which meant anyone could be an enemy.

"How long was I out?" she asked.

"You've been going in and out for about a week," he said.

Too long. "And what of the rebels?"

His face hardened with disdain. "That floating fortress of theirs crashed into the valley below, leaving the Militia to capture the rest. They've been aiding the injured for the past few days, while many others have fled elsewhere. They hope to rebuild, but much time will be needed for that."

Not as much time as it took for them to prepare for such an assault. Reed bit her lower lip, nearly drawing blood. Those damned mercenaries ruined everything. If they hadn't infiltrated and crashed their ship, the rebellion would be mounting a full-scale attack on the capital, maybe even have taken it. The king and his daughter would be killed and Parliament destroyed, laying the foundation for a new government ruled by those freed of the kingdom's iron grip. She needed to get moving and return to their base on the western coast. Otherwise, her foolish generals would think her dead and tear the rebellion apart, claiming the vacant position of commander. Reed tried to stand, but her legs collapsed under her weight as she fell hard onto the floor.

"Take it easy." The man tried to ease her back into the makeshift bed, but Reed instinctively jerked away and snatched one of the daggers resting by her feet. Holding the pointed steel at him, the man took a step back and displayed his empty palms as a sign of peace. "I don't mean you any harm. You may be fully awake, but your body still needs to rest. Take things too fast, and you're bound to hurt yourself again."

Reed lowered the dagger, placing it back in its sheath. "Sorry. I'm just a bit on edge."

He nodded. "Understandable. I'll get you something to eat so you can regain your strength." Getting up, he disappeared through an open doorframe with the door stripped from its hinges.

Reed looked over to the table where the man had been working to see the head of a rocking horse beside a small pile of wood that no doubt used to be the rest of its body. Studying the room a bit more closely, she noticed some of the furniture had been stripped of its wooden frames. When the man returned, he held a bowl of porridge.

"Best I can offer at the moment," he said. "Not much has been on hand with the market being destroyed."

"It's more than enough," said Reed. "Thank you." Taking the bowl, she shoveled the goopy substance into her mouth. It was bland and hard to swallow, but better than nothing. The stranger watched her eat with a sympathetic gaze. It was not how she usually presented herself, but she wasn't among her generals or soldiers. Only a stranger who perceived her as a woman befalling misfortune. Once she finished eating and her stomach was full, she felt drowsy and melted back beneath the quilted blanket.

"You should continue to rest," advised the stranger. "It's been quite some time since you've eaten a proper meal. Your body will want time to process the food." Pacing back to the table, he grabbed the small pile of wood along with the horse head and carried them out of the room.

Reed rested her head on the pillow and closed her eyes. The stranger was right. She needed to rest and regain her strength if she was to make the journey west. Drifting off into sleep, she pictured the shocked faces of all her generals upon her return. She wasn't sure what their next move would be, but she had plenty of time to think about it during her coming travels.

*

The smell of smoke tickled Reed's nose. Something was burning. Sitting up, she realized much of the furniture had vanished. Outside one of the windows, trails of smoke drifted through the air. Reed climbed to her feet and ambled over to see the stranger standing before a blazing fire with his head bowed in sorrow. Through the flaming tongues, she could see the silhouettes of two figures lying on a large bed of wood. Making her way outside, she joined the man's side as he watched it burn.

"A funeral pyre," she said.

"The mesa's ground is tough to dig through without proper equipment, and there's not much room for cemeteries. Burning is the only way anyone finds peace here." His gaze remained on the fire, glistening in its immense light.

"Who were they?" she asked.

"My wife and daughter." His voice cracked as he forced out the words. "Died during the attack. With everything here in ruin, I figured I'd go ahead and burn most of our possessions along with them." Holding the wooden horse head in his hands, tears streaked down his weathered cheeks. He dashed them away with the back of his hand before tossing the horse head into the flames. Sparks erupted as it landed on the pyre.

Guilt tugged at Reed's heart, but she shunned it. The attack on Danforth was necessary for winning the war. Her uncle always told her there would be casualties. Their sacrifice gave their cause purpose. It didn't feel that way standing next to the man as he cremated his family.

"When I saw you lying in the streets," he said, "I couldn't help but think of my daughter and how I failed to save her. I thought that maybe helping you would ease the pain in my heart."

"Did it?"

"I'm not sure yet, but you're alive. That's something good that came out of it." He turned to her, wearing the expression of a broken man. "I never did ask for your name."

"Ana," Reed replied. It was her mother's name. The first to come to mind other than her own.

"Mine's Samuel," he said. "You have family here?"

She shook her head.

"Well, you're welcome to stay as long as you need or until I figure out what to do with myself." He lumbered back toward the house.

"I won't be staying long," Reed said over her shoulder. The man acknowledged her with a slight nod as he continued forward. Bowing her head, Reed mouthed the words of the Rebellion's Creed in memory of Samuel's family. Their sacrifice would not be in vain, despite knowing, deep down, that their blood stained her hands.

5

Several days had passed since Gwen left Laminfell with Mushi. Every so often, on their travels, he would call for them to dismount and carry supplies on foot. This was one of those times. Thankfully, Gwen no longer wore the ragged orange dress. Mushi gave her clothes more suitable for travel. Second-hand trousers with different patches of cloth sewn in to cover the holes and a blue tunic hiding her feminine frame. If it weren't for her long hair, which she tied into a ponytail to keep out of her face, someone could mistake her for a boy. The weight of the supplies flung over her shoulder grew heavier as she wiped the sweat from her brow. Complaining was futile.

"The horses need a break from carrying our weight," Mushi would say. Gwen claimed that if the horses needed a break, then they should all rest. "We can't keep stopping. We have quite a distance to travel and little time."

He hadn't told her where they were headed or why they needed to go so far west. At least the journey allowed her to view the sights of the western plains. A sea of grass stretched across the land like in the open field at Nabal. The blades danced in the wind under a cloudless sky. At dawn, when the sun broke through the horizon, the grass glittered with the reflected light of the morning dew. She pictured herself living out in the open land. No bustling cities or noisy towns to disturb the serenity. Just her and the continent.

"How are you holding up?" Mushi asked, still hidden under his cone-shaped hat. After all this time, Gwen had yet to see his face. Even when they slept, he wore his hat, and all she could peek from underneath was his pointed brown beard.

"Just fine," she lied. She wanted nothing more than to drop the supplies and climb back onto her horse; however, she noticed that he made her walk a certain distance each time they dismounted. Perhaps her training had already begun, and this was part of it. They continued hiking until Mushi finally allowed her to mount her horse. Her legs ached as she straddled the saddle and trotted up beside him. "That was a bit further than the last few times."

"What do you mean?" Mushi said, feigning ignorance.

"Every other time, we traveled on foot for about two thousand paces. This time was for three thousand."

He smirked. "Need to see if you're getting stronger. Push your limits a bit."

"So, my training has already started." She gave him a sideways look.

She felt his gaze as the hat turned toward her. "You're as sharp as I've heard. Reminds me a lot of Noreen."

Gwen was taken aback. "You knew Noreen?"

"Back when we were kids." His head tilted up toward the sky, reminiscing. "I would sneak out of the barracks at Danforth to share supper with her family. She's something like a sister to me."

Gwen's heart ached with woe as she recalled witnessing the guildhall collapse, with Noreen most likely inside. "I can relate."

A somber silence lingered in the air as they rode.

"She's still alive," he said. "I made sure of that during the attack."

Gwen gripped the reins tighter as a smile tugged at her lips. "Thank you. For that and for stopping the Militia from capturing Anden, Wesley, and Damian."

"It's not the first time I've had to get those boys out of trouble." A heartwarming smile broke through the brim of his hat. Not something she'd ever associate with someone called the Hand of Death.

"Back at Laminfell, you mentioned something about a Gray Phoenix. What is that?"

Mushi stared at the road ahead, stroking his beard. "The Gray Phoenix is an old moniker. Nothing to concern yourself with, princess."

"Please, call me Gwen," she said. He nodded in

acknowledgment. "And about the cloaked figures?"

"I'll be honest with you, Gwen," he said gravely. "The fact you're a target of theirs concerns me greatly. These are not a band of thuggish bandits or idealistic rebels. I fear their goals to be of a sinister nature."

"Why not warn the kingdom in some way? Let the Militia handle it?"

"These people are crafty and stick to the shadows. The war with the rebellion has acted as a curtain for them to move behind the scenes unnoticed. You want to know what the Gray Phoenix is? It's the protectors in the shadows of the kingdom, fighting off the things that haunt nightmares."

His words chilled her skin like a winter breeze. "And you hope to teach me how to fight these things?"

"As a queen, you'll face many hardships. One of those is battle. Your father was a fool never to teach you how to wield a sword. He was always optimistic that he'd be able to unify the continent in peace, but that is optimistic thinking indeed."

Gwen looked at the blade dangling from her saddle. The lifeless face of the rebel soldier burned itself in her memory, as well as his blood trickling down the steel. Her hands trembled. "If you do intend to teach me how to use a sword, may I ask you a question?" His silence was an invitation to ask. "Does it get easier? Taking someone's life?"

The Hand spoke bluntly. "Depends on the person. For some, it doesn't. Others just grow numb."

"Have you grown numb to it?" she asked.

"With a title like the Hand of Death, how could I not?"

6

To the rest of the continent, the Holy City of Illios was considered sacred ground with its grand architecture and statues of religious figures to display a sense of greater purpose, but that only pertained to the upper level. The lower level they currently proceeded through was like any other mud-ridden slum Anden stumbled upon in his travels across the continent. Gaunt and hungry-looking men and women wandered about seeking sanctuary on behalf of the Lucius Ambulate and ended up tossed into the gutters. Atop his horse, he could see Titus' Basilica towering above all, with statues of the Seven Saints lining its roof. Even from so far below, Anden felt their gaze fixated on him, and the surrounding foundation of brick and stone made him feel claustrophobic.

A crowd gathered around a shriveled old man shrouded in a worn, tattered cloth common to the pundits serving the Ambulate. He was feeble, leaning on a staff to stay upright, but his voice reverberated through the air with conviction. "Stay strong, brothers and sisters." The geezer's long, white beard shook as he flapped his lips. "The Lucius Ambulate may have cast you out while evil seeps through every crack of the continent, contaminating these very streets, but do not fret. The Emperor watches over us all, and I, as his servant, am here to help you through this troubling time."

Damian reined his horse closer to Anden, a hood shielding his face. "What do you think that's about?"

"A discarded hermit spouting nonsense," replied Anden.

The old man continued to rant. "We may be suffering, but find hope that it will all eventually end. Soon, we will be guided from this broken world into the light of paradise."

Anden was never one for religion. He already knew what a shithole the world was and never liked the idea of death being a gateway to a better place. He'd seen men die, and the only place they went was a hole in the ground.

They dismounted at a rundown inn where a portly woman with a mole lodged above her left eye greeted them at the door. "Hope you boys don't mind sharing a room. We only got one available."

"We'll make do," said Wesley. He tossed the woman a silver coin and flashed his dazzling smile.

The woman took the silver and delicately tucked it away in her breast. She tried mirroring Wesley's smile, but the missing teeth made it less dazzling. Upon entering the inn, the first thing that struck Anden was the smell. Rotting meat and soured milk saturated the dining hall as beggars scraped together crumbs from those who could afford food. Some turned an eye toward them, measuring the possible weight of their coin, but quickly lost interest after catching a glimpse of Damian's sword strapped across his back and Wesley's pistols at his hip. Walking in single file, they headed up the stairs to their room to discover a cramped space with a singular bed cushioned with straw.

Wesley plucked three strands from the mattress. "Shall we draw for who gets the bed?"

"You two can draw," said Damian, unrolling his sleeping pouch on the floor at the foot of the bed. "I'm used to roughing it."

Shrugging, Wesley removed one of the strands and presented them to Anden. Anden pulled one, and they compared the two strands. While a bit crooked, Anden's proved to be longer than Wesley's.

"Seems the Holy City has blessed you," he said.

Anden didn't feel blessed touching the bed. The straw mattress barely cushioned him from the wooden frame. He might as well sleep on the floor.

"We shouldn't waste any time investigating the murders," said Damian. "It's probably best to question some of the locals. Find out what's public knowledge, if any stories differ, and if so, where the dots connect."

Anden agreed. "I'll head into the upper level and see what I can gather from the barmen. If there are tales to be told, they'll have heard them."

"I'll keep my ear here in the slums," said Wesley. "It's the ones wandering the streets who typically find the bodies first."

Damian nodded, wincing slightly. "I'll remain here for the time being. Would be a hassle if someone recognized me." He nursed his side as he eased himself onto the floor.

Wesley watched him collapse with a suspicious gaze. "It'll also give you more time to recover."

"Just a lingering pain. I'll be fine." Damian waved them off to head out.

Leaving the inn, Anden ventured out from the gutters and into the upper city. The contrast between the two levels was night and day. Every building was immaculate, with enough room to not feel closed in, and the people strolling the streets wore fine-colored silks. The men shrouded themselves with shawls while the women adorned their heads with veils in a ceremonious manner. Every person he passed gave him an ostracizing stare, but he ignored them as he made his way to the tavern, The Burning Sapphire. It was a fancy establishment with a glimmering chandelier hanging from the ceiling and a bar crafted from mahogany. Bottles of every liquor found on the continent lined the wall behind the bar like trophies, and the patrons all drank from elegant glass chalices. Anden figured the place had never seen a bar fight, or else they wouldn't allow for such brittle containers. Many of them flashed a hostile glare as he strode up to the bar with his torn tunic, scarred chest, sandaled feet, and tattered hat. The barkeep even gave him a rotten look upon his approach.

"Street vermin aren't allowed in this establishment," he spat, standing tall with his nose pointed upward like a noble looking down on a peasant. "Go back to the mudhole you crawled out from."

"Is that how you treat all your paying customers?" Anden flashed a few silver coins, placing them on the bar.

The bartender begrudgingly palmed them. "What will it be, then?"

"Whiskey. The good stuff."

"Any particular taste?"

"Surprise me," said Anden with a smirk.

The bartender pulled a bottle from the shelf and poured the whiskey into a stout chalice, sliding it across the bar. The glass was cool to the touch, chilled by the block of ice sitting in the auburn liquid. It felt strange not having an iron tankard in his hand. Taking a sip, Anden smacked his lips in satisfaction. Smooth at the beginning, but it had a hell of a kick once he gulped it down. "So, I recently strolled into town, and there have been whispers of some grisly murders taking place here. Care to shed any light on the matter?" Anden felt a shift in the air as the other patrons continued to scowl at him from their seats.

The barkeep cleaned a glass with a rag, trying to keep the conversation casual. "Afraid I don't know what you're talking about."

"That so?" said Anden in a skeptical tone. Taking out another silver coin, he slid it across the bar in an inconspicuous manner. "Because I've heard stories outside the city claiming otherwise. I figured someone on the inside would at least know something more."

The glass slammed onto the bar, blocking the coin from moving further. The barkeep leaned close, his face darkening with animosity. "Well, I don't. So, I suggest you finish your drink and take your stories elsewhere."

Anden retracted the coin and finished his drink in a single swig. Standing up, he tilted his hat to the barkeep. "Thanks for the drink."

He didn't offer a response as Anden headed out the door, much to the delight of the other patrons. Back on the streets, Anden could feel a watchful gaze stabbing into him like an itch on the back of his head that wouldn't go away. The citizens of the upper level now avoided him completely, going as far as to cross the other side of the street. Something strange was going on, but he couldn't put his finger on it. The ring of a bell caught Anden's ear, directing his attention to a middle-aged man riding in an open carriage with bodies stacked in a mangled pile pulled by a massive bovine.

"Death is always near," the corpse collector sang to himself, "as the ringing grows more clear. The piles of bodies grow higher and higher and only make more work for the steer." He chuckled to himself as Anden hurried to meet him at the crossroads. He had a patchy beard, long, dirty fingernails, and a lump sagging out the left side of his nose.

It seemed he took as much care of himself as he did his cargo. "Oi, mister. Got any packages for the trolley?"

"Not today, unfortunately," said Anden. "I was wondering if you could answer some questions."

"Got no time for questions," said the corpse collector. "Need to be passing on through, or else the fancy folk will complain about the smell, and I'll get in trouble."

Anden took out the silver coin intended for the barkeep and flipped it into the man's filthy hands. "Then, how about I give you some company as you pass through? Give you a chance to answer my questions."

"Alright. Hop on up."

Anden climbed onto the cart next to the man, much to his own regret. The stench of the corpses in the back was less than pleasant, but nothing compared to that of the corpse collector himself. From the odor of death in Kelveux to the smell of shit in Danforth's sewers, nothing made Anden want to vomit more than the stench permeating from the man sitting beside him.

"What is it you want to know?" asked the corpse collector.

"I was wondering if you could tell me anything about the supposed murders taking place around here—"

"Shhhh!" The man wagged a finger in Anden's face. "Can't talk about such things here. Wait until we're in the gutters."

Anden did his best to hold his breath as they continued through the upper level and down into the gutters. Finding a secluded alley, the man halted the carriage. Anden hopped off before it came to a complete stop, desperate to distance himself from the smell.

"Sorry about the delay," said the corpse collector. "Talk of the murders is frowned upon by the Ambulate and all the fancy folk. Loren Visconti has even got his spies stalking about and keeping an eye out for trouble. 'Specially since more and more of the refugees come crowding the streets down here."

Anden understood why he felt a strange sensation of being watched earlier. Due to his appearance parading around the upper city, he marked himself a prime target for suspicion. "So, there are murders taking place in the city, and the Ambulate wants it kept quiet."

"Aye. Visconti doesn't want speculation to run out of control. I can understand why." His face contorted with disgust. "Gruesome stuff these murders have been. Five dead already. Picked them up myself, I did. Hardly recognizable. Nothing but husks of skin with their faces burned off and eyes missing from their sockets. Gruesome, I tell you."

Anden envisioned the decrepit face of Vargo with voided sockets. A terrifying sight. "You picked up the bodies?"

The corpse collector nodded. "That's right, I did."

"You remember any of the locations where you picked them up?"

The man scratched a group of hairs sprouting from his cheek.

"Last one I picked up was in a dead-end alley just off Briar Road, I believe. Fancy folk weren't too happy about that one. Caused quite a stir."

"And where is it that you drop the bodies off?" Anden asked.

"At the morgue, of course." He gave Anden a critical stare. "Why all the questions? You a merc of some kind? Hoping to make some coin by catching the killer?"

"I guess you could say that."

"Well, mister merc, I'd be careful if I were you. Whoever is committing these murders is a twisted bastard. Not to mention the Ambulate may not like you probing into such business. Although, if you could take care of the problem, Visconti might be thankful."

"I'll take that into consideration." Anden tossed the man a few more copper coins. "Thanks for the info."

"Happy hunting, mister merc." Whipping the reins of his ox, the corpse collector hauled his decaying cargo back onto the streets. His bell continued to ring, signaling to others that the ferryman of the dead was on his way.

Returning to the inn, Anden found Damian still resting on the floor with Wesley sitting on the bed, face filled with disappointment. "Have trouble gathering info, too?" Anden asked.

"Anything useful, at least," sighed Wesley. "Murder around here seems as common as the Ambulate's service due to scarcity of food and other resources. For them, nothing strange seems to be going on. You?"

Anden downed the last bit of liquor in his flask. "It's the complete opposite for the people up top. One mention of the murders, and I got nasty looks. Apparently, the Ambulate wants things kept quiet. Although, I did cross paths with the corpse collector, who was kind enough to share a few words. Said there have been five victims so far, each one eviscerated in a horrendous way. Last one he found was in an alley off Briar Road."

Damian tapped a thumb against his chin, brooding. "It would benefit us to take a look. Might find some clues."

Anden nodded. "Wesley and I can take a look tomorrow."

"No," said Damian. "I'll go tonight. Time with the Core has sharpened my tracking skills, and there'll be fewer people around to interfere."

"You sure?" asked Wesley, eyeing the arm nursing his side. "You still look to be in pretty rough shape."

"I'll be fine. Remember, Mushi believes these murders might be linked to those strangers in the cloaks. The faster we find the killer, the better."

"Be careful," warned Anden. "The Ambulate has spies littered about the city. I'm sure I've already caught the attention of some of them."

Damian grinned. "After avoiding the Militia for five years, you think I'll let a few pundits catch me?"

7

"You're more than welcome to stay longer if you like," said Samuel.

Reed finished adjusting the twin daggers across her waist and strapping the boots to her feet. "I'm grateful for your kindness," she said, "but I've already spent too much time here. I need to head back west." Nearly two weeks had passed since the attack, and her remaining generals most likely assumed her to be dead. She needed to get to an outpost and send word to them before they took foolish action. It also wasn't safe to spend more time in the Militia headquarters. If anyone recognized her, she would be thrown behind bars and no doubt hanged soon after.

"There should be a caravan of refugees heading to the Holy City. You could travel with them at least to the Western Gate."

If memory served well, Julius Yates headed an operation for the rebellion in Laminfell. Using his resources, she could send word to the rebel base and procure a ship to hasten travel along the Blade's Trench. She gave an appreciative nod to the weathered, aged man. "What do you plan to do?"

Samuel glanced about at the ruins of his home. Having burned a good portion of his belongings, little was left to lay claim. "I'm not entirely sure."

Outside the window, Reed could still see the burned pile of wood and ash where he had cremated his family. "You could come with me on the caravan," she suggested. "Start a new life out west."

His lips curled into a broken smile. "I don't know if I'm ready for that yet. Still need to pick up the pieces of my current one."

"Take care of yourself, Samuel."

"You as well, Ana."

Without looking back, Reed marched out of the damaged home onto the cobblestone roads of the city. She pulled the scarf tucked beneath her jacket over her face. Rubble and despair lay in the aftermath of their attack. Many of the remaining citizens picked at the shattered pieces of their lives, unsure where to go or how to rebuild. Others crowded the streets carrying only necessities as they prepared to travel elsewhere in hopes of starting anew. Such imagery of grief and suffering reminded her of the tales her uncle would tell of King Lucius II's rule. The common people struggled to survive and provide for their families while the wealthy nobles continued to live a lavish lifestyle, even using people as slaves to continue garnering valuable resources and wealth. Reed diverted her gaze to the ground before her, only focusing on the next step she took. While it pained her to see these people suffer, her resolve could not be weakened. They needed to keep fighting; otherwise, more people would suffer as time went on.

"There are always casualties in war," she whispered to herself.

In the main square, the statue of Cain Bezok had toppled over, along with the guildhall further up the road. Seeing it fall from the heights of her ship filled her heart with joy, but witnessing it from the ground amongst the people, that joy felt tainted with guilt. Militia soldiers herded those seeking to leave the city into carriages like cattle. People piled onto each other into masses of flesh. Reed reluctantly shoved herself in, unable to sit comfortably without ending up in someone else's lap. The smell was also foul, as no one had the ability to bathe for days. With their carriage filled, one of the soldiers signaled to the coachman, who whipped the horses' reins. As they trotted off and the carriage jostled down the jagged path descending the mesa, Reed was slammed with a mixture of elbows and shoulders. It nearly drove her to the point of unsheathing her daggers and taking the horse for herself, yet that would draw unwanted attention.

Reaching the base of the mesa, the jostling of the carriage ceased along with the random series of blows. Peeking through the crowd, she saw the remains of the airship scattered about the valley in a cemetery of metal. Reed wondered whose bodies lay amongst the wreckage. Elliot Durham? General Watts? Did the crafty assassin

Vargo end up meeting his end with the demise of their ship? She hoped so. A man as dangerous as him was better dead following their defeat, or else he could bargain to change sides. Elliot was right to distrust a sellsword. Then, she remembered the mercenaries who brought down their ship. Anger seethed within her soul as she hoped their corpses lay charred and rotting in the wreckage. If it weren't for them, she would be witnessing the kingdom's fall, her goals achieved. Instead, she rode west alone in a carriage packed with refugees whose sorrowful faces only made her feel more shame.

8

Mud caked the bottom of Damian's boots as he trekked through the rain toward the northern end of the city. At such a late hour in the night, hardly a soul was out, except for the refugees forced to weather the outdoors due to their lack of coin. He kept an eye out for any suspicious figures tailing him, but no one seemed to notice or care. The burning pain in his side forced him against a nearby wall serving as the foundation of the upper city above. While his wound from his battle with Vargo had been tended, infection still tainted his body. The wound itself took on a sickly yellow color while the surrounding skin burned a vibrant red. He could tell it was serious but omitted any mention of the ailment to his companions, for they would delay the investigation. If these murders were linked to these strange cloaked figures, who were able to recruit a man like Vargo, nearly kill Wesley, and seriously injure Mushi, then his condition was insignificant compared to the threat they posed.

Ascending to the upper level, he hunted down the street labeled Briar Road and paced its length until he found a small dead-end alley littered with a few rotting barrels and a carriage with a busted wheel. He first investigated the carriage. From the array of shelves built to swivel out the back once the latch door opened for display, Damian figured it belonged to a merchant of sorts. The wooden board at the front serving as a bench to rein the horses had a slight bend to it, indicating the merchant was of ample weight. A weight that grew too strenuous for his own carriage and, by striking the right bump in the road, caused the wheel to come undone. While abandoned with a broken wheel, the carriage was still in decent condition, unlike the barrels deteriorating with years of rot. A recent incident having taken place only days ago and most likely having nothing to do with the murders. At the far end of the alley, Damian sifted through the barrels, discovering the smattering of a dark substance staining the brick road. Kneeling, his nostrils flared, breathing in a curt sniff. A hint of blood, smoke, and something else. A strange smell that eluded Damian's knowledge. Rubbing his finger against the substance, he took another whiff.

This time the smells singed his nostrils, and although faint, he could make out the musty scent of incense. An ingredient in ceremonies of death. Studying the surrounding area, he noticed the print of a boot or shoe outlined in a similar substance. The toe pointed toward the larger stain, indicating that the person who left it was most likely the killer dumping the body. Damian searched for more prints, expecting to find another to reveal the killer's path through the alley, but none existed.

"It's unwise to wander the streets at such an hour," called out a voice in the night. Damian spun around to see the old man in tattered robes preaching on the streets when they first entered the city. His white beard hung from the shroud of his hood as he shambled forward into the alley using his staff. It stood a head taller than his reclusive frame and curved into a semi-circle with a strange dream catcher pattern woven into it. "During dark times such as these, people may grow suspicious of someone clinging to the shadows."

"Says the man equally cloaked in darkness," replied Damian.

"Most people in this city consider me a senile old man raving in the streets. A harmless hermit." His eyes glowed in the darkness like lanterns as he studied Damian. "However, a young lad like yourself wielding a finely crafted bastard's blade? Many would grow suspicious indeed."

Damian tugged at the hood of his jacket, shielding his face as the man drew closer. "Plan on calling the authorities?"

The elder chuckled. "Unlike most here, I believe all, including outcasts, should be welcomed within the walls of the Holy City." Turning around, he hobbled into the street. "Come along," he shouted over his shoulder.

Damian remained in the alley, hesitant to follow.

"I can help heal that wound of yours."

He blinked a look of shock. "How did you—"

"You favor that side when you walk," the stranger stated plainly. "Now, come."

Damian followed the elder through the city, descending back down to the lower level. Along one of the walls was an archway with a staircase leading into an underground cavern. Entering it, the elder lit a few lanterns dangling along the walls. As he lit more, Damian could see the light reflecting off the metal of mechanical contraptions, both finished and unfinished, sprawled across a workbench. Containers of herbs, powders, and liquids were neatly organized on an overhead shelf.

"Who are you?" Damian asked in awe.

The elder set his staff down and climbed into a chair. "My name is Arios, pundit to the Lucius Ambulate. At least, until I was exiled." He motioned for Damian to sit beside him. "Now, come and let me see what we're dealing with."

Damian did as the man bid and lifted his shirt to show him the infected wound.

"Emperor be praised," said Arios. "The wound has festered and badly. Anyone else might consider you on the path to death."

"But there's something you can do?"

Arios sifted through vials and containers, inspecting each one.

"Lucky for you, I've become quite adept at curing ailments for the less fortunate who arrive at the basilica's doorstep and are turned away." He mixed a few vials of liquid and placed the mixture into a machine that spun around at an alarming speed.

"I've never known a pundit to utilize engineer constructs," said Damian.

"Hence my exile." Arios plucked a few leaves from an herb and ground them with a powder in a bowl. One of his hands was adorned with strange jewelry crafted of several rings wrapped around his bony fingers and interlinked by a small chain. "Believe it or not, I was actually a candidate for loren, but Visconti tarnished my reputation, claiming these constructs to be the work of dark magic. A divergence from the path of the First Emperor. It was nonsense, of course. His accusations were fueled by fear of losing the election." The juices from the herbs combined with ground powder into a paste which the elder scooped into an empty container. Stopping the spinning contraption, he removed the vial of liquid and handed it to Damian. "Drink that."

It held a bitter taste that contorted his face in revulsion.

"It's not meant to taste good," said Arios, "but it'll ease the pain and help cure any illness from the infection." Dipping two fingers into the paste, he rubbed it on Damian's wound. The pressure he applied caused Damian to wince. "Continue applying the ointment every day for the next two weeks. It'll aid in healing the wound properly and prevent further infection.”

Damian lowered his shirt and bowed his head. “Thank you. If you don’t mind me asking, when did you garner an interest in engineering?”

Arios smiled at him from beneath the hood of his cloak. “When my eyes were opened to a new perspective. Tell me, what do you know of the First Emperor?”

“He’s the forefather of the royal bloodline,” explained Damian. “The creator of the original empire that united all people for centuries before the Great Calamity.”

“He didn’t just build an empire.” Arios rose from his chair, his voice gaining strength. “Legend says he forged the entire continent as a foundation for the empire and fought a horrifying darkness wielding a sword adorned in flame that could scorch the entire world to ash. He didn’t just unify people, but rather gifted each of us with a fraction of his power.” He gave Damian a knowing look. “If you’re familiar with the old traditions, you know that of which I speak. We worship him as a god, for no man could fathom possessing the power he held.” The chains on his hand jingled as he raised a finger. “Although, is it more radical to believe such a being was born with godly power or that he was gifted with tools that allowed him to reach such heights? The Lucius Ambulate wants you to believe in one truth, but I’ve come to believe in the other. Hence my fascination with the emerging technologies of modern times. Who’s to say these constructs aren’t but a resurgence of what existed before the Great Calamity in the time of the First Emperor?"

Damian rubbed his chin. "An intriguing philosophy, but such debates are best left to men of the cloth."

Arios receded back into his frail stature, collapsing into his chair. "A wise decision. Now, if you don't mind me asking, why were you snooping about a place wrought with death? If anyone else saw you, they might wrongly accuse you of a crime you didn't commit."

"I assume you're aware of the murders having taken place throughout the city?"

"All are aware, but none dare to speak of it. What interest are they to you?"

"Earlier, you mentioned Loren Visconti accused your contraptions of being the subject of dark magic." Damian's face grew sullen as his gaze shifted to the floor. "Well, I've seen the results of real dark magic, and I have a feeling the acts of these murders run down a similar path."

Arios leaned forward in his chair. "How much do you actually know?"

"There have been five thus far, and each one of the bodies was left disfigured beyond recognition."

"You've spoken to the corpse collector, then. Not many know the true number of the victims. The Ambulate has been keeping details on the matter a closely guarded secret. They want everyone to think these murders are nothing more than refugees killing each other over resources to survive. It's despicable."

"Why is the Lucius Ambulate wanting to keep this a secret?" Damian asked.

"I'll answer your question with another," said Arios. "How many children have you seen running around the lower level?"

Thinking back on it, Damian didn't recall seeing a single child as they entered Illios. Another strange occurrence given most refugees who seek the aid of the Ambulate are families. "What of it? What significance do children have with the murders?"

Arios combed a wrinkled hand through his beard. "Such questions are best left to men of the cloth."

9

Parry, riposte, feint, counter-parry. Victoria's hand ached as she clashed her wooden sword with Kaylin's. Sweat coated her body, and her lungs burned, desperate for air. The Militia captain stood her ground with ease, checking each of her blows with a prideful smirk. Victoria ignored the weariness weighing on her body and pushed further. This time, she would wipe that smirk from her mentor's lips. She hammered away at Kaylin's defenses, swinging the wooden blade with all the might she could muster, but her arms grew weaker with each strike. Kaylin's deflections became lazy, realizing the young princess was tiring. Victoria wouldn't give up. She would collapse from exhaustion before giving up. The hilt jostled in her loosened grip, nearly flying out of her grasp. Victoria recovered by wrapping her other hand around the sword. Taking a step back, she reared a two-handed strike, knowing it would be her final attack. Summoning the last reserves of strength, she felt the warmth of a raging fire emanate from her chest and surge into her arms. Kaylin raised her sword to block, and as their blades connected, the wood exploded into a shower of splinters. The momentum of her swing flung Victoria to the ground, and without the strength to catch herself, she collapsed hard onto her shoulder. The warmth in her chest faded, leaving her exhausted in the grass and gasping for air.

Kaylin stared slack-jawed at the broken sword in her hand for a moment before rushing to Victoria's aid. The Militia captain picked the princess up, setting the girl in her lap. Victoria sank into Kaylin's arms, resting against her chest as she felt her mentor's pointed chin poke the top of her head. "That seems like enough for today," she said.

Victoria spoke between heaving breaths. "What was that? What did I just do?"

Kaylin glanced around at the splinters of wood scattered about their small alcove in the garden. "From the looks of things, it seems you've finally ignited the spark and gained access to your inner potential."

"Really?" Victoria managed a faint smile. "So, all that meditation crap did actually pay off?"

Kaylin nodded. "That it did. Although, you'll want to rest awhile. Your body isn't acclimated to using that power you just tapped into."

Victoria felt a sting of betrayal. "But I thought we trained my body to be in the best shape possible so it could handle it."

"We did," said Kaylin, "but it still has limits. The amount of power you drew upon exceeded your body's current limitations. As a result, it drained you completely and left you not even the strength to sit yourself up."

"Then what good is having access to this inner potential if using it makes me a vegetable?" groaned Victoria.

"That's only because you lack balance. You'll need to learn how to draw upon the exact amount of power your body can handle to utilize it efficiently and not fall flat on your face after one swing of a sword."

"How do I go about that, then? Drawing upon the right amount?" said Victoria, pondering Kaylin's words.

Kaylin dashed a gold strand of hair from her perplexed face. The princess watched as the gears ground away in her mentor's head before she sighed in defeat. "That's not something that's easily put into words. At Danforth, they told us to think of it like a well. The reserve of water deep beneath the ground is similar to the vast amount of potential power you're hoping to draw from. To do so, imagine yourself casting down a bucket to gather the right amount."

"How will I know how much is the right amount?"

"That comes only with practice," explained Kaylin. "No one can tell you what the right amount is. You just have to figure it out for yourself." She looked down at Victoria with an intense gaze. "This is where many Militia soldiers get frustrated and give up. Everything you've faced until now is considered a cakewalk compared to this. I can't stress enough how much trial and error you will go through to draw on the right amount of power and do it consistently. Failing to do so can leave you weak and vulnerable, but mastering this balance will place you in a league few dare to reach."

Victoria felt something placed into her hand. Looking down, she saw her fingers curled around the hilt of the broken sword. "Draw the right amount of power, and every blow you strike can be just as strong as that last one you dealt. With time and consistent training, you can slowly draw more power and get even stronger."

Victoria's strength returned as she raised her hand to study the broken blade. A glimpse of the power stored within her. For the briefest moment, she trespassed into the realm of a Militia captain. It might be difficult to master, but she was ready for the challenge. She had conquered every obstacle before, and this one would be no different. For her father and for Gwen, it needed to be conquered. With Kaylin's help, she climbed to her feet. "Has there been any word of my sister?"

Kaylin's expression turned sullen. "Rumors have surfaced that she might have been sighted at Danforth during the attack. I'm not sure whether or not I hope for those rumors to be true."

Such news troubled Victoria as well. The thought of her sister fighting for her life as the rebels rained hell on the city caused the wooden sword to slip from her grasp. Her sister couldn't be dead. She wasn't. If she really was in Danforth, someone would know for sure. It would not be a rumor. Gwen was still out there somewhere, waiting to be found. "Rumor or not, you haven't given up on her, have you?"

Kaylin wrapped her strong arms around Victoria in a firm embrace. "Of course not. Every day I worry for her safety and wish that when I wake up the next day, she'll be back here in this place. When I enter these gardens, I hope to see her picking flowers again."

"I hope so, too," said Victoria. "And if she's not back by the time I master this balance, I'll go and find her myself." Kaylin flicked Victoria on the forehead, making her recoil in pain.

"That's reckless thinking," she said in a stern voice. "With your sister gone, that makes you next in line to inherit the throne, so you need to stay here. Besides, I'd find Gwen long before you ever get the chance if the need arises." Kaylin scanned the scattered remains of the wooden blades in the grass. "Might as well try to clean up as much as we can. Don't want the gardeners causing a fuss over this mess."

Bending down, they tediously picked up the splinters by hand. Victoria used her shirt as a makeshift pouch to hold them all as she piled them in. Bits of grass made their way in as well, but they would grow back. Stepping out from the alcove, they marched over to the wall of bushes and small trees and dumped the wood chippings. Not as odd of a place to find stray pieces of wood lying about. The only remaining evidence was the broken hilts Kaylin took the liberty of discarding herself.

"I guess it's time for you to upgrade to dulled steel for sparring," she said proudly. "Soon enough, you'll be waving around a sharpened blade with the skill and power of a true soldier."

"Don't get too excited," Victoria teased. "Once I have some real steel in my hands, I might prove to be better than you."

Kaylin wrapped an arm around Victoria, putting her in a playful headlock. "You're at least a decade away from accomplishing that. Worry about finding balance for now, and then we'll measure your skill to mine in a more serious manner." Releasing the princess, she gave Victoria a solid pat on the back. "Now, rinse off before anyone questions why you stink like a hog."

"Yes, ma'am," said Victoria, giving a lazy mock of a salute as she marched out of the gardens and into the ornate halls of the palace.

Ever since the arrival of the ambassadors for the conclave, more people than usual were found loitering about the palace. An increased number of soldiers and servants arrived to help protect and serve the gathering elites ruling over the kingdom, as well as nosey nobles keen on being informed about the current discussions of Argust's interests. Around every corner existed a cluster of people sharing gossip in hushed whispers. Victoria usually paid them no mind, for such talk of politics or economics often bored her. As she climbed the long staircase up to her chambers, her ears caught the echo of whispers carried by the stonework from above.

"Many are claiming that the rumors are true," said a dissonant voice. "The Hand of Death was indeed sighted at Danforth and stood his ground against not only Captain Quinn but Captain Green as well. From what I hear, Green actually retreated."

"He certainly lives up to his reputation, if that's the case," said another voice laced with fear. "Word in the underground is that his bounty totals around 25,000 gold. The last time anyone saw him was two years ago along the coast of Papuri, where several corpses were found with flesh scorched to the bone. After two years of silence, why show himself in Danforth?"

Victoria slowed her pace while climbing the stairs. She didn't want to alert the men of her presence.

"Well, it's obvious, isn't it?" replied the first man. "He's sided with the rebellion, and that, I can assure you, is a scary thought. If you ask me, Ambassador Krawczyk had the right idea in convincing Parliament to unanimously agree on launching an all-out assault on the southern plains. If they were able to build such a fearsome contraption and have such dangerous men as Vargo and the Hand of Death at their disposal, then it's best to eliminate them quickly."

"You may be right, but I've heard other whispers. Ones more ambiguous in origin but nonetheless frightening. Recently, a name has weaved its way through conversations following the conclave meeting, the Gray Phoenix. No one knows what it is or means, but some speculate it has something to do with the Hand of Death. Some claim it's a sort of cult worshipping him as the next emperor."

"Hogwash. That's nothing but unfounded superstition."

"I thought so too, but you can't ignore the strange occurrence of events recently taking place. Princess Guinevere goes missing, the rebels nearly burn Danforth to the ground, the Hand of Death suddenly appears, and word has also come out of a strange series of murders in Illios. These are bad omens and ones we should heed greatly. Not to mention the king—"

Engrossed by what the two voices were saying, Victoria missed the next step and fell down the stairs with a loud clatter. The men went silent before rounding the stairs to see her lying on the staircase, groaning in pain.

"Princess Victoria," one of them called. "Are you alright?" They both hurried down the steps to her aid, but the princess waved them off as she climbed back to her feet.

"Yeah," she said. "My apologies. Not very royal of me to fall down the stairs."

The man with a purple barrette and sideburns stretching down his cheeks spoke, and Victoria recognized him as the superstitious one talking from before. "Well, with so many steps to climb, anyone is sure to miss one here or there."

Victoria gave them a slight curtsy, as she had been taught to do. "Thank you for your assistance. Now, if you'll excuse me, I must return to my chambers."

"Of course, my lady," they said in unison with a bow.

Continuing up the stairs, Victoria found herself intrigued by the men's conversation. She, too, had heard soldiers whisper about this Hand of Death over the years. From their description, he seemed more like a fable than a man, yet it appeared he actually existed and was seen in Danforth, no less. More intriguing and confusing was the mention of this Gray Phoenix. Was there really a cult that worshipped such a dangerous person whose head was worth a great weight in gold? Victoria shook her head, disregarding the notion with a chuckle. The other man was right in calling it an unfounded superstition. The Hand of Death might be real, but the Gray Phoenix sounded like something from the storybooks her father used to read to them as children. Nothing more than a radicalized detail to spice up the gossip nobles shared with each other. On the other hand, the man in the purple barrette did have a point. Many strange occurrences had recently taken place, and none of them were good. Her worries for her sister's safety grew, as she knew deep down that the longer Gwen remained missing, the less likely she was to return.

10

"Preparations are already being made for the attack on the southern plains," said Lawson. He rested in a nearby chair, tapping a finger against the metal of his prosthetic leg. "Despite your efforts, Your Majesty, this conflict with the rebels will not end in peace."

Peter rested in his bed as Mary Katherine held a withered hand. His wrinkled skin hung loosely from his bones, and his silver hair had turned a dull iron color. The king's condition worsened with each passing day, and Blackwood could scarcely remember the last time Peter left his chambers or even climbed out of his bed. He gave a slow blink of acknowledgment, but Mary Katherine was less understanding.

"Don't act so dour," she said. "You practically goaded the others into pursuing this outcome."

"Unlike the rest of you, the state of Danforth is not beyond my imagination. I witnessed the remains of Takata with my own eyes. I saw the field of bodies slaughtered with their houses burned, and that was done by bandits riding horses. The magnitude of destruction wrought by the rebels with that contraption of theirs is unprecedented." The grip on his cane tightened. "We can't let such actions go unpunished. Not again."

Mary Katherine rose from the king's bedside. "I'm fully aware of the crimes the rebels committed. The countless lives they took and even more livelihoods they ruined. They've grown from a thorn in our side into a dagger, and I wish for nothing more than for it to be plucked; however, genocide is never the answer."

"Neither is peace," said Lawson, glaring up at her from his hunched position. "The rebels made it clear. It's either them or us."

"What's done is done." Peter's voice was a whisper, but the words silenced the room. Mary Katherine lowered herself, sitting beside him once more. "Rahm and the others were right. I was foolish not to act based on my worries about Gwen's disappearance, and innocent lives paid the price. The vote is passed. There's no need to argue further."

Blackwood tore his gaze from the chamber's view of the starlit sky over the capital. "Peter is right. There's no point in discussing a matter that's already been decided on. Our concern is Rahm's proposed vote to usurp him."

"We can't allow it to pass," said Mary Katherine. "Victoria possesses a strong will, but she's never been one for politics. If she's crowned, Rahm will only manipulate her through the power of Parliament."

"I wouldn't let that happen."

The light shined in her eyes like the point of a spear. "You wouldn't have a choice. As long as a majority of the ambassadors side with him, he'll do as he pleases. Not long after Victoria's crowned, I'm sure he'll try to relieve you as chancellor."

Lawson turned to Peter with a weary expression. "What are your thoughts on the matter, my king?"

"Whether or not I retain the crown is no concern of mine," said Peter. "I only care that Gwen is found."

Blackwood stroked his goatee in a pensive manner. "I can't say for sure of all the ambassadors, but Rahm has definitely given up hope on the princess. If he has his way, I'm afraid Gwen will officially be considered dead."

"That won't stop me," said Mary Katherine, "and it won't stop Victoria either."

"Like it matters," scoffed Blackwood. "You said yourself, as long as he holds a majority, there's little we can do except incite some sort of civil war."

"Rahm doesn't hold a majority," Lawson interjected. "Not yet. From the interactions at the conclave meeting, it seems Parson is already on his side, and you can always count on Fletcher being in Rahm's corner. Brookshire wasn't fond of the king's decision to gift the southern plains to the rebels, so I'm sure she's with him, too. That leaves him needing one more vote to gain a majority. We still have a chance to stalemate."

Blackwood paced the room, crossing the foot of Peter's bed. "Noreen is unpredictable and too stubborn to be swayed in any way. If he's looking to guarantee a majority, he'll most likely buy Weyman's vote."

"I wouldn't be so sure," said Mary Katherine. "Shortly after his arrival at the palace, he tried convincing me to agree to launch an immediate assault on the rebellion after learning they hired Vargo. He was desperate because he didn't have the coin to buy Weyman's vote."

"Regardless, Weyman will play his games to see who's willing to pay the most coin," said Lawson. "It would be wise for us to ensure he ends up on our side."

Blackwood's face soured into a grimace at the prospect of indulging Weyman's avarice, but it needed to be done. "I have a knack for persuading covetous swindlers like him. I'll negotiate a deal."

"If it buys more time to find Gwen," said Peter, "I'm willing to offer as much as needed."

Lawson tapped his cane against the floorboards in an anxious rhythm. "That takes care of Weyman, but we still need to convince Noreen if we are to stalemate the vote."

"We'd have better luck training a fleshling to be a house pet," said Blackwood. Convincing Noreen would be the greatest obstacle in their plan. Relying on her vote was like gambling on a coin toss, and any attempts to persuade her might end up backfiring. She'd probably already decided on the matter, and if so, their efforts would be in vain.

"If I remember correctly," said Peter, the wrinkles of his brow furrowing deeper with intense thought, "Ambassador Archer spent much time as a young steward studying in the library with Gwen. If she still fosters fond memories of my daughter, then perhaps there exists a possibility of her being swayed."

Blackwood shook his head. "Doubtful. Noreen's decisions are driven by her logic and morals. I don't think reminiscing about her years as a young girl will prove effective."

"It might if the sentiment comes from the right person." Mary Katherine brushed a hand through her oak-brown hair. "One who also shares a close connection with Gwen."

Blackwood gazed at her with his dark eyes. She stared back with a look of affirmation. One that eased the anxiety he felt. "I trust you," he said.

Peter turned toward Lawson. "James, I leave the responsibility of finding Gwen to you."

"I'll have Captain Hardee assemble the best trackers he can find on the continent," replied Lawson, "from the Militia and hunters from the Core."

"I can offer us some more time by using the military campaign to further delay the vote," added Blackwood. "Should allow for the opportunity to find the best. From then on, we'll rely on holding a stalemate."

Peter surveyed each of them. His brilliant blue orbs penetrated the sagging fatigue of his face. "Thank you all for the loyalty and love you've shown my family."

Mary Katherine took the king's hand once more. "It's the least we can do for your service to the kingdom."

He patted her hand, smiling. "Your kind words warm my heart. Now, please, leave me to rest."

As Peter nestled into the comfort of his thick sheets and plush pillows, the three members of Parliament took their leave from his chambers. Mary Katherine offered her arm to Lawson. "Need help getting back to your chambers?"

He gave a polite wave of his hand. "Appreciated, but I'll manage just fine. I may be crippled, but I'm not helpless." The man hobbled off, the clacking of his cane against the floor accompanied by the metallic squeal of his prosthetic's hinges.

Blackwood walked with Mary Katherine. Once they were out of sight from the soldiers guarding Peter's chambers, she interlocked her arm with his. "You think we can pull it off?"

"I'm not sure," Blackwood admitted. "Weyman will be a pretentious prick, but jingle enough coin, and he'll jump through hoops like a trained dog. Noreen is the one I'm worried about. You'll need to tread carefully. She's not fond of being manipulated."

"I'm not Parson," she spat. "It's not my intention to tell her how to vote. Only to offer a different perspective." The sounds of their footsteps echoed down the empty halls. Mary Katherine clutched Blackwood's arm tighter. "Rahm won't sit quietly once he's suspicious of our plans. He'll fight tooth and nail to make sure the vote ends in his favor."

Blackwood was well aware and ready. He would fight Rahm to his dying breath to protect Peter and his family from the rotund ambassador's clutches. "If he's still thirsty for blood after crushing the rebels, I'll be sure to give him his fill."

11

"Come on," said Mushi. "There's something you need to see." He lowered himself over a cliffside, finding a perch on a small ledge. "We need to hurry before the sun goes down. Don't want to miss it."

"Miss what?" Gwen peered over the cliff, seeing a strip of sand at the bottom where the waves met the shore. Glints of sunlight danced on the glass surface of the ocean water as the sun fled beyond the horizon.

"You'll see. C'mon." Mushi motioned for her to follow as he continued to climb.

Gwen gingerly dropped to her knees and dangled her legs until her toes rested on a thin ledge. Glancing down, Mushi descended at a frightening pace as if he'd done it a thousand times. Meanwhile, she clung to the rocks, making sure to have a firm grasp before reaching for another. The wind felt less gentle and more like a whip lashing into her.

About halfway down, he called up. "Hurry, or you're going to miss it."

At his behest, Gwen quickened her pace, but a hand slipped, causing her to fall. A tingle tickled her stomach as she plummeted toward the shore. She expected to splat onto the sand, but Mushi caught her in his arms.

"That's one way to do it," he jested. Setting her down, he guided her to the border of the shore, where the tide stopped before receding away. The sun was nearly gone. A teardrop of light remained, lingering above the water. "Have you ever seen the sun set twice?" Excitement laced his voice.

Gwen didn't fully understand the question, opening her mouth without uttering a word.

Grabbing her wrist, he pulled her to the ground as they both lay flat on the beach. "Keep your eyes on the horizon."

Gwen watched as the golden orb floated just above the surface of the sparkling sea. A vibrant hue of colors stretched across the sky from auburn to a deep purple, then finally came the night with a handful of stars already emerging. It was breathtaking and without a cloud in the sky to obscure its beauty. It all came to an end when the sea swallowed the last teardrop of light, but Mushi was quick to jump to his feet.

"Stand up! Stand up!" he shouted, urging her up as well.

As she shot to her feet, Gwen experienced an immediate sense of déjà vu. The faint gradient of orange and purple filled the sky once more for a brief moment before the sun plummeted into the sea again. Just as Mushi had said, she watched the sun set twice. It was strange, but the simplicity of the trick made it even more charming.

A large grin overcame Mushi's face. "Well, whaddya think?"

"It was beautiful," Gwen said in awe.

"When I was a kid, I'd always come down here to watch the sun set twice. It never gets old. Every time is just as magical as the first."

They stood there in silence, listening to the waves roll in and splash their feet. The chill of the water nipped at Gwen's toes as they sank into the wet sand. The salty smell teleported her back to the palace chambers, where a window overlooked the eastern ocean as the sun rose instead of set. The sky darkened along with the sea, becoming one vast and expansive void.

"I know we've traveled quite a distance," said Mushi, breaking the silence. "If you'd like to wash off, there's a cave past the rock formations down the shoreline. Good little place to swim and freshen up."

Taking a dip in the water sounded blissful. The continuous riding and walking coated Gwen in sweat thicker than mud on a pig. A bath of any kind was much needed. "I think I will," she said. "Thank you."

"Take all the time you need. I'll be here."

She left Mushi on the shoreline and ventured beyond the cluster of large rocks resting along the beach. There, just as he described, resided a cave with a small alcove of water flowing in from the ocean. The moon's soft glow shimmered off the water and onto the cavernous walls. Disrobing, she eased herself into the pool. Chilled by the night air, her entire body shivered, but she quickly brushed off the cold sensation. Gwen waded through the water, able to clearly see her hands and feet kicking about beneath the surface. Only the small ripples of her movement broke the illusion that nothing was there at all. Patterson was right to describe the sea of the western coast to be as clear as glass. Leaning her head back, she wetted the rest of her hair and splashed water over her face. Not wanting to keep Mushi waiting long, she climbed out and put her clothes back on. Passing by the rocks back to the open shore, she saw Mushi standing in knee-high water with the legs of his trousers pulled up to his thighs. Underneath the poncho, he possessed a stocky build with broad shoulders. The scar he revealed at the tavern in Laminfell stretched further across his body than Gwen had originally thought. It consumed his entire left shoulder, spreading across half his chest as well as his arm. Cupping a handful of water, he splashed it on his face, smoothing out his shoulder-length walnut-brown hair. The bridge of his nose held a small bump, making it appear crooked. Gwen realized she was staring for a bit too long as he noticed her and diverted her gaze as he wandered ashore.

"Have a good swim?" he asked, covering himself with his tunic.

"It was peaceful," said Gwen, wringing out her hair.

The soft smile on his lips gave him a kind and casual appearance, but the darkness in his brown eyes hinted at a more savage side deep within. "We should eat and get some rest. Your training starts at the crack of dawn."

"You mean carrying the supplies while hiking wasn't part of the training?"

"A precursor of things to come," he chuckled.

Gwen's head slumped forward as she heaved an exasperated sigh. Lifting her head, she stared at the daunting cliffside with an expression of dread. "Don't tell me we have to climb back up."

"Of course not," he said, grabbing his poncho and hat. "There's a pathway a few paces down the shoreline."

A pang of annoyance struck Gwen. Sure enough, not far up the shore was a path carved into the jagged cliff, similar to the main road leading up to Danforth. She didn't voice any complaints. Just like carrying the supplies on their travels, descending the cliffside was another one of Mushi's tricks. Viewing the wonder of the sunset was a splendid distraction, but she could see through his true intentions. He was studying her, evaluating her physical condition, most likely to determine where best to start with her training. Reaching the top of the cliff, they returned to the village of dilapidated structures overgrown by vegetation. A place scarred by tragedy radiating with an ominous aura that crept under Gwen's skin. One of the ruinous structures was where they made camp. Mushi emerged carrying a bag of rice and a marred metal pot. Starting a fire outside, he boiled water and dumped the rice inside to cook. Gwen surveyed the surrounding area with intrigue, noticing gashes in the wood of the buildings, areas burned black from fire, and rusted arrowheads scattered in the grass.

"What is this place?" she asked. "What happened here?"

"This place used to be a thriving village named Takata," explained Mushi. "It was my home. That is, before bandits raided it, killing everyone and burning it to the ground. Now, it's a place mostly forgotten by the rest of the kingdom, with me as its sole survivor. Being a vice-captain in the Militia, my father dug a secret bunker under our home. When the bandits attacked, he stored me away there while he went to search for my mother. He never returned. When the morning sun rose and everything grew quiet, I climbed out to see nothing but death and destruction. I even found my father's body impaled on a spike."

"How old were you?"

"Eight."

Gwen hugged her legs close to her chest, watching steam seep out from the metal pot. "That's horrible. I assume your mother met a similar fate?"

"I can't say for sure." His shoulder slumped with a weight of grief. "I searched the entire village for her body but didn't find anything. There's a chance she was taken as a slave instead of killed, but it's been so long since then. I'm sure she's met her end by now, if that was the case."

"Was your father the only Militia soldier present?" Gwen asked. "If he was a vice-captain, then surely more should've been around to help fight."

Mushi shook his head. "Can't say for certain. Militia soldiers did show up afterward and found me. Being an orphan, they took me to Danforth to train. They no doubt hoped to turn me into a capable soldier like my father. Back then, I wanted to be someone my father could be proud of, so I trained to be the best."

Gwen watched the glowing embers of the wood burning at the center of the fire, slowly crumbling away to ash. "I understand what you mean."

Mushi removed the lid from the pot. A waft of steam floated out as it unveiled a white bed of fluffy rice. He scooped some into two small bowls, handing one to Gwen. She stared at it, wearing a somber expression. Her appetite waned following the story of Mushi's dreadful upbringing and offenses committed against his village.

As he dug into the food, Mushi's tone shifted from somber to light-hearted. "Don't let a sad tale ruin your appetite. Perhaps I can remedy it with a better one. A story my father used to tell me before bed about the First Emperor's lost daughter."

"The First Emperor didn't have a daughter," said Gwen.

"That's why she's lost," said Mushi with a smirk. "Lost to history. Many know of his son, to whom he bequeathed the original empire, but according to legend, he also had a daughter. One whose beauty no poet nor bard could dare find words to describe. They said it could only be witnessed with the eyes. Of course, such beauty spawned the interest of many suitors, and the First Emperor expected to betroth her to the perfect candidate. To his disappointment, she fell in love with a lesser-born man with a lowly name. He forbade them from being together, but it seems not even the great and powerful First Emperor can stop love. They escaped, far away from her father's grasp, and started a family here along the western plains. Due to her betrayal, the First Emperor had her name wiped from history to be forgotten. My father would often say that family became the bedrock of our village. That their blood runs through our veins."

Gwen let out a small giggle, taking her first bite of rice. "It's an interesting story. If there's some truth to it, you'd be a part of the royal bloodline."

"All fables have a hint of truth to them," he said, "but I think my father embellished that part of the story. No royal blood runs through these veins, I assure you. Just a tongue-in-cheek reason for the people of my village to call each other cousin. Kinsmen of the forgotten blood." He bellowed a hearty chuckle, and Gwen laughed along with him.

"If it's all the same to you, I think I'll choose to believe in that story," she said. "A bit amusing to be able to call the legendary Hand of Death cousin."

"We'll see about that. Now, eat up so we can get to sleep. Got an early start tomorrow morning."

Gwen wolfed down her bowl of rice and even helped herself to seconds. After cleaning up and putting out the fire, they retired for the night. The interior of the derelict building was sectioned off into several uniform square rooms. The wooden frames of the walls were splintered and scorched, and a section of the roof had collapsed, leaving them vulnerable to the elements if a storm ever blew through. Gwen settled into her room next to Mushi's at the far end of the hall. The walls separating them were more like thin paper windows, allowing her to see his shadow on the other side. She curled up into her sleeping pouch, nodding off to sleep.

*

Sunrise barely broke when Mushi woke Gwen with a tap of his foot.

"Time to get started," he said. "Got a long day ahead of us, so there's no time to waste."

Groggy, Gwen struggled to climb out of her room. Her body fought her the entire way out of the building, weighing heavy as a boulder. Venturing to the cliffside, she knew the task he expected from her.

He responded to her pitiful groaning, saying, "I was able to make this climb at the age of six. If you're going to defend yourself in combat, you need to be in better shape than I was as a kid."

Unlike the previous day, she didn't fall; however, it took much longer for her to reach the shore. The sun had fully risen by the time her feet touched the sand. Mushi waited, sitting on a sizable rock with two more of smaller size beside him.

"Every day starting today," he explained, "you'll warm up by climbing down the cliff. Then, we'll start with strength and conditioning in the morning using these rocks. After breaking for lunch, I'll teach you the basics of close-quarters combat."

Gwen's muscles already ached from the climb. He was mad to think she'd even make it to lunch.

Mushi tugged on his pointed beard, smiling as he observed the misery plain on her face. "You said it would be amusing to call me cousin last night. Well, that's something you're going to have to earn. Start by picking up the smallest rock there and carrying it across the shoreline and back."

Gwen hardened herself, accepting his challenge. She was able to hike leagues while carrying supplies. Surely, she could carry a rock in the sand. Bending over, she wrapped her arms around its jagged surface. She lifted it off the ground with all her might and perched it precariously on her shoulder. Digging her feet into the sand, she started walking.

12

"That tastes awful," said Wesley, spitting the drink out of his mouth. "It's like watered-down rum."

"That's what grog is," said Anden, snatching his flask back and taking a swig.

Refugees crowded the gutters of the Holy City as the two men snaked their way through the streets. The passing rain filled the air with moisture, making it humid. A layer of sweat coated Anden like a second skin he couldn't peel off, and the heat of the sun beat down on him. To stay hydrated, he drank the grog sold at the dilapidated inn they were staying at. A bit weak to give him a buzz, but it still contained more kick than plain water.

"I don't know how you drink stuff like that and enjoy it," said Wesley. Despite the sweat running down his face, he seemed unbothered by the humidity. Having worked on a vineyard for the past five years in the Sanduran heat, he was probably used to it.

"Sometimes it's not about enjoying it. Besides, I've had worse shit than this. There was this one tavern that served a drink so dark, I swear the old girl could've run on it." Glancing around, Anden noted the faces of everyone they passed. For almost an hour, they walked, and the people seen crowding the streets were all adults. "Looks like Damian's little friend might be onto something. All this time wandering around and not a single kid to be seen."

"You don't trust that old man, do you?" asked Wesley.

"I hardly trust anyone associated with the Lucius Ambulate," said Anden. "Exiled or not, he still rants in the streets for fools to buy into his bullshit. Amassing a collection of sheep to do his bidding."

"At least he seems to be on our side in helping solve the murders. He also helped treat Damian's wound."

Anden took a swig from his flask. His lips grimaced in disgust, but not from the grog. "I can't stand the smell of that paste he uses, and helping or not, that old pundit knows more than he's letting on."

"I don't disagree. Regardless, the Ambulate seems to be the one holding all the answers when it comes to the murders. If we hope to uncover anything, we'll likely need to infiltrate the basilica somehow."

"Good luck with that. We're barely welcome to walk around the upper level of the city, let alone the basilica."

The crowd started to separate just ahead of where they were

walking. A path was made for a hooded individual in a white cloak accented with red seams around the edge of his sleeves and the brim of his hood. A pundit of the Lucius Ambulate. His presence alone parted the crowd as he approached Anden and Wesley. The pundit stopped in front of them and studied Anden with a careful gaze.

"His Eminence, Loren Visconti, has requested an audience," he said with a cold demeanor. The hood turned to Wesley. "Is he a companion of yours?"

"He is," said Anden.

"Then he will come as well. Follow me. His Eminence is waiting." Turning on his heel, the pundit paced back through the crowd, who made sure to stay out of his way. Anden and Wesley followed, keeping some distance from him as they walked.

"Well," whispered Wesley, "seems that infiltrating the basilica won't be so hard after all."

*

Roaming the halls of the basilica was something Anden hoped never to experience in his life. His nose flared as the musty smell of incense lingered in the air. He hated looking at the endless portraits depicting the wrinkled faces of every geezer who held the title of loren. Nothing more than a bunch of old men given a fancy title, allowing them to call everyone lost sheep needing guidance according to the teachings of the

First Emperor. Anden never bought into any of that crap. The only path he followed was the one he forged for himself, not some relic of ancient history.

"You seem to be on edge," said Wesley, his heavy boots smacking into the tiled floor. "Afraid you'll burst into flames?"

Anden gave him a sardonic look. "If I do, you won't be far behind me."

The pundit guided them to the end of the hall, where they crossed a set of double doors into the expansive sanctum where worship ceremonies took place. Rows of benches lined every angle, facing a raised platform at the head of the room. Towering over everything was a massive statue carved into the perceived likeness of the First Emperor, extending an arm out into the empty space. Whether the gesture was one of compassion or authority depended on interpretation. Beneath the dominating structure sat an extravagant chair shaped like a fire, the tongues of flame wrapping around each other to form the back. In it was an old man adorned in fine red robes with a crown glistening atop his head. His sunken cheeks, narrow eyes, and angular features gave him an eternal expression of condemnation. One Anden didn't appreciate looking down on him.

"Your Eminence," announced the pundit guiding them up the aisle, "I bring you the man you requested along with a compatriot of his."

The man's gaze did not leave the book resting in his lap.

"Thank you, Theo. I'll take it from here." The pundit bowed and took his leave. "Speak your names."

Wesley gave a cordial bow. "Wesley. And this is Anden."

Anden did not extend the same courtesy. Instead, he gave the man a spiteful glare.

"Are there any more companions I should know about?" the man asked.

"No," said Anden.

He snapped the book closed. "Then let's get straight to the point. I am Francis Visconti, loren of the Lucius Ambulate. I am aware of your inquiries into the deaths taking place and would like to know why you have such an avid interest in them."

"Murders, you mean," corrected Anden.

Visconti's angular face turned hard as stone with a grimace. "The only murders we know of are those committed by riffraff swarming the gutters of the lower city. Since arriving, they've killed each other like savages over food, coin, or whatever else they find appropriately more important than human life. Your accusation stating otherwise threatens to disturb the populace. If you haven't noticed, many of the locals haven't taken kindly to the city being overrun with refugees."

"Oh, I've noticed," said Anden, "but isn't it the duty of the Lucius Ambulate to offer sanctuary to those in need? Not cast them out into the street like vermin?" Wesley gave him a sideways glance, warning him to watch his mouth.

Rising from the chair, Visconti kept a calm demeanor, but the tone of his voice cracked the air like a whip striking flesh. "The Lucius Ambulate is doing all it can, but our concern cannot be limited to the endless waves of refugees entering our gates. We have an entire city, a community of people, to care for. When have a sellsword's concerns ever branched beyond the amount of coin he will be paid? Is that the true nature of your presence here?"

"Yes," interjected Wesley. "We came in response to rumors of strange murders taking place in the Holy City and hoped to make some coin by investigating and capturing the perpetrator."

"Where did you hear such rumors?" asked the loren.

"Are they true?" countered Wesley. "With all due respect, Your Eminence, we came seeking coin, and if there are no murders to solve, then there is no coin to be made."

Visconti narrowed his vision through the slits of his eyes. "I'm afraid you're wasting your time. As I said, the only murders happening here are the refugees killing each other in the streets."

Anden opened his mouth to speak, but Wesley placed a firm hand on his shoulder to silence him. "Such a shame," he said. "To travel all this way and only be met with disappointment. If it's all the same to you, Your Eminence, we will stay in the city for a bit longer to rest from our long journey. In that time, we could maybe help clean up the streets of the lower city. Mitigate some of the killings that are being twisted into stranger tales than they really are."

Visconti stroked his chin with a finger. "The Lucius Ambulate does not need assistance in handling these matters. As soon as you're rested, take your leave of the city." He returned to his chair, waving a dismissive hand. "Go now. I have other matters to attend to."

Turning around, Anden and Wesley paced back up the aisle toward the set of double doors.

"You're not going to question him about the children?" Anden asked in a whisper.

"No, because you already pissed him off enough," said Wesley. "Not like he's going to be that big of a help to us, anyway. One thing we know for sure is that the mere mention of the murders sets him on edge. Meaning something is definitely going on around here."

A sudden crash erupted throughout the sanctum as a mess of candelabras clattered to the floor. Standing over them was the starved frame of a young boy with fear in his eyes as he glanced up at them.

"What are you doing?" shouted Visconti. The echo of his voice filled the room in a whirlwind of fury. "You know the sanctum is off limits. Theo!"

The pundit from before came tumbling through the doors. "Yes, Your Eminence."

"Get this child out and make sure he is properly reprimanded."

"Of course, Your Eminence." The pundit grabbed the boy by

the arm and hauled him off down a side corridor.

Anden glanced over his shoulder at Visconti, who composed himself by smoothing out his robes. "Excuse the outburst. Children are often difficult to keep an eye on. Especially when they wander into places they shouldn't."

"Curious," said Anden, turning around. "That's the first child I've seen since entering the city. By the looks of him, he seems rather thin. The offspring of a refugee. What are the likes of him doing here?"

Visconti reopened the book in his lap, turning his attention away from the two men. "As I said, the Lucius Ambulate is doing all it can in regard to refugees arriving at our doorstep. We are not a house of endless resources. We can help those who need it most."

"At least you're doing something," said Anden. Spinning around, he continued up the aisle and through the set of double doors, leaving the sanctum of the basilica. Wesley followed close behind him as he marched down the hall decorated with portraits. He took a hefty swig from his flask. "I think we've figured out where all the children are being kept. It's here at the basilica, and I have a hunch as to why. All the victims of the murders are most likely children."

"That's a bold claim to make," said Wesley.

"Think about it. We may not know exactly how everything started, but imagine this scenario. Refugees come swarming into the city following the war against the rebellion. The Ambulate can't take them all, so the excess has to remain in the gutters of the lower city.

Many have to struggle to survive, with a number dying every day to starvation or other means, and the weakest of that group are children. If I was a killer looking to hide my trail, that's whom I'd target." Anden glanced up and down the hall, making sure no one was around to hear them. "If the bodies were as mutilated as the corpse collector claimed, it wouldn't take long for people to become worried and for rumors to start spreading. My guess is, after a few murders, the Ambulate decided to take in exclusively children to protect them."

"And despite that fact, the murders continued," said Wesley. "Meaning the Ambulate wasn't doing its job."

"Or," added Anden, "someone within the Ambulate is responsible for the murders, and they haven't figured out who."

Wesley scratched at his beard. "That would explain their desperate attempt at keeping the details a secret and barring anyone else from investigating them. If people were to learn that someone within the Lucius Ambulate was mutilating children, it could bring down the entire institution."

Anden nodded. It was for this reason that he never trusted men of the cloth. They were people who placed themselves on a moral pedestal higher than the rest, but everyone had a sliver of darkness lurking behind them. And those who place themselves closer to the light tend to cast a larger shadow.

13

The countless days of riding along the desolate countryside were slow and agonizing. For one reason or another, they barely managed a full day's travel. If they didn't stop for the horses to rest from hauling the massive number of refugees, then it usually was for the children and elders to not piss themselves and make the smell of the carriage even more unbearable. At times, Reed wondered if it would be faster for her to ditch the caravan and travel on her own. Faster, perhaps, but certainly not safer. The Militia soldiers escorting them killed a few fleshlings stalking about the past few nights, and where a few were spotted meant a horde was not far. Before they encountered such a tragedy, the red-tiled roofs of Laminfell came into view. As soon as they crossed the bridge into town, Reed abandoned the carriage and navigated the intersecting roads between walls of cottage homes, searching for Julius' establishment. An inconspicuous brewery called

The Ship in a Bottle.

Walking along one of the roads, she eventually reached the docks. Various ships made port, but the most troubling one had its hull reinforced with iron, a cylindrical metal tower spewing steam, and countless Militia soldiers scurrying about on the deck. Reed's scarf concealed the frown contorting her lips. Too large a force for simply patrolling the seas of the Trench. She continued down the road until happening upon a building with brick foundations stretching down the length of the street with two separate chimneys and a model ship hovering above the doorway. Reed suspiciously peered through one of the windows only to see a dark room. No flicker of light or noisy patrons having a drink. Something seemed off. A bell rang as she opened the door, but not a soul was around to hear it. Empty liquor bottles lined the shelves behind the bar, dirty glasses remained on the tables, and a thin layer of dust resided on the stools neatly pressed against the bar.

"If you're looking for liquor, you won't find any here," said a gruff voice. In a dark corner of the room where the light from the windows could not reach, Reed saw the faint glow of tobacco being smoked from a pipe.

"Such a shame," said Reed. "I guess that means the man left in charge hasn't been doing his job."

The embers crackled as the man took a drag. Exhaling, the cloud of smoke caught some of the ambient light and lingered in the air like a mist.

"Where is Julius Yates?" she asked.

The wood of the chair scraped against the floor as the man rose from his seat and stepped into the light. His hair was a frayed, disheveled mess, along with the rest of his bruised face. The pince-nez resting awkwardly on his broken nose was warped with a crack across one of the lenses, and dried blood stained the trench coat he wore. "Who's the one asking?"

"Someone who's been through as much shit as you, apparently." Reed removed the scarf from her face.

Julius choked on the smoke from his pipe. Sent into a fit of coughing, he took out a red handkerchief to cover his mouth and catch any stray globs of phlegm leaving his lungs. Composed, he looked at Reed with intense awe. "You're supposed to be dead," he stammered.

"Is that the official story?" Reed sat on one of the nearby stools and propped her feet on the bar, whipping her raven hair over her shoulder.

"It's certainly the one people choose to believe," said Julius.

"That have anything to do with why you look like you lost a bar fight?"

He collapsed back into his chair and sucked on his pipe. "Things went to shit as soon as word spread about the rebellion's fall at Danforth. Many believed you and Elliot to be dead, and with that came the loss of reputation."

Reed gazed at him, her emerald eyes glittering with curiosity. "How so?"

"When Durham sent me here, he tasked me with finding a way to monopolize the distribution of Laminfell's famous beer for profit to help fund the rebellion's cause. It wasn't too difficult a task, with some negotiating, bribing, and a little strong-arming here and there. The tricky part of the whole operation was actually distributing the product. Resting at the midpoint of the Blade's Trench, it's faster to travel by water, but many ships were raided by pirates. Obviously, it was bad for business, and with us already at war against the Militia, it didn't seem worth starting one with pirates as well. So, we struck a deal. We paid them a fee for safe passage along the Trench, and as the rebellion grew, so did their respect for that deal. After what happened in Danforth, they found it opportune and profitable to not only render our agreement void but also to distribute the alcohol themselves."

Reed rolled her eyes. Pirates were considered the bandits of the sea and merchants of the underground. Usually, such criminals were hunted by the Militia, but in times of war, they leveraged positions between both sides. While a sellsword's loyalty might extend to the depths of one's pockets, a pirate's swayed like a boat against the current. It was unpredictable, as all they cared for were the spoils plundered when the tides changed.

"They killed my men," Julius continued, "beat me within an inch of my life, and left me here to wallow in my sorrow as a broken man."

"Did Durham know about this deal?" she asked.

He sucked on his pipe, blowing the smoke out his nose. "Of course."

Lowering her feet off the bar, Reed marched across the room toward the disheveled businessman, ripping the pipe from his lips. "It was foolish to make a deal with pirates. Frankly, I think you got what you deserved." She tapped the pipe against the table, spilling the ash onto the floor. "But you're right about one thing. Traveling by water is much faster. Which is why I came to see you in the first place. I'm in need of a ship to reach the western coast."

"Weren't you listening? I told you the pirates took everything. I don't have a ship to offer." He reached for the pipe, but Reed moved her hand, keeping it from his grasp.

"Who are these pirates?" she asked.

He glared at her through the broken glass of his spectacles. "The Trench Runners. Captained by a ruthless man named Russel."

"And do these Trench Runners make port here?"

"Frequently. In fact, if they kept to our schedule, they should be loading up a shipment today."

Reed tossed the pipe into his hands. "Then, grab a pistol. We'll see if we can negotiate, bribe, or strong-arm them into giving us a ship."

*

The wooden boards of the deck creaked as Reed marched across the docks. Julius followed, nervously glancing about and puffing on his pipe stuffed with fresh tobacco.

"Do you see any of their ships?" she asked.

"There," he said, gesturing toward a ship flying no flag atop its highest mast. "We'll need to be cautious. That's the Silent Whisper, Russel's own ship."

"Good. You'll have the chance to repay him for his betrayal personally."

Every piece of wood lining the hull was worn with rot from a long history of sailing. An abundance of barnacles caked the bottom where the ship met the river, giving it a foul smell of molded seawater that reached the back of Reed's throat, making her gag. Sailors loaded barrels, gawking at her as she strutted past them. Beside the plank leading onto the ship, a man rested on one of the barrels while skimming a piece of parchment and drinking a bottle of alcohol. From the girth of his gut, she was surprised the barrel managed to hold his weight. Tentacles of braided black hair formed a thick beard decorated with various colored beads.

"Look who washed up on the docks," he chuckled. He was as grimy as the ship he sailed on, undressing Reed with a lecherous gaze. "And who's this fair-bodied wench you brought with ya?" Julius glanced at Reed while sucking his pipe. "Don't be rude, Yates.

Introduce us."

Reed gave him permission with a raise of a brow. "This is Reed Skokna, commander of the rebellion. Commander, this is Captain Russel of the Trench Runners."

"A ghost in our midst," said the pirate. "Word along the Trench is you died in a blazing inferno at Danforth."

"I've heard," she said, "and because of my apparent demise, you betrayed a deal made with the rebellion. As it turns out, I'm not dead, and this betrayal will not be easily forgotten. However, I am willing to make an exception if you can provide us with a ship for sailing west."

Russel erupted in a patronizing cackle. He raised his bottle, pointing in the direction of the Militia ship. "Ya see those strapping boys in blue across the docks? That's the second ship I've seen hauling heaps of them up the river toward the western coast. That little stunt you pulled really pissed the kingdom off. Both Freeman and Ivarson are preparing to march through that speck of land ya bartered from the old king, and by the looks of it, they don't plan on taking prisoners. So, if ya plan to threaten me, you'll need something better."

"How about this?" Julius stepped past Reed and produced a small single-shot pistol from the sleeve of his jacket. He pointed the barrel at the pirate as most of his hand concealed the weapon from the sight of any onlookers. "Give us a ship, or I'll shoot you dead, bastard."

Russel set down the bottle of liquor. Grinning, he raised his hand while lifting a single finger into the sky. "You should be thanking me, Yates. Out of all the stripes, I let you live out of appreciation. It's from your hard work that my boys and me profit. Now, you and your commander are going to waste your second chance at life."

Reed slowly reached behind her back, gripping the ebony hilt of her dagger. She could sense something was off. The pirate captain seemed too confident and lax, having a gun pointed at him by a man more than happy to pull the trigger. Keeping an eye on his raised finger, she prepared to strike at a moment's notice.

"Excuse me," a voice interjected. They all glanced over to see an old fisherman with a large straw hat sucking on the stem of a wheat plant. "I was hoping someone could help me haul in the day's catch. It's heavier than these old bones can bear on their own."

The captain unfurled all his fingers before relaxing his arm. "I'm sure these two would be more than happy to help ya, old man. I have my own business to tend to." Picking up the bottle, he sauntered up the plank onto the deck of his ship, leaving Reed and Julius on the dock with the fisherman.

Reed removed her hand from the hilt of her blades as Julius slid the pistol underneath his jacket sleeve. They followed the old man to his boat, but when they arrived, there were no fish to be found.

"What's the meaning of this?" said Julius. "Where's your fish?"

"It was just an excuse to get you out of that pickle you found yourselves in," the fisherman explained. "If I hadn't defused the situation, that pirate would've signaled his sniper to shoot both of you."

"What sniper?" Julius asked.

The fisherman removed the wheat from his mouth and used it to point toward the crow's nest looming over the ship. Standing there was a man holding a rifle, scanning the surrounding area. Now it all made sense to Reed. All the captain needed to do was lower his finger, and both of them would've been killed. Julius ground his teeth on the stem of his pipe as smoke blew out his nose.

"Russel is a careful man," said the fisherman. "Always ensures he has the upper hand."

"We appreciate the interruption," said Reed. She shot an emerald glare at Julius. "Next time, we'll be sure to be more careful."

"What was it you were hoping to gain from such a dangerous man?" the fisherman asked.

"A ship to head west," she responded. "We need to get to Bushgrove."

The old man's brow wrinkled with curiosity. "Looking to partake in the Carnival, I assume."

"Yes," said Reed.

"Interesting thing to nearly get killed over, but with the war going on again, I guess every day could be our last." He placed the wheat stem back into his mouth. "My ship isn't fast, but she'll get you there in time for the celebration."

Reed stared at the small fishing boat floating in the water. It wasn't much, especially compared to the Militia's frigates, but it was all they had. If what the pirate said was true, they could hopefully reach base camp before the Militia found it.

"Alright," said Reed. She turned to Julius, who still smoked his pipe in frustration. "You coming along?"

He breathed out a cloud of smoke. "Might as well. Got nothing left here."

They climbed into the boat as it teetered and loosened the tether to the dock. The fisherman lowered the sail as they drifted up the river, heading west.

14

Gwen swung a fist, only to meet air. She swung again, followed by a kick. Mushi danced out of the way, avoiding the blow. The sand made it difficult to find solid footing and move quickly, but he glided across the beach unhindered. He wasn't even attempting to spar with her as he held his hands behind his back. Gwen delivered another kick, but he sidestepped it and swept a foot into her leg, knocking her to the ground.

"You're getting better," he said. "Your movements are less stiff."

Gwen spat out the sand in her mouth and combed out the grains stuck in her hair. It only took two days for her long, brown locks to annoy her to the point of cutting them. Now, the tips of her hair hovered over her shoulders in a similar fashion as her sister's. "I still haven't landed a single hit on you, and you're barely trying."

He bent down to meet her with a warm smile. "I've been training since I was a boy. You've only just started. Yet, you're progressing faster than most. Give it time." Rising, he marched off down the shoreline.

Gwen climbed to her feet, brushing the sand off her clothes and skin. She could already feel a slight change in her physique. Her arms no longer felt like flimsy noodles dangling from her shoulders. They had a firmness to them. Following Mushi, she asked, "How long does it usually take to complete Militia training?"

"Years," he said bluntly, "but you're just learning the fundamentals. Once you understand those, you can reach higher levels on your own, which is a great transition into your next lesson."

They scaled the winding pathway back up the cliffside. Upon reaching the top, Mushi sat at the edge with his legs crossed and instructed her to do the same.

"From now on, we're going to meditate at the end of each session," he said.

Gwen's brow furrowed in confusion. "What's meditation going to do? I thought you were training me to fight."

"How much do you know about the old traditions?"

"Not much when it comes to fine details, but they're methods passed down since Cain Bezok founded the Militia. Every soldier is trained in the way of the old traditions, but not all of them can fully complete them. Those who do gain access to extraordinary abilities. At least, that was the way of things before REV implants were invented."

Mushi nodded in approval. "But do you know where the power

to perform these extraordinary abilities originates?"

Gwen didn't answer.

He gazed out at the afternoon sun lingering over the horizon. "Inside each of us lies a dormant power. The Lucius Ambulate believes it to be a gift from the First Emperor, a fraction of his power bestowed upon us when he united everyone under the original empire. According to their translations from the ancient text, they called it nin-nir. When one establishes a connection with this power, they can tap into it and perform those extraordinary abilities."

"And this connection is established through meditation," said Gwen, sitting beside him on the ledge of the cliff.

"Exactly," he said with a wink. "Forging the connection typically requires an awakening from within oneself. You need to strip yourself down to your very core, but what this means for each person is different. Also, because this power comes naturally from within, you don't have to worry about it slowly decaying your body over time like a REV implant."

"Can the connection ever be lost?" Gwen asked. She would hate to go through such an effort only for the connection to falter over time.

Mushi tugged at his beard. "It's certainly possible. Think of it like a bridge. Once built, it takes a great effort to destroy. Although, if not properly maintained, I suppose it could slowly dull and fade. Believe me, though, it's much harder to build the connection than maintain it."

Gwen took a deep breath. "Okay. What do I do?"

"First, straighten your back. Then close your eyes and focus on your breathing."

She erected her back and squared her shoulders. Her father had taught her how to hold a proper pose when she was a girl, so it felt natural. Closing her eyes, she entered the dark void of her mind. The sound of the crashing waves beat against her ears as their salty aroma filled her nose. She rested her hands on her lap and felt the individual threads sewn together in her trousers. Pushing away all those distractions, she focused on the rhythm of her breathing by sucking in, holding, then exhaling.

"Good," whispered Mushi.

Gwen continued that breathing pattern. A numbness flowed through her body, making it heavy. It felt as though she was melting into the very stone of the cliff and becoming one with it. The sound of the waves grew distant. The salty smell disappeared. She floated in the abyss of her mind, an empty landscape of nothingness. Silent. Peaceful.

Why did you leave, Guinevere? A voice penetrated the tranquil void. The words were harsh, like a clap of thunder. *Why? Do you not understand the responsibility you bear for this family and the kingdom?* It was her father's voice, scolding her. *You can no longer act like a foolish little girl. You must prepare yourself to become queen one day.*

Clenching the cloth of her trousers, she shook the intrusive thought away. Her mind went blank again as she refocused on her breathing, but it didn't last long. Other thoughts surfaced as well. The cloaked figure from Nabal rose out of the darkness, leaking with bloodlust that weighed heavily on her chest, choking her. She wasn't sure whether she was even breathing anymore. Then, everything turned crimson as blood trickled down the length of her sword. In the reflection of the steel was the lifeless expression of the rebel soldier she'd killed in Danforth. A life she had taken. A tear streaked down her cheek as her breaths quickened and stuttered. She started to hyperventilate.

Mushi's arms wrapped around her in a comforting manner. "Breathe, Gwen. Breathe."

She opened her eyes and saw the distress in his. "I'm sorry."

"No need to be. I can tell you've been through a lot on your travels."

"All these thoughts came rushing in…"

"And you tried warding them off," he finished.

"Yeah."

Mushi unwrapped his arms, patting her on the shoulder. "Next time, don't try to fight them. If your mind wanders, let it, even if the thoughts are not pleasant. Meditation is meant to be a time of self-reflection. It allows us to face the things that trouble our minds the most. These troubles serve as obstructions in the connection. They're issues you need to overcome and resolve within yourself."

"How do I resolve them?"

He shook his head. "There's really no answer to that. You need to come to terms with yourself. Find acceptance, I guess, in whatever manner you can."

Gwen hung her head in disappointment. Something told her she would have a lot of obstructions to deal with to forge the connection with her dormant power, or nin-nir, as Mushi phrased it. He placed a finger under her chin, lifting it up.

"Don't look so glum," he said. "Sometimes talking about these things can help. If you have any you're willing to share." He flashed that warm smile of his, which brought Gwen comfort.

"During the attack on Danforth, I killed a man. A rebel who was about to kill a Militia soldier. I stabbed him in the back with my sword and pierced all the way through his chest." Gwen dug her fingers into her arms in discomfort. "Those lifeless eyes and blood pouring from his mouth. It haunts me that I was the one who took his life."

"So, that's why you asked that question on the road. You were wondering if you could become numb to the sensation you feel."

Gwen faced him with glassy eyes. "I don't want to become numb to it, despite the pain it brings me. I just want to know how to live with the guilt. Wear it like a scar that reminds me of the pain instead of haunting me like a ghost."

"That's a good thing," said Mushi. "The fact you feel remorse means you have a kind heart, just like your father. The first person I killed was a thug who had a knife to Anden's throat. I never regretted taking his life to protect my friend, and I'd do it again a thousand times. In a way, I guess I have." Opening his hand, he stared into his palm. "The blood never does wash away, even for someone like me. I just choose to ignore it. Whenever you feel guilty about something, you usually ask for forgiveness from the person you wronged. The thing is, taking someone's life means you can never ask them for forgiveness. No matter how guilty you feel, they'll always be gone."

Gwen hugged her knees to her chest, burying her face between them.

"To live with the guilt, you'll need to come to terms with that and accept it. You may not be able to ask forgiveness from the rebel you killed, but you can forgive yourself. In my opinion, that's all you can do. Otherwise, it may haunt you until the end of your days, and you'll remain afraid to pick up a sword, even in self-defense."

Lifting her head, she rested it on her knees and pondered his words in silence.

"It's getting late," he said, rising to his feet. "I'll fetch us some dinner. You can continue meditating if you want or rest for the day." He strode off, leaving Gwen on the cliffside.

She watched the tide roll in along the shoreline as the sunlight painted a golden hue across the sky. Crossing her legs and straightening her back, Gwen closed her eyes. Breathed in. Held it. Exhaled. The face of the rebel soldier emerged within her mind with clouded eyes, an absent expression, and covered in blood. She remembered the sword trembling in her hands and her stomach turning itself over as she vomited on the cobblestone road. Then, she remembered the Militia soldier coming to her aid. The blood rushing down his nose from being pummeled on the ground as he thanked her for saving his life. Behind him stood the woman holding the sobbing young boy. Thanks to her actions, they lived. While the rebel's life might be lost, theirs would continue. She didn't want to become content with the act of killing, but recognized it to be necessary under certain circumstances. His blood would always stain her blade, but his face no longer reflected in its steel. Instead, she saw herself, calm and resilient.

15

The chill of the steel pressed against the back of Victoria's neck sent a shiver down her nape. "You're focusing too much on the power of every swing," said Kaylin, removing the blade from her neck. "It makes them linear and easy to read." After a round of sparring, Victoria was drenched in sweat, but not a drop could be found on her mentor's spotless white tank top.

Victoria huffed a breath of frustration. Trying to draw on the correct amount of power from within while fighting was like trying to look left and right at the same time. It was impossible, and splitting her focus made her movements in combat sloppy. Where once she actually forced a few beads of sweat on Kaylin's brow, now the Militia captain barely seemed winded. It was like being at square one again. Years of training down the drain. The disgruntled look on her face prompted a response from Kaylin.

"I told you this would be the hardest part of your training," she said. "You haven't lost all that progress you made. You just need to adapt."

Kaylin was right. With the years spent handling a sword, all those moves should be trained into the memory of her muscles. It should be like an instinct, requiring little thought. She didn't need to split her focus between fighting and drawing from the potential power within. Relying on her body's instincts, she could focus completely on trying to fill the bucket with the right amount of water from the well. Clutching her sword tightly and hardening her face with determination, Victoria beamed at Kaylin with a fierce, blue gaze. "Let's go one more bout. I want to try something."

Kaylin readied her blade and nodded, wearing a proud smile. "Bring it on."

With steel raised, they clashed once more. Victoria refrained from focusing on decisions of movements and strikes. Instead, she let her body feel the flow of the battle and trusted her instincts to maneuver her body. She moved like a dancer, having practiced the routine thousands of times over. Parry, riposte, feint, dodge. No thought, just action. Her mind drifted within herself where she imagined a well. At the bottom resided a reserve of water, and in her hands, a bucket. Lowering the container down, its weight grew heavy as it dipped into the liquid. *The right amount.* Victoria strained to pull the bucket out. At first, it seemed too heavy, but after breaking the surface of the water, she managed to hoist it back up. As the bucket ascended, so did a familiar warmth rise into her chest. Grabbing it with her hands, she allowed the water to flood her body as the warmth extended into her arms and legs. Feeling a sudden surge of strength, her focus returned to the duel with Kaylin. Pouncing forward, she lunged at the Militia captain with incredible speed. Kaylin raised her sword to block, and sparks ignited as their blades locked together. Victoria charged ahead, pressing the dull edge of her steel hard into Kaylin's, forcing her back. Her mentor's eyes widened with shock before shoving the princess off. Victoria felt the warmth fade from her body, but she was still able to move. She had done it. She drew on the right amount of power. Now, she only needed to do it again.

Too late.

Kaylin retorted with a lunge of her own. Victoria barely managed to dodge the thrust, batting the blade away, but the Militia captain responded with a quick flurry of slashes. Victoria's wrist twirled her sword into a deadly vortex, checking each of her mentor's strikes. Such a fierce exchange of blows required all of Victoria's focus. She couldn't afford to escape into the recess of her mind and picture the well and the bucket. More sparks erupted as Kaylin's strikes grew stronger, finally knocking the sword from Victoria's grasp. The princess rubbed her hand, throbbing with pain. Looking up at Kaylin, she noticed her chest heaving with heavier breaths, a singular bead of sweat falling down the side of her face, and a small strand of hair just out of place. Subtle differences, but that meant her mentor actually put effort into that brief exchange.

"Sorry about that," she said, dropping the blade to her side. "Got a little carried away. You really caught me off guard with that lunge of yours. I wasn't expecting you to be able to push me back as you did." She patted the princess on the head. "Seems you've already discovered the right amount of power to draw on."

"Maybe so, but it takes too long. I didn't even have a chance to try again once you were on me."

Kaylin pressed her forehead against Victoria's, her hazel eyes glistening with delight. "Trust me. You made a lot of progress just now. Be proud of it."

Victoria cracked a smile. "Alright. At least it got you a little serious."

Pulling her head back with a wink, Kaylin pinched her finger and thumb together, leaving the smallest space between them. "Just a little."

A few of the bushes rustled as Ben Green stepped through the foliage into the hidden alcove. An expression of twisted amusement stretched across his face upon seeing Victoria and Kaylin. His olive gaze studied the dull-edged blades in their grasps as he curled his lips into a mocking smirk. "Would you look at this? The heir presumptive playing soldier with none other than our most illustrious member of the Phoenix Militia."

Victoria scowled at him, taking a readied stance with her sword pointed forward. "I'm not playing."

"So, you intend on joining the Militia?" he teased. "Is your father aware of this ambition? I'm sure he wouldn't be very supportive."

"What the princess does with her spare time is none of your concern," said Kaylin. "You should leave."

His smirk was replaced with a toothy grin, beaming more amusement than before. "You're seriously training her?" He shook his head, spitting out a scornful chuckle. "I can't believe you'd waste your time with such a thing. Don't you have more important matters to attend to rather than teach a silly little princess how to awkwardly wield a sword?"

"Teaching the princess self-defense seems pretty important to me," said Kaylin.

Ben crossed his arms and tilted his head as if to look down on her. "Then how about a demonstration?" He stepped into the small clearing and faced Victoria. "Come, princess. Show me what you've managed to learn."

"Victoria, don't—"

Victoria didn't hear Kaylin speak. She already took off, charging toward the arrogant Militia captain. Her sword slashed to and fro, hitting only air as he effortlessly weaved around her strikes. Jabbing her sword in a vicious thrust, he caught the blade in a gloved hand and shoved it out of the princess' grasp and into her gut. With the wind forced out of her lungs, Victoria collapsed to the ground in pain. Ben Green leered at her from above.

"Pathetic," he spat. "Although, what else should I expect, having been taught by a hack?" He tossed the blade aside, which Kaylin stepped on as she marched toward him, anger burning in her eyes.

"Green, you've gone too far! That is the princess of the kingdom."

"I'm well aware, but I issued a challenge, and she accepted. Princess or not, you can't allow her to go through life without dealing with the consequences of her actions."

Climbing to her feet, Victoria managed to regain her breath. "You have no right calling Kaylin a hack," she shouted. "You and your men failed to retrieve my sister from Lundur. She would be right here with me if it wasn't for your failure. I've also heard that when coming face to face with the Hand of Death, you tucked your tail and ran. Kaylin wouldn't have just put up a fight, but probably beaten him if she was there."

She might not have struck him with a blade, but her words cut deep. Winds of fury gathered to unleash a storm upon her as his brow creased with a scowl and his lips thinned into a hard line. If Kaylin wasn't there, he would've no doubt struck her, but her mentor's presence didn't deter him from cracking the whip of his tongue.

"Listen well, you pompous little wench. It was Edward who called for a retreat at Danforth. I was fully prepared to fight and capture both the Hand of Death and the Burnt Coat, putting an end to these rumors leaving everyone's lips of the Gray Phoenix."

Victoria's ears perked up at the mention of the Gray Phoenix, remembering the conversation of the two nobles gossiping on the stairs. She wondered what significance that held for Ben to mention it.

He turned to Kaylin with a knowing look. "As for your claim about Captain Gunnway, I'd ask her how she happened to 'earn' her title as leader of the Militia's first division. It would no doubt open your eyes to the kind of fraud she is."

"That's enough." Kaylin grabbed Ben by the arm, but he immediately ripped it free.

"What's the matter?" he said, stepping closer toward her, their faces inches apart. "Afraid that the princess won't see you as the righteous angel you groomed her into believing you are? Think once she's crowned queen, she'll think it best to relieve you of your position after finding out the truth?"

"I won't be crowned queen," interjected Victoria. "Gwen is still out there, and she's the rightful heir to the throne."

Ben scoffed. "Grow up. Your sister is dead!"

A small smattering of blood splashed across the grass as Ben fell onto his back. He cupped a hand around his nose, crimson leaking through the cracks of his fingers. Kaylin stood over him, fist still extended from the punch she'd delivered. Ben rose to his feet, removing the hand from his nose. Blood spilled down his face, over his lips. Lunging forward, he socked Kaylin in the gut, causing her to bend over in pain, followed by an uppercut to her jaw. The blow didn't topple Kaylin, but left her staggering. Ben charged, tackling her through the foliage out into the main area of the gardens.

Victoria chased after them, pushing through the bushes. Reaching the other side, the two Militia captains continued hammering away at each other with their fists. The speed of their movements made them blurs. In some instances, Victoria thought she was seeing double, an afterimage of where they once stood, along with their real selves in their current position. At least what she thought was their current position. Her eyes seemed to be constantly lagging behind, never in the moment of what was taking place. While she struggled to see what was going on, she could certainly feel it. Every impact reverberated through the air around her, colliding with her body as if she, too, were being punched.

"Enough!" a voice boomed throughout the garden, causing their fight to cease.

Ben and Kaylin stood opposite each other, panting and drenched in sweat. The entirety of Ben's lower face was covered in blood from his nose, while Kaylin's left eye swelled with a nasty bruise. Blackwood marched toward them, anger hardening his face. He even frightened Victoria into paralysis.

"What is the meaning of this?" he demanded.

Kaylin relaxed from her fighting stance and swiftly bowed. "Forgive us, Chancellor. Captain Green and I just got carried away with a sparring match."

Ben spat out the blood trickling into his mouth. "You should consider finding a replacement, Blackwood, or else our first-division captain might disgrace her position more than she already has."

"You should both consider yourselves lucky I don't relieve you of your positions this instant," threatened Blackwood. "Acting in such a disgraceful manner and in front of the princess, no less. Is this what you think the kingdom needs in such trying times? Away with both of you."

Ben begrudgingly stalked off, leaving the gardens. Blackwood continued on his way, the heels of his shoes clacking loudly as he stomped through the courtyard of the gardens. Kaylin turned to Victoria, rubbing the area around her bruised eye.

"Sorry you had to see that," she said. "I shouldn't have lost my temper."

"You were awesome," replied Victoria in awe. "I didn't know you could move like that, and the way you smashed him in the face. If you ask me, I think he deserved much more than he got."

A rueful laugh escaped Kaylin's lips as she patted the princess on the head. "I agree, but you mustn't say anything about what just happened to anyone. Got it?"

Victoria nodded. "What did Ben mean when he said you 'earned' your title as first-division captain? Why did he call you a fraud?"

Kaylin sighed, more dejected than she was when Blackwood yelled at her. "What he's referring to happened years ago, back when I took the Exams."

"So? You told me you scored as the highest-ranking candidate that year."

"I wasn't the only one," said Kaylin. This caused Victoria's jaw to go slack. "That year, I technically tied with another candidate. From the words you traded with Ben, it seems you're familiar with him to some capacity."

"The Hand of Death?" gasped Victoria. "He served in the Militia?"

"For a time. I didn't really interact with him until the Exams, and our interaction reached its climax when the academy leaders decided to pit us against each other in a duel to decide who would officially be named the top candidate that year. Many other trainees and high-ranking officers gathered to watch the highly anticipated match. He was the best fighter I'd ever seen, wielding a sword as if it were a part of his own body. His technique was disciplined yet unconventional, making his movement unpredictable. We fought until exhaustion. I wasn't sure whether or not I could win."

"But you did," said Victoria. "Otherwise, you wouldn't have been named the top candidate."

"Yes… And no." Kaylin averted her gaze in shame. "While exhausted, neither of us seemed to back down. As I could feel my strength fading, I charged at him for one final clash, but before reaching him, he dropped his sword and raised his hands in surrender."

"He gave up? Just like that?"

"Just like that."

"But that doesn't make you a fraud. He conceded. You won."

Kaylin shook her head. "Not everyone looks at it that way. Some view it as a tainted victory. That he let me win." Her mentor's expression weighed heavy with shame. Victoria could see it in her eyes; it wasn't the criticism of others that ate at her. The only validation she sought to prove she was worthy of her position was her own.

Growing weary of the somber mood, Victoria tried to change the subject. "Speaking of the Hand of Death, I overheard some nobles whispering about the Gray Phoenix, saying it was some sort of cult that worshipped him. Ben mentioned it too when talking about his encounter at Danforth. Is it real, this Gray Phoenix?"

The lines in Kaylin's face sharpened as she turned to Victoria. "The Gray Phoenix is nothing but a rumor, so it should be treated as such. Forget you heard about it. Now, go clean yourself off. We're done for the day."

Kaylin marched off before Victoria could utter another word.

While she agreed that it was nothing more than a rumor, the fact that Ben Green had mentioned it, followed by Kaylin's curt response, only piqued her intrigue further. Ben made it sound like it was a rumor worth snuffing out. One that should never have seen the light of day. But why? Perhaps it had something to do with the people supposedly involved. The Hand of Death and the Burnt Coat were considered two of the most dangerous criminals on the continent. The thought of them working together, whether or not true, probably filled many with fear. It certainly did for her, especially in regard to her sister's safety. Ben was wrong to claim Gwen was dead. If they were to find her sister, he had to be.

16

Blackwood marched down the palace halls away from the gardens with anger seething from the marrow of his bones. No doubt Green prompted Gunnway to beat his face into a bloody pulp, but the first-division captain should know better. The suggestion of removing Peter from the throne made the political landscape throughout the continent a floor of thin ice to navigate, and fighting between Militia captains could cause that floor to crack or, worse, collapse completely. The kingdom needed to appear composed while deliberating a monumental decision. If people discovered they were tearing each other apart, everything would devolve into further chaos. Blackwood took a deep, calming breath as he smoothed out his hair. Order needed to be maintained.

Turning a corner, he collided with Natalie Parson, nearly

sending her to the floor. The red-haired devil stared at him with curious bewilderment. "Oh my," she gasped. "You're certainly wounded up. I haven't seen you so on edge since our little split."

Blackwood had not the time nor patience to endure a sadistic conversation at the expense of his dignity. "My apologies. I have somewhere urgent to be." He stepped to hurry past her, but Natalie cut him off.

"Off to devise more of your little schemes?" She folded her arms, pushing her supple breasts together as she leaned in closer in an attempt to make him uncomfortable. It worked as Blackwood stiffened his posture and diverted his gaze to the locks of scarlet hair at the top of her head. "You never could help yourself."

She was close enough for him to smell the perfume she often sprayed on her skin. The sweet smell of a spring morning when the flowers blossomed. At one time, he cherished the scent, but now, it wrinkled his nose in disgust, forcing him to take a step back. "A habit I regret to my dying day that influenced you."

"You've always known me to be an observant woman." She waltzed her fingers up Blackwood's arm, but he coiled away at her touch. "Smart play using the southern plains to delay Rahm's vote, but what do you hope to gain? You're only delaying the inevitable."

"Guinevere is the rightful heir to the crown and, until proven dead, must be found."

"The girl is long gone," said Natalie. "I know you care for the old man, but you must realize with or without his eldest daughter present, he is dying. He's no longer the leader he once was."

"That still makes him a better leader than any of us."

Her gaze darkened into a deep crimson. "When did you develop such blind loyalty for that foolish king?"

Blackwood responded with a dark glare of his own. "Around the same time you betrayed your loyalty to me."

Natalie shook her head in disappointment. "Then, take this as condolence for my betrayal. Whatever you're plotting, drop it. Rahm likes to scheme just as much as you, and the more you make him fight for this, the farther he'll make sure you fall."

"I doubt it'll be much more than I've already fallen," said Blackwood as he forced his way past the ambassador with a light brush of his shoulder. He didn't look back to see whether or not she glanced at him with contempt or continued on her way. He didn't really care, as a more pressing matter required his attention. One that didn't enjoy waiting.

Reaching his office, Blackwood opened the door to see Ambassador Slik Weyman seated in the chair across from his desk. The man absently picked at the grime beneath his nails, rings glistening on his fingers.

"Chancellor," he said. "I've been waiting for some time to answer your summons, and time is more valuable than coin."

Fixing his suit, Blackwood closed the door. "Pardon my delay.

More obstacles than usual barred my path."

Slik watched him take a seat behind his desk through slitted eyes. "I'll try not to hold it against you."

Blackwood scooted his chair closer, leaning a heavy elbow on the desk. "Then allow me to waste less of your time. I wish to discuss your stance on Rahm's vote to usurp Peter, leaving his youngest daughter, Victoria, to rule instead."

"You're worried if he usurps the king, he'll also aim to usurp you. Then he'll have a naïve girl as a puppet wearing the crown to pursue his machinations." A sly smile crept across his shallow cheeks. "You need me to help you stop that or slow it down, more like. With half the votes already seeming to be in his favor, all you can hope for is to stalemate. Buy time."

"Time is more valuable than coin," echoed Blackwood. "I need just enough to ensure Guinevere is found."

"How much are you willing to offer?" the ambassador asked.

Blackwood leaned back in his chair, folding his arms. He kept his expression hard as steel, not showing a crack in his demeanor. Peter might have given him sovereignty to distribute as much coin as necessary to ensure Slik's allegiance, but he didn't intend to let the ambassador bankrupt the crown. "Five hundred gold emblems."

"You can't be serious?"

"I will remind you that the crown is currently financing the reconstruction of Danforth."

The ambassador's face soured. "That may be helpful to Noreen, but it does me little good. You want my vote, you'll need to up the price."

"And if I don't?"

"Then I walk out your door along with my vote."

Blackwood pursed his lips. "And give it to Rahm for free? I thought you were an opportunist."

"Rahm will pay a hefty sum to have the deciding vote on his side," said Slik. "More than five hundred gold, that's for sure."

Blackwood stroked his goatee, eyes trained on the ambassador, unmoving. "Where do you suppose he'll get such coin? Apparently, you bled him dry at the last conclave. Sure, he could rely on the other ambassadors supporting him, but let's look at that list. Fletcher is a dear friend to him, but a righteous man with morals who won't sully his hands with such corruption as yours. Brookshire is expending the cost to burn half of her original division to ash as a counterattack against the rebels. Parson, well, her division seems to be taking on much of the refugees from Danforth. She hardly has the coin to burn. Also, you're not the only deciding vote. Noreen is up in the air as per usual, and I'm sure Rahm is gambling she'll side with him since Danforth was brought to ruin by Peter's inaction. That makes spending coin he doesn't have on you worthless. On the other hand, I value you at five hundred gold emblems."

Slik's smile curled into a foul grimace. Blackwood read his

bluff. The ambassador had most likely already talked to Rahm, hoping to guarantee his victory in the vote for a large pile of coin; however, Rahm had no coin to offer. At least for now, knowing Noreen could sway either way. Slik weighed his choice in silence, tugging at his collar in discomfort. Clearing his throat, he forced the words from his mouth, "Fine, but I want five hundred gold for every vote. If you do manage a stalemate, I'll need a retainer. Otherwise, you and Rahm will both be offering me nothing, and if there's no coin to be made here, I'd rather return to my estate."

"Fair enough," said Blackwood. "Five hundred for every vote going forward should the stalemate hold." Rising from their seats, the two men shook hands. "Should Rahm change his mind at any point and give you an offer, we can renegotiate your payment."

Like a disheveled child, the ambassador stalked out of Blackwood's office. Once the door closed, Blackwood collapsed into the chair and buried his face in his palms. He managed to gain Slik's vote and at a discounted price, no less. Three votes to Rahm's four. If they were to stall for more time, they needed to convince Noreen to join their side as well. There was little for him to do in that regard other than stay out of it. Mary Katherine would work her magic as she always did. If she managed to turn him into a half-decent man, perhaps it was possible to sway the young ambassador in the vote as well.

17

The boat undulated with the waves as Reed and Julius traveled along the Blade's Trench with the elderly fisherman. Every so often, one would smack into the hull and shower them with a spray of water. Seated at the bow of the ship, Julius took the brunt of the shower as his coat darkened with dampness along the back and shoulders. He kept his hands cupped around the bowl of his pipe, protecting the soft glow of the burning tobacco. Being the remainder of what he had to smoke, the man didn't intend to let it go to waste. Reed rested against the mast of the small ship, taking note of the tangled mess of netting lying nearby. It looked as worn as the fisherman and stiff in its form, making it unusable for netting any fish and a stark contrast to the pole, with a fresh line propped against the stern beside the fisherman as he manned the rudder.

"What kind of fisherman are you?" she asked. "You look well beyond your years for hauling in a decent catch with a net, if you even use one anymore. I doubt you can make a living from catching enough exclusively on that pole."

The fisherman smiled, pulling the wheat stem from his lips. "At one time, I made a living selling scores of freshly caught fish, but now I just catch them for myself as I travel up and down the Trench."

"How far have you traveled?" asked Julius. The smoke escaping his mouth drifted over to Reed, who waved it away.

"Let's see…" he said, scratching his cheek. "I've probably made my way from one end to the other about five times now."

"And all you do is fish?" said Reed.

"I stop at the ports here and there to talk to the locals, but for the most part, yeah. I sail and fish because I can. I have that freedom."

"Must be nice to live such a simple life," said Julius, exhaling another cloud of smoke that Reed again waved away.

"Could you be a little more aware of where you blow your smoke?" she said, glaring at him over her shoulder. "This man's freedom is only an illusion, anyway."

The fisherman hid behind the brim of his straw hat. "What makes you think it's an illusion?"

"You may choose to sail up and down the Blade's Trench as many times as you'd like, but only because those with power allow it. The Militia, or even pirates, could forbid you from sailing if they so choose by destroying your boat or taking you prisoner. Their invisible hand always looms over you, giving the illusion of freedom. When in reality, you are at their mercy."

The fisherman placed the wheat stem into his mouth, pensively sucking on it. "So, it's the mere presence of a higher power that enslaves us. That's what you're saying?"

"More or less," said Reed.

Another wave smacked into the hull, sending a spray of water across the deck and jerking the boat in a sudden manner. Both Reed and Julius braced themselves not to be tossed around. The fisherman remained still, unmoved by the motion of the water. He removed the straw hat from his head and unveiled the scar of a branded sigil on his forehead. The tissue formed a circle pierced by a singular line horizontally, almost similar in appearance to a third eye.

Julius rose from the bow and leaned against the mast on Reed's left side, squinting through the broken glass of his spectacles. "That mark. You were a slave."

"Many years ago, yes. As a young man, I was captured by bandits and sold into slavery, mining coal and other minerals on the archipelago islands. Eventually, I was moved to the mainland to construct a series of railways for the kingdom, interconnecting major cities for faster transport."

"My uncle mentioned those to me," said Reed. "They never finished due to the rebellion's efforts constantly sabotaging the construction sites."

The fisherman nodded, tracing the circle with a finger. "Slaves working on the islands do not receive a mark. If they escape, there is nowhere to go and no regular people to hide amongst. Only slaves moved to the mainland were branded, so they could be found in the event of an escape. Back then, everyone recognized this mark and wouldn't hesitate to call on the Militia upon spotting it. Only the rebellion offered any sort of solace for us. They freed me from my bonds working on the railways and offered refuge. Richard Skokna was even among the group that freed me."

"You met my—" Reed stopped herself. "You met Richard Skokna?"

"Met him and also served with him," said the fisherman. "Richard was a true revolutionary, an inspiration. The charisma and leadership he showed rallied many people to join him in his cause against the injustice and corruption sweeping the continent under Lucius' rule, including myself." A soft smile crept across the man's wrinkled lips as she shook his head. "Those were the days. Back when the rebellion held true to its values and stood for something."

Reed scowled. "Doesn't it still?"

The fisherman placed his straw hat back over his head, concealing the mark and casting a mask of shadow over his face. "The rebellion's ideals died along with Richard. When his brother, Boris, took his place, its purpose became more focused on vengeance. You see, Boris loved his brother, and when the kingdom had him assassinated, he swore revenge at any cost. He constructed that infernal creed of his, and that's when I knew the rebellion wasn't worth fighting for anymore."

"But Boris expanded the rebellion," said Julius. "He recruited nobles, engineers, and former politicians. Through his efforts, he allowed them to contest with the kingdom and Phoenix Militia. A feat many considered impossible."

"The same people who allowed the kingdom to become corrupt, you mean," spat the fisherman. "And they corrupted the rebellion as well. What happened at Danforth proves my point. Richard would never risk an attack if it possibly involved hurting civilians. His aim was to strike the kingdom and the Militia, and that's what he did. Now, the rebellion will level an entire city just to prove a point."

"The rebellion is fighting a war," said Reed. She could feel the rage boiling in her blood, listening to the fisherman's words. "A war to release the people from the kingdom's grasp and obtain the power to rule over themselves. Give them a chance at true freedom."

The fisherman erupted into a fit of laughter. "True freedom? I'll tell you what. King Peter has done more for the people of the continent than the rebellion since Richard's death. Because of him, people like me no longer have to fear others seeing the mark on my forehead. He even offered them peace and opportunity at this true freedom you speak of, and what did the rebellion do? They betrayed that trust, burned a city to the ground, and ruined the lives of hundreds who now have to live as refugees."

Reed thought about the massive number of people she rode with into Laminfell. Women, children, men, and elders—all distraught and unsure of what would become of their lives going forward. The despair tugged at her heart as she watched those who stayed at Danforth pick up the shattered remains left in the wake of the rebellion's destruction. She remembered Samuel burning the bodies of his family, unable to move on.

"There are always casualties in war." Reed didn't even think about the words. They escaped her mouth of their own free will. A defense of their actions. Her actions.

The fisherman's lips soured. "Sounds like words straight from Boris' mouth. Content with nothing but bloodshed until he felt satisfied that his brother's death had been avenged." He spat the wheat stem out of his mouth and into the breeze, where it landed on the surface of the river, traveling downstream. "The binds we place on ourselves restrict our freedom more than any other person could. Those were the words Richard Skokna shared with me when I told him the mark on my head could never let me be truly free. He was right. I allowed this mark to continue defining me as a slave until I wrapped a red headband over it and fought as a rebel against my oppressors, and now I wear a hat as a humble, old fisherman traveling along the river. You claim my freedom is an illusion. That someone could destroy my boat or take me prisoner, but I can always find another boat, and while my body may be imprisoned, my soul will always reside here on these waters. I found my freedom. It seems to me, you have yet to find yours."

Julius took a drag from his pipe, returning to his seat at the bow. "A compelling little speech, but I think I'll find my freedom within a nice cottage on the beach and enough coin for a comfortable life."

Reed peered over the side of the boat into the water. Her reflection was distorted by the ripples. Growing up, her uncle taught her it was her father's will to destroy the kingdom and the royal bloodline, establishing a new government ruled by the people. He never told her it was him that created the creed she often recited before bed, dreaming of one day spilling the king's blood just as they had done to her father. His anger became hers. It was what bound her to lead the rebellion, despite never meeting Richard. All she knew came from the memories of brief mentions shared by her mother and what Boris had told her of him, which now seemed mostly fabricated, according to the fisherman. Being elderly, he could be misguided by age and faulty memories, but he proved to be right about the transformation of the rebellion itself. Hurting the innocent civilians they claimed to be fighting for was a misstep down the wrong path. An act of injustice brought about by a corrupt ideal. The Red Rebellion had become the very thing they swore to destroy.

18

Why did you run away? Victoria's voice cried out to her. *Why did you abandon the palace? Abandon me?*

Her father soon followed. *How can you be respected as a queen if you run away? Your name will join Harrod the Coward's in the history books. Is that how you want to be remembered? Answer me, Gwen. Gwen!*

"Gwen." Mushi's calm voice snapped her back to the beach. This time, clouds filled the sky, blocking the sun from her view. "You alright?"

She sighed, collapsing flat onto the shore. Grains of sand shifted around and stuck to her clothes and hair. "I keep hearing voices every time I meditate. It keeps me from focusing."

Mushi reclined back, nestling his arms into the sand. "Whose voice?"

Gwen sat up and crossed her legs. "It's nothing. Just another obstacle to overcome."

"Gwen, avoiding the obstacle is not the same as overcoming it. Remember what I said about talking through things?"

Her shoulders fell limp as she hung her head in shame. "It's my father and sister, mostly. They keep yelling and berating me for leaving the palace."

The Hand of Death pursed his lips. "So, you feel guilty for running away?"

"I didn't run away," Gwen snapped. Her glare was as sharp and jagged as the cliffside she climbed every morning. "I left on a journey to learn about the continent, its people, and cultures. If I'm going to be their queen, I need to understand them."

"How long did you expect your journey to take?" he asked. "By itself, traveling the continent would take a considerable amount of time, but to understand each region's customs means spending more time amongst them. Some could argue a lifetime."

Gwen stared at the vastness of the sea, watching the endless series of waves roll in.

"You need to be honest with yourself. Sure, things may have changed when you realized the dangers you were in, but originally, you never intended to return to the palace, did you?"

"Of course I did," she said with a harsh edge to her words. "It's my duty to become queen."

"Duty." He spat out the word in a dismissive manner, lacking any conviction. A hollow shell devoid of any meaning as he uttered it. "At one time, it was my duty to stand by and watch as the Militia prepared to execute a trusted comrade, a friend. Fuck duty. It doesn't bind us to anything. If it did, you wouldn't have left in the first place."

Gwen felt a flash of irritation. "Tell me, then. Why did I leave?"

"For the same reason you enlisted Anden, Wesley, and Damian into helping you return to the capital. Fear. It just turned out the fear of what awaited you out here, beyond those walls, overtook your fear of the throne. Nothing more than a scared little princess."

She shot to her feet, anger flooding her veins. Sand flew through the air with some spattering across Mushi's body. "And you're just a vagabond who's killed hundreds of people on some wild goose chase for these cloaked freaks that, according to you, the rest of the continent doesn't know exist. Yet, they pose an existential threat. If you don't believe in duty, then what drives you to pursue such a senseless endeavor?"

His expression remained apathetic, unfazed by her anger or the sand kicked up in his face. Standing, he stared at her with the hint of darkness she sensed when first looking into his eyes. "The conviction of believing it's the right thing to do. Before I became a vagabond, as you so aptly described, I was a friend of your father's. He always talked about you. Said you not only had the mind but the heart of a strong leader the kingdom needed. Having now met, I can see he was right. You have a sharp mind, a kind heart, and you're a quick learner; however, you lack the proper conviction. When things get tough, you cower and run. A half-assed sense of duty won't compel you to become a strong leader—hell, not even a strong person. You need to have the conviction to face the world believing in yourself and your choices, no matter what they may be."

Gwen's spark of anger flickered out as she stood on the shore like a scolded child, speechless.

"That's enough for today," said Mushi. "It's your turn to prepare dinner. I'll be waiting outside the hideout." Pushing past her, he made his way toward the pathway in the cliff.

Dejected, she ambled toward a boulder where three makeshift fishing poles rested. Picking them up, she cast their lines into the water and stabbed them into the sand, standing them upright. Now, all she could do was wait. As a beautiful gradient filled the sky, painting the clouds a myriad of warm colors, she was disappointed for them to block the glowing orb's descension beyond the watery horizon. She could not lie on her stomach to quickly rise and watch the sun set twice. It would've sweetened the sour taste left in the wake of her and Mushi's argument. She curled up on the beach as the tide rolled in, desperate to reach her toes. His words lingered over her. She needed to be honest with herself. Shame and guilt gripped tight around her heart, forcing a hand on her chest. The amount of pain her father had to be enduring all because she ran away without a word or reason. The pressure she forced onto her younger sister, who had to take up the mantle as queen in her stead. The weight of a kingdom and its people. It was her responsibility to bear, and she ran away in fear. The breeze brushed Gwen's hair over her face, hiding the tears creeping down her cheek.

"I'm sorry," she whispered into the night. "It was selfish of me to leave as I did, but I was scared. Scared I'd never live up to the expectations you had for me. Scared that I'd fail as a queen, as a daughter, as a sister. I didn't want to fail our family."

She wished her words of confession could be carried across the continent to her father and Victoria, but they were only met with the crashing tide. If it was conviction she lacked, she would need to find it washed up along the shore. Wiping her eyes dry, Gwen noticed the lines were taut and giving a bend to the poles. She reeled in her catch and trekked up the winding path in the cliffside. Mushi awaited her, sitting next to a fire that burned with fierce flames. Impaling the fish with sticks, they each hovered over the lashing tongues of heat. Gwen stared at the meal with guilt.

"You were right about me being afraid," she said. "I guess I lashed out because I didn't want to face the truth. I'm sorry."

"Don't sweat it." His face glowed in the light of the fire. "Just understand the only reason I responded harshly is that only facing the truth head-on will allow you to unlock the power of nin-nir."

Gwen forced a smile. "Back on the beach, you said you were friends with my father. How did you meet?"

"When I did serve the kingdom, my work required me to report to your father directly," he explained. "His eyes always shined with a certain excitement when speaking about you or your sister." His dark eyes glowed with the reflection of the fire as he stared at her. "You shouldn't feel guilty. He's proud of you. Always has been."

"Do you agree with him? Do you think I can be the strong leader the kingdom needs?"

He looked up at the stars twinkling in the night sky through the gaps in the clouds. "I think you have the potential to be more than that. With proper conviction, I think you could be the light that pierces through the darkness surrounding the continent. A beacon for the people just like the Lucius Ambulate preaches the First Emperor to be."

Gwen wasn't sure about all that, but appreciated his kind words. Pulling a fish from the fire, she cracked it open with her fingers and ate the white meat inside. "I'll try not to let you down."

At the conclusion of their meal, Mushi doused the flames as they retired for the night. Gwen, however, did not immediately fall asleep. Instead, she crossed her legs, straightened her back, and closed her eyes to meditate.

"I may have run away before, but no longer," she whispered to herself. "When I return home, I'll set things right and be the queen you thought I could be. I will be the light that pierces the darkness."

Inhaling deeply, a warmth ignited her gut. It was weak, but with every breath, it grew stronger. The heat numbed her body and melted her skin into the floor. The sensation kept growing, radiating with more heat until it finally exploded. A rush of energy surged from Gwen's core throughout her body. Fire raced through her veins to the tips of her fingers and toes, making them tingle. Opening her eyes, a bright yellow orb obstructed her vision for a brief moment before disappearing. Her head grew light, and the room started to spin as her vision blurred into darkness.

19

The plate of half-eaten food filled Victoria's heart with sorrow as she took it from her father's lap and placed it on a nearby table. He hardly ate a full meal anymore, leaving him a husk of his former self. Gone was the strong leader and king she knew her father to be, replaced by a frail old man. He raked the crumbs out of the scraggly silver beard that covered his bony chest.

"I'm glad you were able to keep me company over dinner," he said. "I hate not seeing you as much lately."

"It's alright," she replied. "I know you've been busy." With the conclave taking place, there wasn't a moment where either Blackwood, Mary Katherine, or Lawson weren't visiting him. In the rare times none of them were present, he slept.

The wrinkles around his cheeks deepened with a smile. "Thank

Helmond for me. Despite the increased number of mouths to feed, he still maintains a pristine quality."

"I will," said Victoria, forcing a smile. She climbed into the bed beside him, holding his brittle hand. "Father, I was wondering if I could ask you about something. Curious whispers throughout the palace halls among different people."

A thin finger caressed her cheek. She turned to see her father's gaze glowing in the faint candlelight of the room. "What is it, Victoria? What whispers have you heard?"

Victoria nervously laughed. "I feel like a silly little girl asking about this, but the thought can't leave my mind. A while back, I overheard some nobles talking about the Hand of Death appearing in Danforth, and they mentioned something about a Gray Phoenix, believing it to be some sort of cult. I didn't think much of it because it sounded ridiculous, but more recently, Captain Green mentioned the term as well. He said if he had captured the Hand of Death, then the rumors of the Gray Phoenix would never have surfaced." The more she spoke, the grimmer her father's expression became. "It's more than a rumor. The Gray Phoenix is real."

Her father licked his lips and sucked at his gums in prolonged thought before clearing his throat. "Yes, but it's not what you have heard it to be."

"What is the Gray Phoenix, father?"

His grip tightened around her hand. "I hoped such a thing

would be forgotten in the years to come, but it seems that's not the case. At least I can offer you the whole truth, but you must promise me not to tell anyone of this." His blue orbs glowed with an intense stare as he mustered what little strength he had in his voice. "Promise me, Victoria."

"I promise."

His hand relaxed. Sinking into the pillows, he gazed up at the ceiling. "For some time, it has been evident the number of fleshlings and bolgias stalking about the continent has increased over the past few years, if not decades, to an unprecedented degree. Where they once only ventured just beyond the entrance to the Demon's Cavity and down the Forked Tongue to Kelveux, they've now spread throughout most of the continent in large hordes never before thought possible. Reports seemed to come in every week of them killing herds of cattle or even residents of small villages. We realized something needed to be done."

The air grew cold, biting into Victoria's bones. Talk of the demonic creatures spawned an ominous presence that loomed over them. Memories of her mother's death flashed through her head. The twisted, rotting corpses silhouetted against the flames of their destroyed carriage as the creatures tore flesh from bone. Pools of blood nourished the soil and sullied her dress. Soulless, black sockets stared at her with ravenous hunger. She thought those nightmares had long been forgotten, but they merely hibernated in the recesses of her mind.

"Isn't that why the Hunters' Core exists?" she asked. "To kill these creatures?"

"The Core does hunt and kill them for a price, but their efforts do little in dwindling the creatures' numbers. Through text offered by the Lucius Ambulate and other historical documents, we discovered no mention of the monsters existing until the fall of Harrod the Tyrant, when Edward usurped him. It was years later, following the conflict, that the first sighting was documented on the far outskirts of Kelveux. We determined it meant they were either in hiding for hundreds of years—perhaps since the Great Calamity—or something brought them here. Either way, we found it important to determine these vile creatures' origins in the hope of also finding a way to be rid of them for good. So, we assembled a secret task force. One we named the Gray Phoenix."

Victoria was in awe of what she heard. A secret task force assembled to hunt down the origins of the monsters plaguing the kingdom. Somehow, the idea of it being a cult seemed more believable. "And the Hand of Death was a member of this task force?"

Her father nodded. "As was the Burnt Coat. There were four members in total. All skilled warriors, weaponizing different proficiencies in search of the dark spawns' origins. With the war raging, we kept their existence a secret from the public so as not to spur further fear or superstition. It was the right decision, given some of the things they found." Her father shuttered beneath the covers. "The atrocities they uncovered not only from the monsters but from misguided individuals hoping to further their understanding of the creatures as well were vile sins against mankind. They uncovered a darkness we never knew existed and wished it never did. At times, I fear fighting that darkness for so long finally caused one of them to snap."

"The Burnt Coat," said Victoria. "You're referring to when he killed his own men."

"No man ever leaves the abyss unchanged. Unfortunately for him, it seemed to drive him insane. He claimed voices in his head tried to influence him and that his own men attacked him first, but there was no proof. So, he was to be executed; however, the other members went rogue and helped him escape before disappearing. We scrambled to keep their identities a secret, not wanting people to lose faith in the kingdom for allowing a group of dangerous individuals to go rogue and possibly join the rebels. The Burnt Coat was the only one made a public criminal, having been a former Militia captain. The others were given bounties released only to the underground. We figured mercenaries from various guilds would be able to hunt them down for a fair price, but one of them mounted a hefty sum by leaving a wake of corpses in his path."

"The Hand of Death," breathed Victoria. Her father gave a slow blink in acknowledgment. "Since those two were spotted in Danforth, rumors are surfacing, spawning from the fear that they might return."

"Whether or not they plan to return is pure speculation." Her father leaned closer, his voice stern. "Although, you should understand this. The tales and fables you've heard or read about regarding witches, necromancers, dark magic, and twisted, immoral rituals are real. Unlike the Core, these men were not hunting monsters. They hunted the ones who made them."

A cold sweat moistened Victoria's hands, turning them clammy. The thought of Gwen being rumored to even be in the same city as these people spooked her.

"I did not tell you or Gwen about this because I did not want to instill such fear in you," he said. "I also did not think it would be a problem for you to bear, but I may be wrong in the coming days."

Victoria noticed his face darken with sorrow. "What is it, father?"

"I'd rather not speak of it, but it is a reality nonetheless." She felt her heart sink as he continued to speak. "I don't know what else you have heard, but some of the ambassadors think I am unfit to rule over the kingdom. A vote will soon be held to determine whether I should be relieved of the crown. If that is to happen with your sister absent, you will take her place as heir and rule as queen."

Shock stabbed Victoria through the heart, and fury shot her off the bed. "They can't! You can't! Making me queen is like giving up on Gwen. It's like saying she's dead."

"I know," he said, "but we're working to make sure that doesn't happen—"

"I won't stand for it. I won't go through with it. I won't accept becoming queen."

"Victoria." A bit of strength hardened her father's voice. "If Parliament decides it, you won't have a choice. That is the reality."

Tears filled her vision, causing her eyes to become glassy. Her worst fear was coming true. People were starting to give up on Gwen, even their father.

"It might be your reality, but not mine. We will find Gwen. We will!"

Without another word, she stormed out of her father's chambers and escaped into the palace halls. She could hear her father's weak voice calling after her, but she ignored it. She marched down the hall in a blinding rage. Her march turned into a sprint, wiping her eyes dry. No more weeping. She needed to be strong. Even if everyone else gave up on Gwen, she wouldn't. Her sister was still out there somewhere on the continent. She had to be, and Victoria wouldn't rest until her sister was found.

20

Embers fluttered through the air like lightning bugs in a desolate wasteland of fear and chaos. The terrified screams of people running for their lives were overcome by the thunders of cannon fire and gunshots. Noreen's lungs burned, and her legs ached from the long descent from her office in the guildhall to the front gate. The soldiers urged her to keep moving toward the underground bunkers, but the ambassador was petrified with shock. Seeing Danforth burn filled her soul with despair, but she could not pull herself away from looking at the destruction. The hellish glow of the flames rose high into the blackened sky. The silhouette of a massive flying fortress penetrated the clouds of smoke, heading straight toward them. One of the soldiers screamed at Noreen. The muscles in his neck strained, and his veins bulged with effort, but she did not hear him over the eruption of the cannons overhead. Flashes of light followed by rain dipped in fire tore into the stone of the guildhall and shook the ground beneath them with a vengeful tremor. Noreen's body found the will to move again, and she sprinted away from the collapsing building. Debris fell all around her as a large chunk slammed into a soldier's skull and shattered it into a bloody mess of brains. Some of it splattered onto her clothes. In a state of panic, she tried to wipe it off and tripped over herself, falling face-first into the ground. The other soldiers kept running, fearing for their safety as more debris continued to fall. The rest of the guildhall crumbled, hurdling toward the ambassador. She crawled to her feet to reach safety, but it was a vain effort. The speed of the stonework falling was greater than her legs could muster. Aware of the inevitable, she closed her eyes, hoping it would be quick.

A sudden force slammed into her, but it was not from above. Rather it came from the side, propelling her at an angle with such speed, the wind loosened her hair from the intricate braided bun it was woven into. Opening her eyes, she no longer found herself near the base of the towering guildhall. Instead, she lay on the cobblestone of the southern road, a safe distance from its ruins. Standing over her was a strange man wrapped in a ragged quilt and wearing a cone-shaped hat made from straw. Stepping past her, he marched down the road as if nothing had happened.

Coughing up some of the dust from the collapsing stone, she forced out the words, "Thank you."

The stranger paused for a moment, glancing over his shoulder. "You don't need to thank me. I'm just doing my best to keep the promise I made." Beneath the brim of the hat, Noreen could make out the faint details of a face she had not seen for years. The outline of his slightly crooked nose, the harshness of his brow, and subtle lines that spread across his cheeks from forcing a smile throughout most of his life.

She uttered the name in a whisper, "Mushi."

Noreen awoke in a fit of panic. Heavy breaths heaved her chest and shoulders. Her neck glistened with sweat. Yet another nightmare. She wiped a hand over her weary face, lying back down on her bed. Turning on her side, she stared at the oval mirror at the far end of the room, melancholy plain on her face. She wished that nightmare was only a dream, but it, in fact, served as a memory haunting her subconscious. Out of everything she witnessed that night, Mushi remained the constant focus of her dreams. The boy her family shared their table with for meals, who teased her incessantly. The man who was to serve as her protector when she became an ambassador, but ended up a criminal instead. They called him the Hand of Death for slaughtering hundreds in cold blood. So, why? Why was it that he saved her? It had to be more than some silly promise he had made when they were foolish teenagers. Years had passed, and so much had happened. None of it made any sense, and that was what bothered her so much.

A sudden knock at the door peeled Noreen away from the

reflective glass. She hastily wrapped her messy blonde hair into a bun and tossed a robe over her nightgown. Opening the door, she was surprised to see Mary Katherine standing at the threshold.

"Pardon the intrusion at such an hour," she said. "I hope I'm not interrupting anything."

"No, ambassador," Noreen replied. "I actually was just having some trouble sleeping."

"As was I. There seems to be a never-ending list of things to lose sleep over. Do you mind if I come in?" Noreen gestured for her to enter. She strolled into the room wearing a shawl over her nightgown and hair tied in a ponytail hanging over one shoulder. "Perhaps a bit of conversation will ease both our minds."

"Of course," said Noreen, closing the door. She suspiciously eyed the ambassador crossing the room toward the bed. Noreen kept a distance, opting to sit in the chair near her vanity. It wasn't a sleepless night that brought Mary Katherine to her chambers. No bags darkened the underside of her eyelids, nor did she seem drowsy in any way. She had planned this.

Mary Katherine studied the bed before giving a sideways glance. "It's nightmares, isn't it? Haunting your dreams every time you close your eyes." She no doubt noticed the sweat staining Noreen's sheets and wetting her face.

"You speak as if you're familiar with the ailment," said Noreen.

"Only through observation. Believe it or not, the chancellor suffered nightmares following Vargo's assassination attempt. He shared the same look in his eyes that you have now. The want of sleep, but afraid of what awaits you on the other side."

Noreen guarded herself by crossing her arms and legs. "If it were my choice, I'd be on a farm tending to the horses. Instead, I'm greeted by a city engulfed in fire and the drum of cannons raining down from above."

"I can only imagine," said the ambassador. Her attention turned to the book resting on Noreen's nightstand. "Have you received any word from Captain Quinn about the efforts to rebuild?"

"Most of the injured soldiers have recovered, but many of the citizens have abandoned the city. The buildings may be rebuilt, but it'll be years, maybe a decade, before Danforth thrives as it did before."

"It won't be the only one to face such challenges. Other cities in history have gone through rebirths following large-scale disasters. Papuri after the last eruption of the Crescent Mount as well as Illios when the original city crumbled to ruin due to massive landslides." Picking up one of the books, her eyes skimmed over the cover. "But it seems you've already been reading up on such history. You've always been an avid reader, even as a young girl."

Noreen wondered in what direction Mary Katherine was trying to steer the conversation. "Knowledge is important in our line of work. The more we understand the mistakes of our past, the less likely we are to repeat them."

A smile tugged at the corner of the ambassador's lips. "A lesson I'm sure you passed onto Gwen during your shared time in the palace library. She also developed a knack for reading."

That was her angle. An appeal to empathy using the missing princess and their shared history. "Her interests aligned more with adventure. A curiosity with the wonders to be found on the continent than its history."

"But curiosity can cause us to expand our knowledge into realms we initially did not expect," Mary Katherine countered. "Gwen's learned more about the continent's history than you might give her credit for."

"And what of her sister? Where do her interests lie?"

Mary Katherine took a deep breath. "Victoria is a brash young woman born with her father's warrior spirit. She seems more interested in swords and combat than books and politics."

"More of a Militia captain than a budding ambassador."

"A fine way of putting it."

Noreen narrowed her sky-blue eyes, adding a subtle sharpness to her words. "Is that why you've come to my chambers at this late an hour? You want me to believe the king's youngest daughter will prove inadequate to rule because she's too militaristic?"

Instead of appearing shocked or offended, the ambassador's face grew sullen with disappointment. "No. You misunderstand my portrayal of the princess. She's no tyrant in the making but rather easily manipulated through political ploys."

"Manipulated by Rahm, you mean."

"Yes." A hint of desperation tainted Mary Katherine's voice, but she did not try to hide it. "Something I do not wish to see happen."

"I doubt Blackwood would allow such a thing."

The ambassador's glossy gaze turned harsh with a glare. "You're young, but not naïve. If Rahm usurps Peter, Blackwood won't be far behind. That opens a path for him to become chancellor and do as he pleases, provided he maintains a majority in Parliament."

"And what do you hope to gain from stalemating him?" asked Noreen. "The king could die tomorrow, and all this effort would prove meaningless."

"It gives us time to find Gwen. She's the proper heir and more suitable to handle politics than Victoria. Peter will continue to cling to life as long as the possibility of returning Gwen home remains. Of that, I'm certain."

Noreen sat in prolonged silence. Finding Gwen would ease her heart, but was it worth keeping a dying old man on the throne whose fragile hands could barely keep the kingdom aloft? As a father, the king had a right to worry about his daughter's safety, but Parliament still had a duty to uphold order throughout Argust.

"You want Gwen to be found, don't you?" Mary Katherine continued. "From what I've heard, you two became close friends during your time together."

"I do consider Gwen a friend," Noreen admitted, "but I can't act solely on personal desires. It's our duty to think of what's best for the kingdom."

Mary Katherine's expression hardened with determination. "I think finding Gwen is what's best for the kingdom, and I'll leave it at that. I can't force you to vote with us. It's your decision to make." The ambassador shuffled over to the door.

Noreen's voice brought her to a halt. "Out of the cities you mentioned struck by disaster, you forgot one. The only one to never rebuild. Takata."

Mary Katherine lingered by the door with a sympathetic gaze. "Danforth will not end up like Takata."

"I know," said Noreen, "but Papuri and Illios were struck by natural disasters. Danforth's case is more akin to Takata's than any other. Destroyed by the evil in men's hearts."

"What are you presuming, ambassador?"

"Only that twice in the history of the modern kingdom have entire settlements been wiped out. Both during King Peter's reign. Rahm might be right to usurp him."

"Do not think of me like Blackwood. I'm not asking you to help us for Peter's sake. I'm asking you for Gwen's." Stepping through the threshold, the door closed behind Mary Katherine with a gentle *thud*. In the silence of the chambers, it resounded off the walls like the rumbling of thunder.

Noreen remained in the chair, her arms and legs still crossed in a guarded fashion. Her fingernails dug into her skin as she clutched her arm in frustration. Why could things never just be black and white? They were always gray, the answers murky as mud. Her heart wanted Gwen to be found, but her mind found the concept illogical. She was gone, and the king was dying. That meant Victoria would most likely be crowned, so why stall the inevitable? She turned around to look back at her reflection again. She knew why a pang of hope pricked her heart. It was the same reason Mushi rescued her from the collapsing guildhall. Like him, she had made a promise and wished to uphold it, even if it was illogical.

21

Atop the basilica, away from the poor, famine, death, and despair, Illios looked as divine as a holy city should. The sea of buildings with their columns and towers shined as a beacon for those who felt lost or misguided. The countless statues of historical and religious figures served as inspiration for others to find purpose in their lives. Damian looked at the statues of the Seven Saints lining the rooftop beside him: Edmond Dracon, Michael Satner, Boris Gutùenr, Titus Eliethaénr, Alexander Qlytho, Nero Authirna, and Cain Bezok. All of them great men and greater warriors. Through their efforts and their king's, they shaped the foundations of the modern kingdom. Damian respected their legend, hoping to leave a mark on history just as they had. He somewhat accomplished his goal, but his mark was more like a stain. They called him the Burnt Coat for his treachery, and history would only remember him as a monster. Rolling up his sleeve, he stared at the tattoo of a sword across his forearm, reminding him of the oath he took as a member of the Core and the failures as a Militia captain he hoped to rectify in due time. His gaze returned to the city skyline, for it seemed he was not the only one to fall from grace. Anden's theory of someone within the Ambulate being the culprit behind the murders seemed quite plausible. Not only were they exclusively keeping children locked away within the halls of the basilica, but the residue of incense he found in the alley also pointed in the direction of a pundit being the culprit.

All throughout the night, Damian loomed overhead, keeping a keen eye out for any suspicious activity. While many of the pundits slept, a few patrolled the perimeter wielding lanterns to ward off the darkness. It didn't take long for Damian to learn their patterns and tendencies while on watch. One of them even snuck away for a few hours with another hooded figure possessing a slender frame. An affair of sorts, breaking the vow of chastity all pundits were supposed to make upon their initiation. Not that he cared if they kept their vows or not, but the man's absence did create an opening in the basilica's security. One most likely used to sneak the victims out of the basilica, living or dead.

As dawn bloomed over the horizon, the pundit eventually returned to his post, trying his best to appear as if he hadn't left for a second. With nightfall fading, Damian's watch ended on an uneventful night. He climbed down from his perch and dropped into a narrow side street where no one was watching.

"Takes some vigor to scale such a structure," said a familiar voice. Damian turned around to see Arios leaning on his staff. "How's your side doing?"

Damian opened his jacket and lifted his shirt, revealing the scar of a healed wound without a trace of infection. "Never felt better. Thank you again for your help."

"It's my pleasure," said the elder. "And how goes your little investigation?"

"Still in its infancy," Damian replied. He marched down the street, heading back toward the lower city as Arios hobbled behind him.

"Did you find an answer to the question you posed to me the other night?" he asked.

"You mean how the Ambulate is keeping the children locked up in the basilica like livestock? Frankly, I'm not sure why you couldn't just tell me that in the first place."

"It's one thing to be told the Ambulate is caring for the children and another to see it for yourself. I'm sure you caught a glimpse of Leopold's exploits with Miss Fuller standing guard atop the basilica all night."

Damian glanced over his shoulder. "So, you're aware of that?"

"The whole basilica is aware of it. I can't tell you the number of thrashings he's received from Visconti himself for breaking his vows and leaving his post, but it seems more blood pumps through one head than the other."

"Why doesn't Visconti simply remove him from his duties?"

"The Lucius Ambulate may still possess a powerful presence over the continent, but its influence is fading. With the rise of engineers and their creations, many people's fascination with the past dwindles as they turn their curiosity to the future. Visconti's aversion toward this change doesn't help. Sure, many are willing to follow the teachings of the Ambulate, but fewer are willing to uphold them and study the ancient texts. Leopold may break his vow of chastity, but he's a good lad who does as he's told and is willing to do what most are not these days. Visconti may be a traditionalist, but he's not a fool either. He needs all the pundits he can get."

They descended a broad, stone stairway leading to the lower city. Damian slowed his pace as the elder struggled to climb down the stairs. More light filled the sky, causing the buildings and statues to cast long shadows, blanketing them in darkness. "I had no idea the Ambulate was headed toward such a state of decline."

"At times, I wonder when that decline began," said Arios. He was slow to descend the stairway as his staff hit the next step before shuffling his feet down. "It's easy to point to recent events, but in my opinion, I think the catalyst for the Ambulate's downfall was when people started to view it as a form of faith."

Damian stopped, turning to face the elder. "What do you mean?"

Arios groaned as he slid his hands down the length of his staff, lowering himself onto one of the steps as a seat. "It's quite a discussion, so I hope you don't mind if I take a while to explain. Little to nothing is known of the time before the Great Calamity. It's been described as a cataclysmic disaster that shook the ground with unyielding anger and erupted in a torrent of fire and brimstone. A veil of smoke blanketed the sky so thick and dark, not even the faintest light could pierce through as ashes showered the continent like snowflakes of death. Floating remnants of the shattered mainland waded in the roaring sea. Civilizations fell, reverting to ages before when people only sought survival. Knowledge of the time prior faded into obscurity as various tribes and kingdoms sprouted, hoping to emulate the once mighty empire. It wasn't until Kronos the Conqueror united them all under one rule again that the Lucius Ambulate was formed in that time of peace."

"I knew the Ambulate was old, but I didn't know it was that old," said Damian.

"That's because it wasn't the Lucius Ambulate you're familiar with. The founders were not even men of faith. They were scholars with a singular interest: the ancient text. The only surviving remnants of the age before the Great Calamity, our link to a past long forgotten. Even with years, decades, and centuries of study, we've only managed loose interpretations that grant us insight into the legends we know today as the First Emperor and the original empire he ruled over. However, this knowledge became a power used to sway people into adopting certain beliefs based on these loose interpretations and transformed the Lucius Ambulate from an academy of scholars into the house of faith many have become familiar with. That's where the Lucius Ambulate's descent began. When its primary focus ceased being the true understanding of the ancient text and instead became obsessing over the interpretations handed down over the centuries."

Damian lifted the hood of his jacket over his head as the sun continued to creep upwards over the city. "An interesting tale, but I don't see what that has to do with the children or murders taking place."

"My point is that the Lucius Ambulate journeys down a stray path," said Arios, climbing back to his feet. "I'm sure you've already put together that someone within the Ambulate might be responsible for the murders. Why else would you feel the need to keep such a sharp eye on the place?"

"If all the victims have been children," said Damian, "and the Ambulate keeps them held in the basilica, then yeah, I'd say I'm pretty sure."

"Your suspicion is well founded, I assure you."

Damian glared at him with his cold gray eyes. "You seem to know quite a bit, old man."

The elder's eyes glowed with an intense stare from beneath the shroud of his hood. "That's because I know Visconti. He's a man of self-preservation. A man who seeks to be revered for years to come after his passing as loren and has no wishes to see the Ambulate fall while his hands still clutch onto it. I do not know who is behind the murders, but do not be surprised at how deep the rabbit hole may go."

22

In the past month or so since arriving on the coast, Gwen grew accustomed to the taste of sand thanks to her daily sparring sessions with Mushi. This was the first time in a while, however, since she received a mouthful during her strength training carrying the rocks. She hadn't even made it to the largest one yet, and her body gave out. Her arms and legs went limp, and she was unable to pick herself up. She lay in the sand like a washed-up fish baking in the scorching sun. She didn't understand what had gone wrong. Waking up this morning, she felt right as rain and made the climb down the cliff in record time. Mushi couldn't contain his surprise as she narrowly kept up with his pace. The endless days had finally paid off, or so it seemed.

Mushi hurried over, picking Gwen up and resting her against the large rock she'd dropped. "What's wrong?"

"I don't know," she said. Gwen willed her body to move, but not a single muscle flinched. She felt drained, exhausted. "I was feeling fine a moment ago, and now it's like my body has shut down."

He measured her with an intense gaze. "Rest for the time being until your strength returns."

Slightly irritated, she rested against the rock. The inability to move caused her to focus on the small details. The bumpy surface of the rock digging into her skin. The heat from the sand warming her hands. The breeze caressing her face. The sun glowed in the sky above, cooking her in its intense heat. Beads of sweat raced down from her armpit to her hips. She wanted to wipe it away but couldn't. Mushi sat atop the rock, not saying a word. He only stared at her as if trying to peer into her very soul. Minutes passed, and she regained the ability to close her palm. Then lift her arms. Slowly, enough strength returned that she could stand.

"Feeling better?" Mushi asked, hopping off the rock.

Gwen bounced on the balls of her feet, threw a jab, then a kick. The fatigue she felt waned. "Yeah, I think I'm good to go." She bent down to pick up the rock again, but Mushi stopped her.

"Actually, I want you to try that one." He gestured to the large boulder displacing the sand a few paces away. It was the largest of the rocks Mushi had assembled.

"There's no way," said Gwen. "I fell flat on my face trying to carry this one. That one will crush me."

"Just give it a try."

From the smug look on his face, she knew he wouldn't let her off the hook. Gwen approached the boulder, stretching out her arms and legs. It was too wide to carry in its current position, so she squatted down and lifted one end off the ground. It was easier than she expected as she stood the structure upright. It towered over her by a few feet and cast a long shadow along the shore. Wrapping her arms around it in a hug, Gwen took a deep breath and summoned all her strength. Her muscles tensed as she strained. The boulder didn't budge at first, but after a few moments, she freed it from the sand. Her mouth hung open in awe as she managed to balance it on her shoulder.

"That rock weighs about five hundred and fifty kilos," said Mushi with a smile.

"This is incredible," said Gwen. "Is this the result of the power you spoke of? Nin-nir?"

"It seems like it. Now go ahead and drop it."

Gwen set the boulder back down on the beach with a massive *thud*. Once her muscles relaxed, she grew lightheaded and lost strength in her legs. Swaying with the ocean breeze, she fell again, but Mushi was there to catch her this time. Her body went entirely limp as he gently laid her on the sand.

"What happened?" she asked in a daze of confusion. "I feel exhausted again."

Distress lingered on Mushi's face as he tugged at his beard.

"This is very strange. Usually, when the connection is forged, one must actively draw from it, like casting a bucket down a well. It's a natural safeguard because utilizing too much power can strain the body, making it weak, and even kill someone if they're not careful. You seem to lack this safeguard, subconsciously drawing from it like a broken faucet." The distress turned into a brief moment of fear, then resolve. "This can be very dangerous, Gwen. You need to learn how to regulate the flow of power through your body, or else performing the simplest of tasks will cause you to go catatonic."

"Has this ever happened to anyone else?"

"You're the first, as far as I'm aware," he said. "Have you regained enough strength to stand?"

Gwen rotated her shoulder and wiggled her legs. "I think so, if you don't mind helping me up." He grabbed her hand and pulled her to her feet. Wobbling a bit, she leaned on him for support as he guided her toward the formation of large rocks near the cave. "So, how can you teach me to regulate it if this has never happened before?"

Mushi fished out a small device from his trousers. "From now on, I want you to use this when we spar." Holding it up, he pushed on a trigger, and a flame sparked to life. "The lever controls the amount of fluid feeding the flame. Your goal is to keep it lit while fighting. Press too lightly…" With a sharp flick of his wrist, the flame was snuffed out. "And the flame will extinguish. Press too hard…" He pressed down hard on the trigger with his thumb, and a column of fire exploded out of the device, nearly tearing her from his shoulder. "And you'll get burned. It's imperative you learn to focus on the amount of power you're drawing on and limit it when physically straining yourself. Otherwise, you'll constantly drain your body of its strength. Possibly to the point of dying if pushed too far."

Reaching the rock formations, Gwen was able to stand on her own. Mushi handed her the device. She placed her thumb on the trigger and lit the flame. Unlike his other methods, this exercise was more than a simple challenge. From the seriousness of his voice and the intensity of his gaze, Gwen understood the severity of the consequences if she were to fail. If one of the cloaked figures attacked her and she fought back only for her body to give out and go limp, it would mean certain death. Facing him, she took a battle-ready stance, keeping the flame steady. "Ready when you are."

For the rest of the day, they sparred. Keeping the flame properly lit while also focusing on a fight proved challenging. It either dashed away in a thin trail of smoke from dodging Mushi's strikes or exploded into a fireball during an intense moment. They took breaks more often than usual, as she tired frequently, but Gwen pressed forward until the sky darkened. They watched the sun set twice before heading back to camp, where Mushi prepared dinner. Managing to capture two rabbits, he roasted them on a spit. Gwen joined him by the fire, staring at the base of his neck.

"What's that thing dangling around your neck?" she asked.

"What do you mean?"

"I could see something dangling there today while sparring. What is it?"

"Oh," he said, reaching into his tunic. "You mean this?" He unveiled an object wrapped around a string as a necklace. The firelight shimmered off its metal surface. Gwen squinted her eyes to see it was a plain silver ring. "It's a keepsake. A promise I made with myself."

"Is it meant for someone special?" She found herself leaning in close for an answer.

"You could say that." Tucking it back into his tunic, he didn't add anything more and let the sounds of the crackling flames fill the air.

Gwen couldn't help it. Her curiosity bubbled to the surface. "So, who is she?"

"Didn't your father teach you it's rude to be nosey?"

"Come on," she said. "You can't dangle something like that in front of me and not expect me to be curious. A ring must mean you have a special lady in your life."

Mushi stared into the fire, watching the embers dance as they floated toward the sky. "Her name was Catherine. Cathy, for short. She possessed the beauty of a noble but the mouth of a girl raised in the country." He chuckled softly. "She was a fiery one. Could put anyone in their place with just her words." His face held a warm glow that captivated Gwen, bringing a smile to her lips as well.

"Where is she now?"

The warmth faded from his face, turning cold. "She's dead. Has been for a while."

"I'm sorry." Gwen's heart ached seeing the pain in his eyes. It was as if she'd reopened an old scar. One that festered, making him ill. "How did she die?"

Mushi continued to stare into the fire, rotating the hunk of meat cooking overhead. "I'd rather not talk about it."

Gwen respected his wishes, not pushing the matter any further.

"What about you?" he asked in an uplifting tone, seeking to change the subject. "Anyone special in your life? Romantically, that is."

"Not really." Being stuck in the palace never provided her with many opportunities to pursue romantic interests. At least not ones she was actually interested in. The only men outside her family or Parliament she ever spent time with were sons of wealthy nobles. They weren't the pick of the litter either. While a good number of them were handsome, the absurd size of their ego and poor attitude to those around them quickly deflated any sense of attraction.

"You still have plenty of time," said Mushi, snatching one of the rabbits from the spit and tearing into it. "A woman of your beauty and status won't be short on suitors. I'm sure you'll find the right one, eventually."

"I hope so." She grabbed the other rabbit and tore into the

tender meat as well. "I don't know what would be more shameful, running away from the throne or having the royal bloodline come to an end with me?"

"You've still got your sister to rely on in that regard."

"Emperor bless the man who ends up with her. You thought Catherine was feisty, but I'm sure Victoria could give her a run for her money."

"Now that's something to see," he said with a chuckle.

The two of them shared a laugh in each other's company, as they did every night. Beside an open flame and stuffing their faces until their guts were full.

23

Perusing the shelves of the palace library was like glimpsing into the past for Noreen, each book containing a different memory. A wealth of knowledge at her disposal. Lessons of their past to learn from and hopefully never repeat, but that seldom ever happened. Finding the appropriate gaps, she slid the borrowed books back into their place. Mary Katherine was sharp to recognize their contents through the titles alone. Having faced disaster before, Noreen did seek answers from the cities of Papuri and Illios. First, with the volcanic eruption of the Crescent Mount in 614, and then the mass wasting in 832. Unfortunately, neither account offered specific information regarding the cities' reconstruction. It only mentioned years of struggle and strife before reclaiming the glory they held before falling to ruin. Not the most uplifting of outlooks. As for Takata, no official records existed, forcing her to rely on rumors and stories the young Mushi shared with her as children. Not that it mattered. She sought guidance on how her city could crawl out from the pit of destruction, and Takata remained there to this day.

Navigating the labyrinth of shelves, Noreen ran a finger along the endless rows of embroidered spines. With everything going on and her indecision on how she would vote at the next conclave meeting, she needed an escape, a distraction. That need made her wander from the vast section of historical literature into the realm of folklore and fiction. The place where Gwen's interest in reading originated. Noreen usually had no interest in such tales, as they were nothing but fantasies containing no substantial knowledge useful for her practices. Now, she yearned for a bit of escapism. It was a strange feeling. Scanning the lines of tomes, she had no clue where to start. History had a set start, whereas fiction possessed countless beginnings. One of the books caught her eye. Images depicting the four elements of nature decorated the spine. Pulling it off the shelf, the mural of a man standing in a forest with his arms outstretched, surrounded by a swirling vortex of water, fire, air, and earth, splashed across the front cover in a grand, artistic display. Printed in silver lettering read the title, *The Ballad of Purah the Enlightened.*

Noreen cocked a curious eyebrow at the title. Purah was not a figure of fiction but a famed disciple of Cain Bezok, member of the Sanction of Saints and founder of Danforth. It wouldn't be the first time a fictitious legend was crafted from the deeds of a historical figure. How much was fictionalized intrigued her. Thumbing through a few pages, Noreen quickly realized the story served as a metaphorical journey of enlightenment, mentioning mythical creatures and powers of magic. Nothing historical in the slightest, but that was exactly what she needed. Placing the book under her arm, she strutted to the shelves' end, where the room opened up into a study with tables and chairs. Seated at one of the tables was a young woman scribbling on a large piece of parchment with a thick tome beside her. The slouched position and hand pressed against her forehead reminded Noreen of Gwen slogging through dense literature all those years ago when they first met. Curious, she glanced over the woman's shoulder, who was too absorbed to notice her presence. The large stretch of parchment was a map with scribbles drawn across the continent in strange patterns. Looking at the text, Noreen recognized why the young woman struggled.

"Schusterman was a brilliant navigator but a terrible writer," she said. "Always made things a bit too wordy and difficult to decipher."

The young woman spun around, shutting the book and folding the map in a flustered manner. Noreen was shocked to see the freckled face of Princess Victoria Clougher. The woman's shocked expression relaxed as recognition sank in. "Sorry, Ambassador Archer. You scared me."

"My apologies," said Noreen. "I shouldn't have snuck up on you like that. I just… I couldn't help myself. You looked so much like your sister when she had trouble slogging through a few of these books."

"You're right to say it's hard to decipher," she said. "There's so much information. Too many numbers and charts, and it all has to be so precise."

Noreen unfolded the map, giving it another scan. Both Danforth and Lundur were clearly marked, and from them stemmed numerous hand-drawn lines branching in various directions. "And what's spurred this interest in navigation?"

The princess' head wilted with embarrassment, her face hidden behind the strings of dirty blonde hair. "I'm trying to find Gwen."

Noreen measured her with a sympathetic gaze, sliding into a nearby chair. "How so?"

Victoria pulled the map closer and placed a finger on the first location. "Gwen was spotted in Lundur the following morning after her disappearance. More than a week later was the attack on Danforth, which some rumors say she was present during." Noreen had heard similar rumors, but there was little evidence to support them other than hearsay from a couple of soldiers—and people's memories of a life-threatening event can be hazy with fear and adrenaline. "The reports from Lundur say that whoever kidnapped Gwen escaped somewhere south. If we assume it took them about a day's journey to travel from

Alastair to Lundur, that distance could be used to measure the average length of travel each day. Using Danforth as a second reference point, I've been trying to triangulate where they went, but—" She bit her lip in frustration.

"There are too many unknown variables," Noreen finished for her. "It's clever but inaccurate. Using your little method, they could've gone to Sandur, White Horn, Kelveux, and anywhere in between. Besides, even if we assumed the rumors were true about your sister being in Danforth, we can't say for sure they returned to the same location afterward when we don't even know why they would be there, to begin with."

"But it's at least something," said Victoria. "It's a starting point with what little we do know and could lead to further clues." Squeezing her hands into fists, she pressed the knuckles into her temples. "We need to find her. I don't want to take Gwen's place as queen."

Noreen was unsure how to respond. Her fingers nervously clutched the leather binding of the book under her arm. "Your sister wasn't too keen on the prospect of becoming queen one day either," she said. "When I first met her, the stress from the mere thought of it nearly brought her to tears. She felt intimidated by the responsibility, believing it impossible for her to bear such a weight. I told her she didn't need to bear that weight alone. I made a promise that when she did become queen, I would follow by becoming chancellor, and we would take on the responsibility of ruling the kingdom together."

"I know," said Victoria. Her hand relaxed, falling into her lap. "She always said you were smart, confident, and that as long as you were by her side, she had nothing to fear."

Noreen's chest tightened with grief. Following her election as ambassador, Noreen's interactions with Gwen dwindled. She had her own division of the kingdom to tend to, and even when she visited the palace, her time was limited due to conclave meetings. Eventually, she became conflicted. A part of her wanted to uphold her promise, but another part faced reality. Gwen would become queen—that was certain—but Noreen becoming chancellor was never a guarantee. Although, after all these years, Gwen still fully believed in the promise she'd made.

"That promise also extends to you," Noreen said. "If you do take your sister's place as queen, I'll help you carry the burden of ruling as well."

"It won't happen." The words were harsh, leaving the princess' lips. "I won't become queen. Not at Gwen's expense."

"I understand how you feel, but you can't ignore the reality of the situation. Even if you don't want to, you won't have a choice—"

Victoria shot out of her chair, shoving the tome and map off the table. "Why do people keep saying that? I should have a choice, and I choose to find my sister." The princess stalked off, leaving Noreen to clean up the mess.

The ambassador didn't stop her, not even with a word. Instead, she picked the tome up from the floor along with the map and placed them back on the table. She couldn't blame her for feeling angry. Her sister was missing, her father was dying, and with his death, she would become the ruler of Argust. A position people envy for the power, but never the responsibility. Looking over the map once more, Noreen studied the various lines of the young woman's attempts to triangulate Gwen's possible position. The method might have been faulty, but the princess' heart was set on finding her sister. Fine. Noreen planned to keep her original promise as well as a new one. She would help make sure Gwen was found—for Victoria's sake.

24

Another hot and muggy day caused Anden's clothes to stick to his skin with sweat. It was unbearable, but he'd rather be outside with a hint of a breeze than crammed in some room with people sweating as much as him. It also would seem less suspicious for him to remain at the inn all day and not keep up his appearance as a lowly sellsword to the Ambulate's spies watching him. They thought they were clever and stealthy, but Anden could identify them by the subtleties of their movement and behavior. The calculated effort to remain close for observation but not too close to cause suspicion. The casual demeanor they presented wandering through the crowded streets while keeping a constant eye on him. There were three in total. One positioned himself across the street and watched the front door of their inn as he came and went. Another watched from above on the balcony of a building in the upper city, attempting to peer into their room. Because of this, they never opened the curtains. The third usually followed him in the streets anytime he went out. As Anden tucked himself into a shady alley gambling on a game of liar's dice, the spy sat in the street peddling for coin like other dozens of refugees struggling to get by.

"You in or not?" one of the players asked, sporting a thick coat of dirt on his face.

The other two players already anted up as well. Anden tossed five copper coins into the center of their circle. The winnings were slim, but he couldn't ask for much from this lot. Scooping each of their dice into their respective cups, they all gave a good shake before slamming them face down. The goal of the game was to guess the right number of dice between all of them. If you thought the player before you guessed wrong, you called them a liar, and if you were right, you won. Lifting up his cup, Anden peeked at the dice. A pair of ones, pair of twos, and one three. Not a great set, but he'd been dealt worse.

The first bid went to the wiry man to Anden's left. Rat Tail was what most called him because of the long, slender ponytail slithering down his back. That was the story anyway, but Anden assumed it was mostly due to the overbite causing his front teeth to poke through his lips. "Three fours," he said. A safe bid to open the game.

The second bid was Anden's to give. "Four twos." It wasn't a stretch to think another pair of twos existed between his three opponents.

The next bid went to the stout, childlike man in overalls to Anden's right, named Wilfred. He chewed his bottom lip while taking another peek beneath his cup. "I'll be going with four fours."

The last player to bid in the rotation was a gangly-looking man with dark, sunken eyes seated across from Anden. His face was thin with concave cheeks, as if he hadn't eaten for days. Like Damian, he was hard to read as his gaze fixated on Anden, never taking a second look at his dice. "Four sixes."

Rat Tail's foot bounced as he mulled over his decision. Tapping a finger on the side of his cup, he said, "Five sixes."

Anden took a swig from his flask as they all turned to him again. Taking another look at his dice, he tried to hide his disappointment behind a stoic expression. Not a single six in his set. To up the bid, he either needed to increase the number of sixes or that of another number. No one else jumped onto his bet with his twos, and neither ones nor threes had been mentioned. Sixes was the right call, but how many existed on the board? He could take a chance at calling Rat Tail a liar, but the gangly man's confidence in his bid convinced Anden he had sixes stacked.

"Six sixes," he said with confidence.

Wilfred chewed on his lip again as he studied the dice. "Liar," he said, pointing a finger at Anden.

With the accusation made, all of them lifted their cups. Anden glanced around the circle and counted all the dice. Wilfred had one six, the gangly man had three, and Rat Tail had one. A total of five sixes indeed made Anden a liar and the loser of this round. Unfortunate, but that was the way of the game. Giddy with himself, Wilfred chuckled as he raked in his and Anden's coins.

Having given the spy enough of a show to watch, Anden tipped his hat to the men. "That was an entertaining game, but it seems my pockets are empty. I should be on my way." Rising to his feet, a firm hand clasped onto his shoulder, forcing him back to the ground. A bearded man in rags stood behind him, blocking his path out of the alley.

"I'm afraid we can't let you leave just yet," said the gangly man. His sunken eyes gazed at Anden, full of greed. "There's still more coin to collect from you." Rat Tail brandished a rusty dagger, and Wilfred slid a pair of brass knuckles onto his thick fingers.

Anden raised his hands in surrender, hoping to calm the situation. "Shaking me down won't produce any more coin. I'm all dried out, and that I can promise you is not a lie."

"We're more interested in the price on your head," squeaked Rat Tail, waving the dagger around.

A sly smirk pulled at Anden's lips. "Well, it's certainly been a while since I've experienced this. I'm curious, though. How much is the bounty now?"

"Five hundred gold," answered Wilfred with merriment.

"Shut it, you big oaf," said the gangly man. He turned his thin face to Anden, scowling. "As for you, don't think of pulling any tricks, or else we'll break every bone in your body."

"Five hundred?" Anden shook his head. "That doesn't sound right. Nor does the threat of breaking my bones. Usually, they just want to kill me."

"Quit your mumbling and come with us peacefully. I'd prefer to deliver you to the Bone Blades in one pretty package."

"Oh," chuckled Anden, "that makes a bit more sense."

"What does?" asked the gangly man.

"The reason for my bounty being so low. I guess my old one doesn't get around as much as it used to. Although, trying to bring me in alive is a foolish mistake, one that does you no favors."

Grabbing the bearded man's arm still resting on his shoulder, Anden flipped him over on top of the gangly man. Their bodies collided, slamming into the ground, piled onto each other. Rat Tail and Wilfred lunged at Anden. Catching Wilfred's fist, he used the stout man's arm as a shield from Rat Tail's knife. The rusted blade penetrated Wilfred's flesh, causing a splash of blood to shoot out and paint Rat Tail red. With a kick to the groin, Anden sent him crumbling to his knees, followed by a swift knee to his face to knock him out cold. Wilfred yanked the dagger free from his arm, slashing away at Anden. Blood splattered off the blade onto the alley wall as Anden weaved around the man's wide swaths. Stepping toward him, Anden caught his wrist and twisted it, forcing the dagger free. Shoving a sandaled foot into Wilfred's face, he tugged at his beefy arm and, with a sharp crack, dislocated it at the shoulder. The stout man collapsed in a fit of pain, wailing with childlike innocence as blood continued to leak out of his arm.

Meanwhile, the gangly man and his bearded compatriot disentangled themselves, climbing back to their feet. They cornered him against the wall with light gleaming from the steel of their swords. Anden regretted not bringing his own weapon as he prepared to fight them off with his bare fists. The roar of a gunshot thundered down the alley as the bearded man's brains erupted out the side of his head. Another gunshot, and the gangly man dropped his sword, falling as a pool of blood began to form from the wound in his leg. People gawked at the scene from the streets as Wesley waved the barrel of his pistol at them.

"Go on now," he said. "Nothing to see. Just some crooked gamblers being delivered for the Emperor's judgment."

Anden greeted him with an unamused expression. "I could've handled it."

"I'm sure, but we're supposed to have each other's back." Wesley's gaze shifted toward the man on the ground clutching his leg and breathing heavily. "If you have any questions, I'd ask them before he goes into shock."

Anden lowered himself to the man's eye level, slapping him across the face to gain his attention. "Alright, shit stain. Where did you hear about this bounty from the Bone Blades?”

The man shook his head. “I don't know. It was months ago. You just matched the description. A beggar-looking man with a silly hat and constantly drinking from a flask.”

“That certainly sounds like you,” said Wesley.

“They're calling you the Drunken Warrior. Want you brought in alive to make an example to anyone who crosses the—” The word stuck in the man's throat as his skin turned pale and breathing more rapid. His pupils dilated into saucers, lost in the eternal stare of imminent death.

Wesley watched as he succumbed to the symptoms of his wound. “And there's the shock. So, what did you do to catch the Bone Blades' attention?”

Anden rose to his feet, stepping over the man and fishing out the copper coins he'd lost from Wilfred's pockets. “Beat up a couple of their men outside a tavern. When Gwen gets back, you should have her explain more of the details.”

Wesley chuckled with a wide grin. “That must've been the trouble she talked about back at Sandur. Still, we've already got enough on our hands with hunting this killer and not raising Visconti's suspicions. Perhaps you should try lying low like Damian for a while.”

Anden ripped the bucket hat from his head and stuffed it into his trouser pocket. “They recognized me because of my hat and flask. As long as I don't wear it and limit my drinking, it should be fine.”

Wesley raised a speculative brow. "We'll see, I guess."

Anden felt naked, wandering the streets without his hat. Typically, it served as a shield from everyone's gaze, but now his face laid bare for all to see. He could even feel the hovering presence of the spy looming behind them several paces. To his credit, the man tried his best to blend in with the crowd, but Anden memorized his gait. A bit stiff in the shoulders with his back straight as an arrow. The walk of a disciplined man. He had definitely witnessed the little skirmish having just taken place, but Anden was confident nothing would come of it. Lowlifes killing other lowlifes for coin—that was how he'd report it to Visconti. Anden felt something hit his shoulder. A soft peck like the hit of a raindrop. Looking over, he noticed a strange fluid stained his tunic.

"What the hell?" he said in bewilderment.

"Must be an unlucky package from a passing bird," said Wesley with an amused expression.

Anden glared at the sky, hoping to catch a glimpse of the fowl that shat on his shoulder. Instead, he was surprised to see the face of a young boy peering from an arching overpass in the upper city. In his hand was a dipper of sorts, dripping with the same strange fluid. Anden glanced over his shoulder to see the spy still following them; however, he didn't seem aware of the boy.

"I need your help losing our tail," he whispered.

"What's going on?"

"Can't really say for sure. Just trust me."

Nodding, Wesley slowed his pace and distanced himself from Anden. Nearing the spy, he turned around to walk in the opposite direction and hit the man in the shoulder hard enough to knock him to the ground. "My apologies," said Wesley.

Anden took off running. Weaving through the crowd, he sprinted through the lower city, putting as much distance and bodies between him and the sight of the spy. Turning multiple corners, he ensured to make his path hectic enough to track, but not so much that he himself got lost. Hiding behind one of the brick foundation walls, Anden glanced around the surrounding area. Moments passed, and the spy was nowhere to be seen. Satisfied, he climbed to the upper city and found the overpass where he spotted the boy.

"Over here," he heard from a nearby stable. In one of the empty stalls, the kid waved him over. Approaching, Anden recognized him as the kid who knocked over the candelabras in the basilica's sanctum.

"The high priest was right," he said. "You really do wander into places you shouldn't."

Bags darkened the underside of the boy's eyes as if he hadn't slept in days. The clothes he wore sagged from his boney frame. From his height, Anden estimated him to be about ten years of age. He nervously rubbed one hand over the other as he spoke. "You're one of the men arguing with the head pundit, right?"

Anden lowered himself to seem less imposing, balancing on

the balls of his feet. "I guess you could say that. What are you doing outside the basilica?"

His eyes scanned their surroundings, making sure no one else was around. "I was hoping you could help me. I don't want to disappear like the others."

"Disappear? You mean the murders?"

"Maybe," said the boy. "I don't know. The pundits take some of us away, and they are never seen again. They disappear."

"How many would you say have disappeared?" asked Anden. "Five?"

The boy shook his head. "More."

Anden's eyes widened as his body froze with shock. The corpse collector said five bodies had been found fitting similar descriptions. Was the Ambulate hiding even more? "The pundit that takes some of you away, is it the same one every time?"

"Sometimes it's Master Theo. Sometimes it's Master Leopold…"

If it was more than one pundit taking them away, then it meant the Lucius Ambulate as a whole might somehow be involved. Did the influence of these cloaked bastards really go so deep? As the kid continued rambling, something on his arm caught Anden's eye. A scar of sorts.

"What's that on your arm?" Anden asked.

The boy looked at the scar before showing it to him. Across his forearm was a series of numbers branded into his skin. 111933. "We were given these when we arrived," he explained. "Said it was easier to identify us."

Studying the numbers unsettled Anden. Something strange was going on, stranger than murder. He released the boy's arm. "You should head back to the basilica, kid. It's dangerous for you to wander the city alone."

"You'll help us, though, right?" Desperation croaked out the boy's throat. "You'll make sure we won't disappear anymore?"

Anden's gaze drifted to the hay scattered across the ground. "I can't make any promises, but we'll try our best. Now, get out of here."

The boy scurried out of the barn as Anden took out his flask. Having been outside in the heat for most of the day, the liquor was distastefully warm. He would have spat it out, but his desire for a buzz forced him to gulp it down. It seemed they might be in deeper shit than originally expected.

25

The day of the Carnival neared as boats filled the port and lined the shore of Bushgrove containing massive amounts of cargo in heaps of barrels and boxes requiring lifts to unload. The groans of the vessels bobbing in the water hardly masked the shouting of sailors aboard their decks and the distant chatter of crowds gathering in the town. The fisherman's boat was a dwarf amongst giants as they weaved through the endless fleet, struggling to find a place to make port.

"There's a strip on the other side of town too narrow for larger ships," said the fisherman. "Might be able to let you off there."

"Never have been to one of the festivals here," Julius said. "Seems like quite an event."

The fisherman nodded. "With the tragedy at Danforth and Militia troops marching along the southern plains, I'm sure many people seek a distraction."

He navigated the boat into an alcove where smaller ships huddled together and guided it into shallow waters for Reed and Julius to jump out.

"Thank you for offering us your boat for travel," said Reed. "It's very much appreciated."

"Enjoy the Carnival." The fisherman grabbed a long shaft of wood and pushed himself back into deeper waters, sailing off into the estuaries.

"What now, commander?" asked Julius.

Reed pulled the scarf over her face, trekking through the water and up a hill toward the busy town. "We try to secure some horses for traveling back to base. There was another outpost set up here, right? Running a similar operation to yours?"

"Lieutenant David Locke," said Julius, nearly tripping down the hill. His wet boots slipped on the soft soil, almost forcing him to climb on all fours. "Based at the Leaky Canteen."

"Let's hope he didn't also make a foolish deal with pirates."

The town of Bushgrove bustled with all sorts of people preparing for the Carnival. People stood atop ladders hanging strings of lanterns over the pathways of the streets, banners were lowered over the crusted walls of the various mud houses, and all kinds of vendors hurried to set up their shops and claim the best spots for potential traffic during the festival. Reed glanced about at the waves of people flooding the streets and considered it a blessing. With Militia soldiers most likely present, they should be able to sneak through town without drawing any attention. Amid the crowd were traveling merchants looking to make a profit from any tourist needing customary items for the celebration. One of the merchants was a spry individual, bouncing from person to person, spouting incessant compliments to charm them into buying any one of the assortments of masks dangling from the hulking pouch on his back. Like a frog crossing a pond of lily pads, he hopped his way in front of Reed.

"Aha," he said. "Even though you mask your face, I can tell from those brilliant green eyes that you are a woman of immaculate beauty." His personality was as vibrant as the bandanna wrapped around his head, and his voice reached a pitch as high as the jingle of his massive earrings. "I can provide you a mask that will lure any potential suitor with seductive mystery. They will be pining to catch a glimpse beneath it."

"Not interested," said Reed, disregarding him with a wave of her hand.

"Would you happen to be selling any tobacco?" asked Julius.

"No," said the merchant. "Only masks." He stepped in front of Reed, cutting her off. "Are you sure you wouldn't be interested in at least taking a look at my selection? I may already have one in mind for you." He pulled out a mask in the shape of a fox's muzzle. "Those eyes of yours strike a fierce gaze like that of the fox. Both crafty and predatory. A perfect match."

A hand clamped down on the merchant's shoulder. Behind him stood a man and woman in dirtied clothes as if they had traveled a far distance. The man towered over the merchant, while the woman was just shorter than Reed. Both possessed oily dark hair, fierce chestnut eyes, and plump noses. Siblings, by the looks of it.

"The lady said she's not interested," said the man, bending over so his lips hovered next to the merchant's ear. "We've been watching you bounce from one customer to the next, but I don't think you've paid the proper fee to sell goods here for the Carnival."

The merchant's face contorted in confusion. "Fee? I've sold masks here for years and have never had to pay a fee."

"Then you're lucky we won't charge interest," said the woman. "This is Harpies territory, so you better produce some coin, or we'll make sure you never set foot in this town again."

"Leave the merchant be," said Reed. "He may be a bit eccentric in his sales pitch, but I doubt the effort of roughing him up is hardly worth the coin."

The man and woman fell silent before riveting their gaze on the red scarf covering her face and studying the rest of her attire. They also glanced over at Julius, noting the red handkerchief protruding from his jacket pocket. The man stepped forward, and she let him grab her arm. "You shouldn't be so careless in showing your colors," he whispered. "Militia are purging us like a plague 'round these parts of the continent."

"So, you're actually with the rebellion," said Reed. "That makes things easier." Like a snake baring its fangs, Reed's hand shot to the handle of her daggers as she pressed the point of the blade into the man's abdomen. "Flinch wrong, and I'll puncture your liver like a skin of wine."

The woman reached for the dagger strapped to her thigh, but Julius stopped her by unveiling the pistol concealed in the sleeve of his jacket. "Not so fast there, missy."

Reed turned to the merchant watching everything unfold with wide eyes. "Go on," she said with a nod. Not wasting any time, the merchant took off down the road, his masks clacking together as he disappeared amid the crowd. Reed returned her fierce gaze to the man standing completely paralyzed. She removed the scarf covering her face. "You know who I am?"

The man nodded, mouth agape in awe. "You're Reed Skokna. Uh, I mean Commander Skokna. Everyone thinks you're dead."

"I've been told." She removed the blade from the man's side. "So, if you're with the rebellion, why are you parading around as part of the Harpies?"

"I told you," said the man, "the Militia are hunting down anyone remotely associated with the rebellion. My sister and I came here hoping to hide at the outpost until it all blew over."

"And how stands the outpost?" asked Julius.

"Abandoned," said the woman. "Not a soul to be found. It seemed like Lieutenant Locke scurried off somewhere."

Julius shook his head in mild amusement. "Never thought Locke to be one to abandon his post, but I guess even the best of men crumble when the Militia shows up outside their front door."

"You're on the run," said Reed. "Still doesn't explain why you're choosing to masquerade as a couple of underground thugs shaking people down for coin."

"It's how we can get by," said the man. "Especially with the Carnival taking place, it's easy to fool some wandering merchants into handing over a few coins so they don't have to fear being bothered by us."

"Our fight is with the Militia and the kingdom, not traveling salesmen trying to make a living."

The woman raised a disgruntled brow. "Is that why we gave up peace, to continue a fight we've already won?"

"Piper, shut it," interjected the man. "She's still our superior."

"Like it matters at this point, Spencer. Fuck her." The woman, Piper, pointed a dagger of a finger in Reed's direction. "We joined the rebellion because we wanted freedom from the kingdom, and we got it. You signed a treaty granting us land and autonomy to govern ourselves. Everything we could've asked for."

"Not everything," said Julius.

Reed spat over her shoulder, "Not the time."

"Oh, that's right," said Piper. "I forgot. 'The sins of the father must be rectified despite whose head wears the crown.' And look where it's gotten us."

Her brother, Spencer, turned on his heels to face his sister. "Piper, that's enough."

"No," said Reed, bowing her head in shame, "she's right to be critical. Attacking the Militia headquarters was misguided. I'm hoping to rectify that wrong by returning to base camp and picking up whatever pieces of the rebellion may remain. If you're looking for somewhere to hide from the Militia, you should come with us. You'll be safe there."

Piper scoffed. "You're marching into a war zone. You'll find nothing left."

"You'd be surprised to see how resourceful we are," Reed said. "There wasn't anything left leaving Danforth or when I found Julius in Laminfell, and here we are."

"We've had more than enough encounters with the Militia down south," said Piper. "Consider this our resignation. Come on, Spencer. Let's leave these two on their suicide mission."

Her brother gave an apologetic bow. "Forgive my sister. We really have been through a lot since the Militia showed up. I wish you the best. Hopefully, you're as resourceful as you say." With that, he turned his back on them and followed his sister into the crowd.

"Well, they painted a pretty picture of what to expect,"

commented Julius. "Sure you still want to head to base?"

Glancing at the ground, Reed noticed one of the masks from the merchant lying not far from her feet. It was stark white in color and sculpted with features of a face devoid of emotion. The only glimpse through its veil was through two holes cut where the eyes should be. Bending down, she picked it up. Julius peered over her shoulder at it.

"Too bad he didn't drop one with a more interesting design," he said.

Reed continued to stare at it, reminding her of all the times she stood before her generals or fellow rebels. How she needed to appear strong and stoic. A fearless leader just like her father, or rather, like the man her uncle described him to be. Regardless, what lay beneath its guise was a failure. One who became a slave to the desires of her uncle and forfeited the freedom of her own people.

26

Gwen's hands throbbed and ached as she smashed her fists into one of the many rock structures crowding the shore near the cave. The skin on her knuckles peeled away as she pulverized the stone with the warm touch of blood trickling through her fingers. She punched, again and again, chipping away at the stone, but fatigue seeped into her bones, forcing her to lean on the structure for support.

"You're letting the power flow through you wildly," said Mushi. "For an efficient strike, you need to focus on where you want it to go." He took a wide stance beside her. Pulling back his fist, he launched a devastating punch at another rock structure. Upon impact, it shattered and crumbled into a pile of rocks. Sand went flying into the air, causing Gwen to shield her face. "Utilizing nin-nir properly can bolster your speed, strength, endurance, and durability. Such control requires a delicate balance, one you've already been working on. Visualize the flame from the lighter. Control and regulate its flow. I want ten consecutive punches tearing chunks of rock from this boulder without you tiring out."

The most she was able to achieve was five. Her hands trembled, and her lungs burned, as she rested for a moment, catching her breath. She looked at the small crater in the stone, splattered with bits of blood. While not obliterating the structure like Mushi, she was able to remove small chunks here and there. Composing herself, Gwen pushed off the structure and held up her hands in a fighting stance. Closing her eyes, she imagined holding the lighter. Pushing the trigger, a flame ignited. It needed to be stable, not too strong or weak. A warmth emanated from her core as the bead of heat swayed and danced in her mind. It spread from her chest out to her limbs, melting away the aches and pains. Soon enough, all she could feel was its comforting heat. Opening her eyes, she focused on the crater in the structure while keeping the image of the steady flame in her mind. As she swung her fist, she forced the energy to flow through her arm and into her hand. Her punch collided with the boulder, ripping out a chunk of rock. *One.* She threw another punch, yielding the same result. *Two.* Her breathing was steady as the rest of her surroundings faded away, including Mushi. All that existed within this moment was the crater in the rock, growing larger with each punch. *Three. Four. Five. Six.* She fell into a rhythm, a trance that could not be broken. *Seven.* More debris flew as an entire side of the structure was reduced to rubble. *Eight. Nine.* One more. She could feel her heart desperate to race with excitement, but she kept calm. The flame needed to remain steady and constant. Rearing her arm back, Gwen unleashed a powerful hook. With so much of its support missing, the top half of the structure collapsed into the sand. *Ten.*

The warmth flowing through her body faded as the aching pain in her hands returned. Fatigue came with it. Her legs wobbled under the weight of her body, but she managed to remain standing. Turning to Mushi, she gave him a prideful smile. In response, he gave three slow claps of approval.

"Impressive," he said, surveying the collapsed structure. "Many Militia captains would be envious of your progress in such little time. It's almost frightening."

"Have I earned the right to call you cousin now?" she asked.

Mushi shook his head, wearing a playful smirk. "Not yet. There's one more test you must face, but that'll be later tonight. For now, rest up."

"Going to have me catch some rabbits for dinner?"

"Not quite," he said before strutting off down the shoreline.

Gwen spent the remainder of the day pacing the beach, allowing the water to splash her feet as she observed the various shells washed ashore. She found one in good condition despite a small crack—the spiraled top and beautiful cream color enamored her enough to keep it. Mushi never returned, even to watch the sunset. It made her anxious about the task awaiting her. As the chill night air settled in, Gwen ascended the winding path up the cliffside to their camp. Upon arriving, Mushi tossed Gwen her short sword while wielding his own weapon.

"You'll be needing that," he said.

Gwen followed him beyond the outskirts of Takata's ruins to an open field. Under the glow of the crescent moon, there was little to see and even less to hear besides the chatter of cicadas. Mushi sat on the ground, resting his sheathed blade upright against his shoulder.

"It's time to see how much you've truly learned." He gestured to a specific area in the open field. "I've scouted a small fleshling horde that's nested here. No more than five or six in total. I want you to see how many you can kill." He produced a small firecracker from his garment. "Use this to draw them out. Light the fuse with the lighter I gave you and toss it on the ground."

Gwen took it from him. She remembered her first encounter with a fleshling. How its clawed hand grabbed onto her ankle, desperate to tear the flesh from her bones. Glancing down, the mark it left still stained her flesh with a faint print. "And what if I can't kill them all?"

"I'll be right here watching you," said Mushi. "I'll kill them before they kill you, but only when you're on the brink of death. So, it would be wise to fight like your life depends on it."

Gwen gulped down her fear as she unsheathed her sword. The ring of the steel stilled the night, silencing the choir of cicadas. Taking cautious steps, Gwen walked out into the middle of the field, where Mushi gestured. Glancing about, not a single creature stirred. In the dead of night, with no fire or torchlight, the allure of the western plains dissolved into a haunted valley. Holding the firecracker between her fingers, she pulled out the lighter and ignited the flame. Staring at the flickering light, her body radiated warmth from her core. Lighting the fuse, she tossed it a few feet away, followed by a sharp snap and flash of sparks, then silence.

The dirt erupted into the air as a gangly creature with rags of pale skin and black holes for eyes shot up from the ground. It charged at Gwen, digging its claws into the dirt and chomping its maw of razor-sharp teeth. She readied her blade, waiting patiently for the moment its ravenous hunger took over. As it drew nearer, it lunged, extending its talons to latch onto her head. Gwen rolled underneath the creature as it landed. Spinning around, her blade cut through the fleshling's neck and decapitated it. Its body tumbled into the grass, spewing out a fountain of viscous, black blood.

The soil beneath her gave way as four more fleshlings surfaced. Gwen scanned her surroundings, keeping a keen eye on each one as they circled her. Two of them charged head-on while the other two rounded her flank. The first two creatures swung their claws at her. She dodged one and parried the other. Distracted, another one attacked from the side, tearing into her back. She grimaced as the crimson streaks trailed down her back and onto her legs. The fourth one rammed into Gwen, pinning her to the ground. Saliva dripped onto her cheek as the fleshling snapped at her. Pressing a forearm to its throat, she held the creature at bay. Rot lingered on its breath as its jagged teeth were inches away from her face. Grasping the sword with her free hand, she pierced the blade through the fleshling's chest. It didn't howl or screech as she plunged the sword deeper. It only continued to gnaw at her until finally going limp. Pushing the creature's corpse off, Gwen stood to face the three remaining monsters. They grouped together, slowly pacing and watching her.

"Come on," she shouted, hoping to coax one into action.

It worked. One sprinted at her in a ferocious dash. Taking a solid stance, Gwen readied herself to counter. Upon its approach, the fleshling feinted a strike, throwing Gwen off balance before digging its claws into her arm. The pain burned with its icy touch, but there was little time to dwell on it. The other two charged as well, weaving back and forth between each other. Their cunning grew with every assault, and the flame in Gwen's mind flickered, causing the warmth to recede. Summoning all her strength, she launched into the air and leaped over the two fleshlings. Her blade carved into one of their spines as she flipped overhead, landing with a somersault. Turning on her heels, she charged toward the other one and hacked away. One of its arms went flying. She chopped into the creature's waist and cut it in half. To finish it off, she impaled the blade through its skull.

Exhausted and bloodied, Gwen collapsed to her knees. The flame died along with her strength. Her body grew cold and numb. She couldn't even lift her sword. Vulnerable, the last fleshling charged recklessly at her. She could see in its voided gaze the tenacity to rip her to shreds and feast on her corpse. There was nothing she could do. She tried to move, but her body was unresponsive. Vaulting into the air, the creature's jaw opened wide to bite into her, but in a splatter of black blood, its head rolled into her lap. The body fell at Mushi's feet as he sheathed his sword.

He bent down, offering to carry her on his back. "Rest easy. I'll take you back to camp and tend to your wounds." Gwen fell forward, her chin resting on his shoulder as he scooped her up for the hike back to Takata. "Four out of five isn't bad. Good job, cousin."

"It's all thanks to your training," she said. All she could muster was a faint smile. It felt comforting to lean on him like this. To know she was protected by such a disciplined yet caring man. He challenged and pushed her limits not just physically, but emotionally as well. After spending all this time together, they learned more about each other, yet some things remained a mystery. "Mushi," she whispered, "how did you earn the name the Hand of Death?"

He glanced over his shoulder with a raised brow, curious as to where the question came from all of a sudden. "I don't think now is an appropriate time to share such a story."

"I know you're a skilled warrior and have killed many people, but the Hand of Death is such a menacing title. Especially from the stories I've overheard Militia soldiers tell. It's like you're not even human. You said you've grown numb to killing, but you're not completely emotionless. You've shown me that much."

"I appreciate the sentiment, but speaking candidly, I hope you never find out why they call me the Hand of Death. It's something I'm not entirely proud of."

She nestled her head on his shoulder in a somber manner, thinking about Damian and the story he told back in Danforth. How he was attacked by his own men but branded a traitor in the aftermath. She remembered the guilt he wore on his face. "We all have things we're not proud of. Doesn't mean we should be viewed as monsters."

"I agree with you, Gwen," he said. "I agree with you."

27

Blackwood's fingers drummed against the stone arm of his chair. His light tapping and the crackling of flames from the pit before him filled the empty chamber. He hated waiting. It did nothing but make his heart pound against his chest and twist his stomach into knots. In his other hand, he unrolled the bit of parchment Slik Weyman had handed him the previous day. He looked at it countless times, and still, the words inked by Captain Ivarson's hand made him nauseous with anxiety.

Ambassador Weyman,

I am filled with both pride and reluctance to say the attack on Danforth has been repaid in full with more than enough interest. The southern plains have turned black with ash and red with blood. Many rebels and rebel sympathizers were killed, and many more were taken prisoner. We did discover the location of their base of operations, but it appeared abandoned. Unfortunately, Reed's body remains unfound, as well as the rest of her surviving generals. Despite this, a devastating blow has been delivered, and I currently sail with our support unit back to Colkirk. For now, I await further instructions from you or Parliament.

I pledge my service.
Captain Tyson Ivarson

Brookshire undoubtedly received a similar letter from Captain Freeman and shared its contents with Rahm. Captain Hardee managed to gather a group of elite trackers, but his search for Gwen had barely begun. As much as he wanted to pray for more time, there was no avoiding it. Today would be the day of the vote to usurp Peter from his throne. He'd bought out Weyman and hoped Mary Katherine's words were enough to convince Noreen.

The groan of the metal door and shuffling footsteps reverberated off the stone walls as the ambassadors finally gathered. Rahm was the first one to reach the bottom of the winding staircase, closely followed by Petram and Natalie. His jowl twitched in an amused smirk, but Natalie was the one to speak.

"Not interrupting your brooding, are we?" she teased.

Blackwood ignored her with an inviting gesture. "Ambassadors, please take a seat. We will begin as soon as everyone assembles."

The three of them sat on the far end of Blackwood's right side. First, Fletcher, brushing off his immaculate uniform, then Rahm's husky frame collapsing into the stone chair, and finally, Natalie sitting furthest from him, seeming a bit disgruntled at his dismissive attitude. The next two descending into the chamber were Slik and Alyssa, looking more gaudy than usual. Along with the rings decorating his fingers, a bracelet jangled around his wrist, glittering with small gemstones. An addition courtesy of the five hundred gold Blackwood had provided. Alyssa strutted toward the chair nearest to Blackwood's right side, holding her head high with an air of pride. Two small chandeliers dangled from her earlobes as she elegantly lowered herself onto the stone. Her tan skin glistened in the firelight as if coated in a layer of oil.

"You seem to have a glow around you, ambassador," said Blackwood.

Alyssa flitted a sideways glance at him. "Thank you, Chancellor. Exfoliation is a wonderful thing. Allows you to get rid of all that bothersome dead skin flaking off your body."

"Indeed."

The distinct tap of Ambassador Lawson's cane against each step cut off the conversation. Alongside him was Mary Katherine, offering her support. As they came into view, the Militia veteran was quick to wave her off, no longer needing her help or, more likely, not wanting to be seen needing it. Mary Katherine sat in the chair directly to Blackwood's left, and Lawson limped his way in between her and Weyman. Blackwood gave him a nod as he eased himself into the chair. Mary Katherine forced a reassuring smile. He could tell she was just as anxious. The last one to join the circle was Noreen Archer. Her expression was carved from stone, not glancing at Blackwood, Rahm, or anyone else. She marched to the only open seat beside Natalie, opposite Blackwood. He studied every little motion. The way she crossed her legs, gently placed her arms on the rest of the chair, and straightened her posture. Her eyes held the same cold stare making her unreadable. It seemed he would have to wait further to find out which way she would vote.

"We've all gathered, Blackwood," said Rahm. He gestured toward the chancellor with his fat hand. "Take the stage, and let's get started."

Blackwood rose, towering over the ambassadors. Keeping his head bent, the shifting shadows masked most of his face in darkness. "As I'm sure you're all aware by now, the campaign against the rebels has reached its conclusion. The southern plains have been purged, and Captain Ivarson, along with Captain Freeman, are pulling back their forces. With that issue officially settled, we shall move forward with the next pressing matter." The words stifled in Blackwood's throat. He didn't want to say them, but he had to. "Ambassador Krawczyk set forth the motion to relieve King Peter Clougher of his title and authority, deeming him unfit to rule. With his eldest daughter missing, the responsibility of the kingdom shifts to his youngest daughter, Victoria. Parliament will proceed with a vote whether or not to support this motion."

Rahm shot out of his chair. "While the rebels have not been completely rooted out from the continent, a fatal blow has been delivered. Our forces cut through the southern plains with little resistance. If similar action had been taken earlier, instead of opting for peace, tragedy could have been avoided. King Peter was once a strong leader, but much time passed, and age caught up to him. In his weary state, he is more concerned with his missing daughter, which we can sympathize with." A glare shined through his spectacles at Mary Katherine. "But we must not let one girl supersede the well-being of the entire continent. It is our duty to protect the kingdom, even if that means from our very own king. A duty heralded by the Sanction of Saints centuries ago." He raised an open hand. "I stand firmly for removing King Peter from the throne."

Natalie rose from her seat, mirroring Rahm. "I agree with Ambassador Krawczyk. King Peter needs to be replaced."

Rahm's gaze flickered to Fletcher, who followed suit. "I admire King Peter for his accomplishments following the horrid rule of his father, but in recent events, he's displayed misguided judgment. It is unconventional, however, necessary."

"'Misguided judgment' are fairer words than I would use,"

said Alyssa Brookshire. She, too, rose to her feet in an elegant display. "The king offered the southern plains to the rebels, and now it exists as a scar of his foolish decision. We are to act as his advisers, yet he did not seek my counsel. Had he done so, we might have avoided setting fire to such a large stretch of land."

Blackwood scanned the four ambassadors standing beside him. "Ambassadors Krawczyk, Parson, Fletcher, and Brookshire stand in favor of usurping the king. How do the other ambassadors stand?"

Mary Katherine glared back at Rahm remaining glued to the stone. "You can stand there and profess to do this for the betterment of the kingdom, but we all know it's for your own personal gain. The king has done more for this kingdom than any of you have and ever will. As long as he breathes, Peter will remain king." She leaned further into the chair, folding her arms.

"Here, here," said Lawson, striking his cane hard against the floor. "The king may have made mistakes, but no man is perfect. He did what he thought was best, just as you all are doing now."

Slik glanced at Blackwood before clearing his throat. "I stand with the king as well."

All eyes turned to Noreen, who scratched her nails against the stone armrest. The chiseled expression she had upon entering the Tomb started to crack. Blackwood could see the struggle to make a choice, debating the matter in her head. Tugging at her bottom lip, she breathed a heavy sigh. "King Peter has made mistakes, and those mistakes bred dire consequences. Consequences that many have fallen victim to, including myself. His mind may be fading with age, but I believe his heart is in the right place. So, I stand against Ambassador Krawczyk's proposal to remove King Peter."

Silence overtook the chamber. Blackwood could scarcely believe what he had just witnessed, the words he had heard. They did it. They stalemated the vote. Rahm's face reddened with anger as many of the other ambassadors remained still in awe. Blackwood swayed, wanting to collapse into his chair in relief, but caught himself. He couldn't relax just yet.

"On the motion of usurping King Peter," he said, "the vote concludes in a stalemate. Another will be held in the coming days following further discussion, but as for now, we are dismissed."

With that, the ambassadors exited in a chorus of grumbles, gripes, and shock. Mary Katherine subtly grabbed the chancellor's hand, squeezing it.

"We did it," she whispered.

"For now," he responded, dropping into his chair in relief.

Allowing him to unwind, she left his side to help Lawson climb back up the winding staircase. As the others filtered out of the Tomb, Rahm remained standing over the pit until only he and Blackwood remained. The ambassador stared into the fire in silence.

"Have something to say?" asked Blackwood.

Adjusting his spectacles, Rahm paced the circle of chairs. "I'm impressed. I didn't think you could sway Noreen after what befell her at Danforth. It seems I put too much faith in any contempt she held against the crown."

"It would appear her love for Gwen trumps any sort of hatred you were banking on."

Rahm scoffed. "She would be the last person I suspected to be swayed by emotion, and acting upon it will bury this kingdom. Nevertheless, time favors me more than you. Hold firm in the stalemate all you can, but the old man is dying. That is unavoidable. One way or another, the crown will pass from his head to his daughter's."

"And we will ensure that it is his eldest daughter who inherits that crown," said Blackwood. "One you and the others will not be able to manipulate so freely."

"A foolish endeavor," said Rahm. "You played this round well, but I advise you to proceed with caution. While you fight to stay afloat, I'm on my way to procuring a vessel to victory in the long run. It's not too late. You can still hop on, or else you'll end up drowning."

28

The wind whipped against Damian's body in a way that reminded him of climbing up toward the rebellion's floating fortress. Like Danforth, being high above the city allowed him to see so much, including his current target, Leopold. The pundit paced the route around his section of the basilica with the lantern raised close to the hood of his cloak. Damian couldn't see his face, but the erratic swivel of his head told him his moment to act would soon approach. Reaching the edge of the basilica grounds, another figure emerged from a nearby bush. The two embraced, and Leopold blew out the light of his lantern before sneaking off with the woman of his forbidden affection. As the two love birds scampered off the basilica grounds, Damian descended from his perch. After Anden's encounter with the young boy, Damian's suspicions spurred him into taking more drastic action. He needed to find out if these "disappearances" were linked in any way to the murders.

Finding one of the side doors, he peered through the nearby windows to make sure no one was wandering around inside. With the coast seeming to be clear, Damian slammed his foot into the door, tearing the latch from its lock. Not a single torch lit the halls of the basilica, but Damian didn't mind. Quite the opposite, in fact. Years of scavenging and hunting in the wastelands of Kelveux, where the sun could not penetrate the constant veil of clouds, forced his vision to adjust to the darkness of night. He wandered the empty corridors keeping a careful ear out for the sound of approaching footsteps and keen eyes for an indication of Visconti's personal office or study. If the Ambulate did possess any information on these "disappearances," they would most certainly be found there. After climbing a series of stairs and traversing more hallways, Damian stumbled upon a door with an interesting ornament of a sword adorned in flames hanging from it. Curious, he opened it and stepped into an expansive study with mounds of paper stacked atop a desk alongside a thick hardcover book with an empty, black cover. Symbols and paintings relating to the Lucius Ambulate decorated the walls. The most profound being the opposite wall itself, painted as a portrait depicting a man wielding a sword glowing with the radiance of the sun and standing over a massive crowd of people as the heavens themselves were split into two. Damian deduced the man wielding the sword to be the First Emperor and that the study belonged to the loren himself.

He approached the desk and opened the book. Each page was

divided into separate columns, and while the columns weren't labeled, they contained different categories of information. Damian scanned the length of the pages. Each was filled with a list of numbers, locations, names, and prices. The locations he recognized to be some of the various islands making up the archipelago off the shores of Papuri. The names listed belonged to wealthy nobles of the region, owners of the mining operations that harvested many of the important minerals used by the kingdom. The list continued page after page, seemingly never-ending and dating back years. Damian couldn't believe what he was seeing. The book served as a method for keeping records of inventory sales. Looking at the numbers, he remembered Anden mentioning the young boy carrying a scar on his arm forming a series of numbers similar to the ones in the book. These were the reasons for the "disappearances." For decades while the war with the rebellion had been unfolding, the Ambulate was taking refugee children in only to sell them off to slavers in the archipelago. While unlawful, it didn't have anything to do with the murders they were investigating. He reached to close it, but something caught his eye. One of the rows at the bottom of the page had been completely blacked out. Neither a number nor a location, name, or price could be seen. Damian flipped through the book, discovering more blacked-out rows until he reached the end of the listings. Twenty-two names had been blacked out in total. More than the number of the murder victims Anden claimed the corpse the collector had retrieved.

Footsteps thudded down the hallway and grew louder as they neared the door to the study. Someone was coming. With nowhere to escape, Damian flung himself into a wardrobe where a few lavish garments hung. It was a tight squeeze for his broad frame, but he managed to fit. Cracking the wardrobe door, he saw two men enter the study. One was older with an angular, hard-set face, and the other was younger, wearing the same hooded cloak as Leopold. The younger one set down the lantern he carried on a nearby stand while the older man furiously thrust himself into the chair behind the desk. The wrinkles on his face deepened with anger.

"You're sure no one saw anything?" he asked.

"Yes, Your Eminence," said the younger man. "Some of the refugees might've caught a glimpse of the body, but the corpse collector assures no one saw the inscriptions."

"Good, and make sure this one doesn't go around telling the sellswords about it. Those irritating bastards are still lurking about. No doubt biding their time for another one of these incidents to take place. We need to make sure not a word of this is spoken henceforth. Understood?"

"Yes, Your Eminence."

The old man pinched the bridge of his nose. "Do you have a copy of the inscriptions?"

The young man took out a folded sheet of parchment and handed it to him. "It's a similar design to the others."

Unfolding it, the old man studied the parchment as his gaze slid to the bottom corner. "111933. I'll be sure to strike him from the records. Make sure the body is disposed of before morning."

"Of course."

"You're dismissed, Theo."

The young man bowed before departing, leaving the lantern on the stand. The old man pried open the coverless book, took out a brush, dipped it in ink, and drew a thick, black line across one of the pages. Blowing the ink dry, he closed the book and placed the piece of parchment in a drawer. Damian kept still, careful not to make a sound, watching the old man leave as he picked up the lantern and headed out the door. Once the man's footsteps faded down the hall, Damian emerged from the wardrobe and rushed over to the desk to tear open the drawer. Pulling out the piece of parchment having just been placed there, Damian unfolded it to see a sketch of strange symbols arranged in a ring-like pattern. He didn't understand what they meant or even what they were, but a disturbing sensation crawled up his back, causing him to shiver. In the corner of the page, he saw the number 111933. Reaching back into the drawer, he pulled out more papers with more sketches of the strange symbols arranged in ring-like patterns. 136110. 147152. 110894. 127874. 100990. As he flipped through the other sketches, the more incomplete they appeared as the ringed pattern turned into messy amalgamations of the symbols. Twenty-three sketches in total. The same number of rows struck from the records in the book. These murders went back further than they had originally thought, and there was hardly a chance of denying that the Ambulate was involved in some way. If they sold children to slavers, who was to say they wouldn't do the same for the cloaked strangers? Hell, maybe those cloaked bastards were members of the Lucius Ambulate. At this point, Damian would almost believe anything. The Ambulate was hiding something in regard to the symbols. He took the most recent sketch and tore a page from the book, stuffing them into his jacket.

*

Damian hid in the darkness beyond the light of the lanterns being held by the pundits standing guard at the entrance of the morgue. Flail chains dangled at their hips, connected to three spiked balls reflecting in the light like stars. While the possession of weapons didn't correspond to capable warriors, the former Militia captain had no intention of starting a fight. He needed to find an alternate way inside. A light tap on his shoulder startled him into action, spinning around with a hand gripping the hilt of his sword. He was shocked to see Arios standing behind him.

"You move quietly for a shambling old man," said Damian, dropping his hand from his sword.

"When you know the city as I do," said the elder, "you can maneuver through it like a shadow." He peered around Damian's wide frame at the pundits guarding the morgue. "It can also help get you into guarded areas unseen."

"Have you heard about the murder?" asked Damian.

"Ah, that's why you want to break in. Another body has been found."

"I want to investigate it for clues that might confirm my rising suspicions of who the culprit might be."

The staff rattled as he extended a bony finger. "It won't be pleasant, but I do happen to know a way in. Follow me."

Damian followed the elder down into the gutters of the lower city directly beneath the basilica. In the foundation of brick and stone supporting the structure was a crack, no bigger than the one he used to enter Danforth. Lowering his staff, Arios shuffled into the crevice. Damian barely managed to squeeze through as his shoulders scraped the stone, causing a light dusting of dirt to powder his jacket. The darkness around them grew so thick that even with his adjusted vision, it became nearly impossible to see. With a sharp tap against the ground, the tip of Arios' staff radiated with light. It seemed to be another one of his constructions.

"Useful little tool," he chuckled.

Damian couldn't agree more. The man's ingenuity seemed on par with Leon's, which was saying something. With Arios as his guide, they continued through the cavern, and the scent of death soon touched Damian's nose. In Kelveux, he learned every creature's death possessed a unique odor. The moldy stench currently filling his breath came from human remains—and many of them. The smell grew so palpable, he could almost taste it. On the other side of the compressed cavern were walls of bones. Rows of skulls lined the walls, with the rest of the skeletal remains scattered across the ground, cracking beneath the weight of his boots. The tunnel of death seemed endless, stretching far beyond his sight on either side.

"I wasn't aware a series of catacombs existed beneath the Holy City," said Damian.

"Another one of the Ambulate's secrets," said Arios. "During the era of King Cypher Clougher, the ground beneath Illios started to crumble and fall to the wayside. It destroyed much of the original city, including many of the cemeteries, which allowed the smell of rot to taint the air. When the new city was built, the Lucius Ambulate took it upon themselves to transfer any remains henceforth underground to mask the smell because a place reeking of death could never retain the illustrious title of the Holy City. What you see now is the result of centuries of work."

"And within here lies an entrance to the morgue?" asked Damian.

"The only two official entrances into the catacombs are through the morgue and the basilica. That little crevice we just snuck through is a result of centuries of negligence."

They headed right with empty sockets from every skull staring as they passed. The shifting shadows from Arios' staff caused their gaze to follow them as if they were intruders. Damian faced hordes of fleshlings, a couple of bolgias, and worse; however, these corridors built from human remains stirred an unsettling feeling within him he hadn't felt since he was a young soldier. It turned his hands clammy and sent a shiver slithering down his spine. He was relieved to reach the end of the tunnel, where a ladder disappeared into a hole in the ceiling.

The exiled pundit hoisted his glowing staff toward the opening above. "The ladder will lead you into the morgue. I hope you find something that makes your journey through such a wretched place worth it and can bring an end to this madness."

"If the saints bless us." Damian ascended the ladder into the hole and toward a trap door. Pushing it open, he peeked into the room above, not seeing a soul in the dim torchlight. He climbed out into a large room with brick columns and rows of tables between them lining either side. Some had corpses sprawled across them, while the others sported dried stains of blood.

One of the bodies was smaller than the others, with a cloth covering the torso. The eyes were missing from their sockets and burned black. The mouth was the same, lips charred, teeth melted, and the tongue a shriveled piece of flesh. Checking the arm, he noticed bruising around the wrist, indicating the victim might have been bound by rope. On the forearm was the scarred tissue of a branded number,

111933. Damian reached into his jacket and pulled out the parchment he had taken from Visconti's desk. Glancing at the corner of the page, he noticed the same number had been written. He turned his attention to the cloth draped over the child's torso. Lifting it, Damian was disturbed to find the same pattern of strange symbols marked on the parchment also burned into the boy's flesh. The air in the room seemed to grow cold as he stared at the sigils. Upon closer inspection, the symbols appeared to be cut into the flesh using a knife or dagger before whatever burning took place. What confused Damian most was the lack of burns anywhere else on the body, given the severity found on the face and torso. The arms, legs, and even throat remained untouched. Breathing in deeply, he caught a whiff of a similar scent as in the alley. The musty fragrance of incense. There was no doubting it any further. This was the work of dark magic, and the symbols no doubt served as the key to figuring out what it all meant. He needed to decipher them.

Crawling back into the catacombs, Arios awaited him, with his staff still glowing. "Found anything useful?"

Damian showed him the parchment with symbols. "Would you happen to recognize any of these?"

The elder grabbed it from his grasp and held it closer to the light. He scanned the page with a pensive expression. "Admittedly, not all of them are known to me, but a few of them I recognize to originate from the ancient text. I've never seen them orchestrated in such a fashion before. Where did you find this?"

"It was given to your old friend Visconti by one of his pundits," explained Damian. "They're also inscribed on the victim's flesh, hence the number written at the corner of the page." He pulled out another scrap of parchment, the one he tore from the coverless book. "It seems the current loren has been doing business with the miners in Papuri. He's been selling the child refugees off to become slaves. No doubt to keep the Ambulate afloat financially."

"The order has been struggling for some time," said Arios shaking his head, "but this is unprecedented. Emperor be praised. I knew the Ambulate had fallen. Little did I know how far into the abyss they dived. If you don't mind, I'd like to take this and study it for myself. See if I can decipher any of it before you try making bold accusations."

"Please do," said Damian. If anything, understanding the sigils would most likely help them learn what the goal of the mysterious cloaked figures might be. One look at the boy's body, and he knew Mushi spoke true. They had to have a hand in this mess. As Damian stood beside the old man surrounded by thousands of skeletal corpses, he wondered what it all had to do with Gwen.

29

After Mushi left at sunrise to Emperor knows where, training was whatever Gwen wanted it to be. She carried the rocks across the shore like any other morning and went for a swim to cool off afterward. Controlling the flow of nin-nir during normal activities grew easier. No longer did it cause her body to go limp with exhaustion. Efficiently using it in combat still proved challenging, as the effort, no matter how successful, always left her feeling drained and weak. Despite all her conditioning, Gwen's body lacked the capability of properly withstanding such an intense surge of power. By the early afternoon, she meditated at the edge of the cliffside overlooking the beach, only to be disturbed by the sound of Mushi's approaching footsteps.

"Where have you been?" she asked, glancing over her shoulder to see him holding two sets of folded clothes.

"Out shopping," he said with an awkward shrug. "You've worked so hard and accomplished such rapid progress, I figured you deserved a break. Bushgrove is celebrating the Carnival tonight, and I thought it might be fun to partake." He unfolded one of the sets of clothes, unveiling a brilliant white dress with a short skirt glowing in the radiance of the sunlight. "I don't really know your taste for these sorts of things, so I got the vendor's opinion. Said it was a more traditional style. Hope it works for you."

Gwen couldn't help but smile. She loved the dress as it reminded her of the one she wore when leaving the capital. The thought of attending a festival also filled her with excitement. "Seriously? This isn't one of your deceitful tricks, is it?"

"Not at all," he chuckled. "Go wash up and change so we can get there when it starts. We have quite a trip across the estuaries."

She snatched the dress from his grasp and hurried down to the cave past the stretch of rock formations on the beach. Not much time was spent soaking in the water. It only took a matter of minutes for her to wash herself and don the new dress. The top wrapped around her chest at a slant, covering one shoulder and leaving the other bare. A gilded band kept it taut around her waist, and the bottom barely reached her knees. Mushi also provided her with a pair of heeled sandals and a bronze choker to wear around her neck. Her reflection in the water with shoulder-length hair reminded Gwen of her sister. How she wished Victoria could be with her to experience the festival.

"Gwen," she heard Mushi shout, "we need to head out!"

Gwen scampered through the jungle of rocks to meet Mushi on the other side. He looked about the same, except his clothes were now made from silk and sported a vibrant red sash around his waist. He also donned a long, black sleeveless vest.

His gaze fixated on her as she rounded the last structure, saying, "You clean up quite nicely."

"Wish I could say the same for you."

He glanced at his outfit, patting himself down. "More into comfort than appearance, I guess. Now, come on before we miss all the fun."

They journeyed south, hiking a good distance toward the estuaries. Upon reaching the bank, a dinghy of a boat awaited them, floating in the water.

"Where did you find this?" Gwen asked as Mushi assisted her into the vessel.

"Scavenged it a while back. Seems the bandits didn't destroy everything all those years ago." He unfurled the boat's sail. Catching the wind, they took off across the water.

She watched him man the helm, brimming with anticipation. "What's to be expected at this festival?"

"A little bit of everything. The Carnival is one of Bushgrove's major festivals of the year." He beamed a toothy grin. "There'll be plenty of things to enjoy. I guarantee it."

The sun had set by the time they reached the port. Ships flooded the docks, leaving no room even for their little boat. Mushi navigated the craft to a naked shoreline, hopped out, and pulled it ashore to ensure Gwen didn't get wet while exiting.

"Best thing about these dinghies is that you only need a patch of land to make port. Oh, I almost forgot." Fishing through a small wooden chest, he pulled out two masks and handed one to Gwen. "It's customary to wear a mask for the Carnival."

Hers was slim and decorated with a bloom of blue feathers in an array similar to a peacock. The nose extended well past her own and came to a point similar to a bird's beak.

"It's pretty gaudy," said Mushi, "but compared to the other female masks, it was tame."

Gwen placed it on her face and stared at him with a twinkling, hazel gaze. "I don't mind. I am royalty, after all."

That sparked a laugh from him. "Very true." He put on his own mask, which covered the majority of his face. The eyes were sunken in, and there was an opening in the center where his nose poked through, mimicking the appearance of a skull. "Shall we?" he said, holding out an arm.

"We shall." Gwen wrapped her arm around his, and they proceeded up the docks and into the city.

The streets were packed with massive crowds from all walks of life. Some wore simple garbs similar to hers and Mushi's, who, she reckoned, were locals. Others wore lavish garments and headdresses, decorating themselves in all kinds of jewelry. Gwen figured them to be nobles, most likely traveling from the northern coast of Papuri. A few hunters could be spotted in the crowd with steel at their hips and tattoos on their arms. She even saw someone with their hair tied in a ponytail reminiscent of the style common to the people in Skovgade, as Helmond would sometimes demonstrate. Lanterns dangled overhead, lighting the various bustling pathways. Music thundered in the distance, along with chattering banter, toasts being made, and an overall festive celebration. Everyone either seemed drunk with merriment, booze, or both. It was a marvel to take in and much different from the celebrations customary in the palace. At those gatherings, everyone in attendance was expected to behave elegantly, but here all realms of debauchery existed. The various masks people wore added their own flavor of mystery and excitement. The removal of direct identities broke down the barriers between nobles and the common folk, mercenaries and soldiers, even thieves and vendors. Here, at this festival, everyone was equal in the sharing of celebration.

"Where do you want to start?" Mushi asked.

Gwen glanced about, taking everything in. There was so much to do, but the rumble of her stomach indicated the first thing needing care. "How about we start with some food?"

"You read my mind."

Sifting through the crowd, they made their way to a bazaar.

Chefs of various specialties cooked meals with a hint of flair. The mixture of aromas made Gwen's mouth water, overwhelmed by the vast number of options. Mushi didn't hesitate, jumping from one station to the next to observe the delicacies offered. After taking a lap around the bazaar, Gwen settled on a bowl of beef and bell peppers while Mushi returned, holding a plate of squid tentacles and oysters. He offered some to her, but she kindly declined. With their meals finished and their bellies full, the duo continued exploring the Carnival.

A little girl wearing a rabbit mask tugged at her mother's arm, pointing at a nearby bushel of flowers. From their red pigment, rounded petals, and elongated stamen, Gwen recognized the flowers to be river lilies. The child continued to pull at the mother's arm.

"Mama," she said, "pretty flowers."

"I see that," the mother responded. She wore a mask in the likeness of a deer sprouting majestic horns from the top of its head. "Would you like to pick some?"

"Ya." The girl clapped her hands in excitement.

Gwen approached the mother and daughter as they picked some of the flowers from the bushel. "I can make a wreath from those, if you'd like."

The child's eyes lit up from behind the mask. "Please do, miss bird lady."

"Are you sure?" asked the mother.

"I don't mind." Gwen bent down on her knees, taking the

flowers and weaving the long stems into a circle with flower blossoms spaced around the circumference. The little girl watched her toil away with an awed expression plain on her face. "I used to make these for my sister when I was younger. Not sure if she really liked them or not because she wasn't interested in flowers like me, but I enjoyed it all the same. You, however, have quite an eye. River lilies are rare to find in the eastern part of the continent. Legend says that Nero, one of the saints, gifted King Edward's firstborn with a crown of river lilies to symbolize a hopeful future. Since then, these flowers have been linked to rebirth and new beginnings." Finishing the wreath, Gwen placed it on the girl's head, stood up, and offered a curtsy. "You look most beautiful, lady rabbit."

The little girl returned the gesture, although a bit more clumsily. "Thank you, miss bird lady." Turning around, the girl proudly displayed the crown of flowers to her mother. "Look, mama, I'm wearing a crown like a princess."

"How fitting." The mother looked at Gwen, bowing her head. "Thank you."

As the mother and daughter took their leave, Gwen turned to Mushi, who watched her from a distance with an amused smile tugging at his lips. He seemed lost for a moment, as if reliving a memory of the past before snapping back into the present moment.

"Don't think I forgot about you," she said, handing him a water lily she'd plucked from the bushel.

He tucked the flower into his sash, the petals blossoming at his waist. "I appreciate it. So, what do you want to do next?"

On the outskirts of the square, in one of the clay houses, a group of people crowded around, shouting and jeering at some sort of spectacle. Gwen tried to peer through them all to see what was going on. "What do you think that's all about?"

Mushi followed her gaze to the circle. "Seems to be an event held by the fighting circuit of the underground. Fighters from all over the continent contend in matches to earn coin and respect. It also draws quite an audience who like to gamble on the winners."

Curious to watch a match, Gwen headed out of the square and forced her way through the rabbling crowd with Mushi close behind her. Squeezing to the front, a wooden barricade separated them from an open space where two men fought. People shouted at the top of their lungs, waving pieces of parchment marking the bets made regarding the ensuing match. Gwen observed the two combatants battle, analyzing their skills and techniques. It wasn't anything impressive. Their strikes were sloppy as they wailed at each other like drunkards in a bar brawl. Each strike thrown, if dodged correctly, left them wide open for a counter, but neither of them seemed to notice. If this was what these fighters had to offer, Gwen figured she might have a chance to test her skills and even win. With Mushi having been gone for most of the day, she didn't have an opportunity to spar, and the desire nagged her like an itch needing to be scratched.

"Can anyone enter?" she asked Mushi.

His eyebrows twitched in subtle surprise. "With the proper amount of coin, yes." Pulling out a small sack, she dumped three gold coins into his palm. "Alright, I'll set you up with an opponent."

He disappeared into the raving horde of onlookers and left Gwen to continue watching the fight. One of the men struck the other with a wide, telegraphed hook, smacking a fist into his jaw. The man's body jerked with the momentum of the blow as he stumbled into the wooden post. The crowd was quick to push him back toward the center, still dazed. All it took was one solid jab to knock him to the ground. Some of the people cheered, and others booed. It was about then that Mushi returned to her side and gave a wink, indicating his mission was complete.

As the loser was dragged out of the ring, an ostentatious man in a lion mask hopped over the barrier into the circle. He motioned for the roaring crowd to go silent. "That was quite a match," he boomed with a resounding voice. "For our next bout, I would like to introduce one of the top fighters from the icy tundra of the south, Kory 'Stone Fist' Simmons!"

Stepping into the circle was a young woman with a lean frame and dirt-colored hair pulled into a braided ponytail. The crowd erupted into cheers as she paced the edges of the ring, facing them all with arms extended wide.

The man in the lion mask silenced them once more with a

wave. "Her opponent is a name I've never seen before, but one welcome to our circle nonetheless. Put your hands together for Erika!"

"That's you," Mushi whispered. "Didn't want to use your real name for obvious reasons."

Smart thinking on his part. Hurdling over the barrier, Gwen entered the ring. The crowd continued to cheer viciously as she twirled around and stepped in the center across from Kory. Studying Gwen's outfit, she raised a mocking brow.

"Sure you want to fight in that?" she said. "Be a shame for it to get dirty and torn. At least take off the mask. Makes it easier to see."

"I'll manage." Gwen took the heeled sandals off her feet and tossed them to Mushi, who remained in the front row.

"All right, ladies and gentlemen," shouted the lion-masked announcer. "Close your bets and do it quickly, as this match is about to begin."

Gwen took a deep breath, settling her nerves. For her, this was nothing more than a sparring session with Mushi on the beach. She'd done it many times before, and this time, the sand wouldn't slow her down.

The man in the lion mask climbed back over the barrier before raising an arm. "Fight!"

Kory wasted no time. She unleashed a flurry of punches, each one a quick jab. Gwen weaved around her strikes, ducking and strafing. While her movements seemed to be an improvement from the previous two fighters, they were lethargic in speed compared to Mushi. Dodging a blow, Gwen delivered two jabs into her abdomen, but she seemed unfazed. The woman's skin was thick, having endured the south's freezing temperatures. Kory delivered a powerful kick, aiming for her head. Gwen raised her arms, blocking it just in time. She wasn't just tough, but strong, too. Gwen tried to distance herself, but Kory closed the distance and unleashed another series of strikes. People in the crowd jeered and taunted Gwen for her defensive strategy as she continued dodging. Envisioning the flame, Gwen deflected one of Kory's punches, leaving the woman open, and countered with another strike to her abdomen. This time, the power from her core surged into her fist as it connected. Kory groaned in pain, but Gwen wasn't done. She swept a kick at her opponent's legs. Kory jumped back to avoid it; however, Gwen pivoted into a spin and followed up with another kick directly into the chest. The woman slammed into the barrier, using it for support to stay on her feet. She stared at Gwen with a look of bewilderment as some of her hair started to disentangle from the braided ponytail.

The audience went wild, starting to chant her fake name in unison. "Erika! Erika! Erika!"

Kory peeled herself from the wall and raised her arms in a guarded stance. This time, she kept her distance. The next strike was Gwen's to make. She hurtled toward the woman, who threw a punch out of pure instinct. Gwen grabbed her wrist and swung a kick at the woman's side. Kory, however, caught her leg and kneed Gwen in the gut. Wind escaped her lungs, leaving her gasping for air. Kory's hand came free from Gwen's grasp and struck her across the cheek, knocking a few blue feathers off her mask. Gwen stumbled back, catching her breath.

"I told you that mask would only get in the way," she said.

Warmth radiated throughout Gwen's entire body as the power of nin-nir surged through her. She charged at the woman again, this time quicker. Her opponent barely had an opportunity to react as Gwen delivered a series of devastating kicks, jostling Kory left and right as she struggled to block each attack. She aimed for the woman's side, but Kory caught her leg again.

"Nice try, but that trick didn't work the first time," she said.

Gwen jumped into the air, spinning her body around, and nailed Kory in the head with the back of her other heel. Both women fell to the floor, but Gwen was the only one to stand. The fighter from the south remained on the ground with a glazed-over look in her eyes. Everyone in the audience erupted into cries of disbelief. Some of the spectators shredded their pieces of parchment, cursing under their breath.

"I think we can say that was quite an upset," announced the man in the lion mask. "She may be new, but I think Erika is a name worth remembering."

As Kory recovered from her daze, Gwen helped the woman to

her feet. "Well fought," she said. "You're tougher than you look."

"Thanks," said Gwen. Her body suddenly felt drained as she stumbled. Kory grabbed her shoulder, keeping her aloft.

"Only one of us should be dizzy after the match," she jested, "and I think I'm seeing enough stars for both of us."

Gwen composed herself enough to straggle back to the barrier where Mushi held onto her sandals. As she approached, he gave her a small round of applause and helped her over the barrier. Leaning on the railing, she watched the man in the lion mask prepare for his next announcement.

"The next match," he said, "is one to look forward to. I feel sorry for the deranged man who requested this fight, but ladies and gentlemen, some brave soul has challenged the current champion of the ring. The man who has dominated the underground fighting circuit for two long years. Spectators know his name, while fighters fear his reputation. I give you: the Butcher!"

A tall man padded with a dense layer of muscle entered the ring. Clasped around his shoulder was the pelt of a large creature with four beady eyes and quills running down the back intermingled with its fur. Black paint had been smeared across his face resembling a mask. On his forearm, Gwen noticed the tattoo of a sword with strange runic symbols. The man was a hunter of the Core, and the creature slung over his back like a cape was no doubt a bolgia he'd probably killed.

"And his opponent," continued the announcer, "is another

newcomer: Kinley."

Gwen was shocked to see Mushi hop over the barrier. "You're fighting?"

"Of course," he said matter-of-factly. "Can't let you have all the fun."

As he stepped into the center of the ring, the man they called "the Butcher" unclasped the pelt and flung it over the barrier. The nearby spectators reared back in fear and disgust as the creature's dead gaze lingered on them. He stared down at Mushi's skull mask, towering almost a full foot over him. Mushi stared right back, his arms crossed in a leisurely pose.

The man in the lion mask climbed atop the railing of the barrier, raising his hands into the air and leaning his head back as he exclaimed, "Make your bets, people! Will the Butcher finally suffer his first defeat, ending his two-year reign? Considering he's up against a no-name fighter, probably not, but who knows? As we saw in the last match, anything can happen here!"

The crowd cheered the Butcher's name as the two men stared each other down without flinching.

The announcer raised a hand into the air. "Fight!"

A moment passed, and the fight was over. The Butcher was sent flying into the barrier, breaking it apart. He lay on the ground, covered with splinters of wood, and struggled to breathe as a hand clasped against his chest. Mushi stood at the center of the ring; his leg still extended from the single kick he delivered. Silence overtook the crowd. The man in the lion mask was also speechless, unable to announce the winner. Mushi strode over to the barrier where Gwen rested. Hopping over, he guided her through the crowd before pausing a moment. He turned his attention to a man holding a box cluttered with pieces of parchment and varying coins of value.

"Our winnings, if you wouldn't mind," he said, holding out a hand.

The man nervously gathered a handful of gold coins, placing them in a sack and tossing it to them. Snatching it, Mushi continued sauntering out of the building and entered the city streets where the Carnival continued to rage on.

"You didn't have to show off so much," said Gwen. "You could've given them a bit more of a show."

Mushi shrugged. "I didn't see any reason to prolong the fight. For being their champion, I could tell he didn't have much to offer."

"That seems a bit presumptuous. That was the pelt of a bolgia he was wearing."

"And you think he killed it by himself? It was just theatrics playing up his nickname."

Gwen crossed her arms behind her back as they wandered around the city under the glow of the lanterns overhead. "So, Erika and Kinley. Those are some interesting names to come up with."

"Old childhood friends from my village," explained Mushi.

"They were originally the ones to show me the trick with the double sunset."

Further up the street, the sound of music grew louder as they approached a square where people were dancing. The band played an upbeat tune with thumping drums, whimsical flutes, and the furious strings of a lute. Those frantically dancing jostled and swayed to the torrential nature of the melody. Gwen drifted out into the shuffle, joining them. She twirled and leaped across the square under the influence of the instruments' rhythm. Mushi remained at the edge, watching her frolic about.

"Come dance," she said. "Loosen up a bit. Enjoy the music."

"I'll pass on this one. Not really my style."

Gwen continued to dance without a care in the world. She felt lighter with each step she took. Her brown hair tossed about as she rocked and swayed her body. The masked faces in the crowd blurred as she spun to the swelling music. All her worries about leaving the palace, the rebel attack, and the cloaked figures melted away. Happiness washed over her as she felt a sense of freedom. With the song coming to an end, reality rushed back to her, and Gwen found herself surrounded by more masked patrons. The next song the band played was at a slower pace. A waltz. People around her paired up, dancing in couples. Feeling a tap on her shoulder, Gwen turned around to see Mushi extend a hand.

"May I share this dance?" he asked, giving a slight bow.

Gwen nodded, taking his hand and placing the other on his shoulder. He wrapped an arm around her waist and proceeded to lead in the waltz. His footwork was smooth and confident. She was taken aback that he knew the steps so well.

"I thought you said dancing wasn't really your style."

"I was referring to the music. I could never do up-tempo. I prefer it when things are slowed down."

"Well, you dance very well."

He smiled. "As do you."

Pacing around the square, they shared the rest of their dance in comfortable silence. Their feet did the talking instead of their lips. Gwen danced with many nobles at the palace during balls her father hosted, but never like this. Those were for show and courtesy. This was something more. The dance reflected the relationship they shared. He, the teacher, guided her along the way, and she, the student, followed in his footsteps without question. In his arms, she felt the same comfort and protection from the other night after fighting the fleshlings as he carried her on his back. With the song ending in a resounding flourish, Mushi released Gwen into a spin and, upon pulling her back in, transitioned into a dip. His hand caught her leg as she dangled above the ground. Their faces were inches apart, the beak of her mask almost touching his nose. Through the holes, she stared into his dark brown pupils. Her heart fluttered a bit as she held her breath. He stared back, looking through her like he was searching for something, but in the end, he couldn't find it.

Standing up, he offered another bow, formally ending the dance. "It's getting late," he said. "We should think about heading back soon."

"Yeah," Gwen breathed.

They returned to the dinghy and sailed across the water back to Takata. The stillness of the night awkwardly lingered between them until Gwen's voice broke the midnight air.

"Thank you," she said. "I had a lot of fun at the festival."

"You wanted to see the continent and understand its cultures. I hope that helped in some way."

Gwen smiled, running a hand through her hair. "It did."

By the time they returned to Takata, it was well into the earliest hours of the day. Mushi retired to his quarters and Gwen to hers. As she nestled into her sleeping pouch, she found it difficult to sleep. Her attention focused on Mushi lying just on the other side of the thin wall separating them. A part of her wanted to reach past it and out to him. She wanted to know the reason behind his inquisitive gaze. What was he searching for in that intimate moment at the conclusion of their dance and didn't find? Was it something about her? Why did she care? She wanted to find out, but restrained herself. Turning over to put the thoughts out of her mind, she forced her eyes closed and fell asleep.

30

The siblings' words held true. South of Bushgrove laid the ruins of a battlefield. Fields of ash blanketed the soil where crops once grew, the corpses of cattle and horses were seen every so often along the roadways, and droves of people were either carted in a cage or dragged along bonded in chains by Militia soldiers whose blue uniforms were spattered red with blood. Reed and Julius managed to procure the shambles of a cart pulled by a mule. With their clothes ragged, worn, and permeating with the stench of travel, as well as the sound of their stomachs yearning for food, the soldiers paid them little attention, viewing them as nothing more than helpless vagabonds. Reed wore the plain white mask left by the merchant to conceal her identity and lay in the back of the cart wrapped in whatever cloth she could find. From a distance, it made her look sickly and dissuaded anyone from coming close enough to investigate further. Julius sat at the helm with his legs dangling behind the mule's flea-infested hide. For the first time on their journey, he didn't suck at his pipe, for he had no tobacco to burn.

"This is a waste of time," he said, whipping the reins to spur their steed, but the stubborn beast maintained its casual gait. "Days of seeing nothing but destruction, and you seriously hope to find base camp untouched? At this rate, we're bound to find a graveyard."

Reed rolled over to look at the back of his head through the slits of the mask. "Just get us there, and we'll see for ourselves. As I said to that girl back in Bushgrove, we're resourceful."

They traveled west, reaching the continent's edge, where she spotted a familiar hillside; however, the tents and huts she was accustomed to seeing around it were gone. Tattered remains of the rebel base camp lay in the wake of the Militia's discovery. Just like the rest of the southern plains, nothing had been left behind.

"What did I say?" Julius said. "Nothing but a graveyard."

Reed climbed out of her cocoon and hopped off the cart. She marched through the camp, barely acknowledging its ruin. Julius followed, confused as to where she was headed with such conviction. Reed stopped at the exact spot where the war tent once sat. From there, she took ten large, carefully measured strides toward a patch of dirt. Watching her, the businessman cocked a suspicious eyebrow at the strange behavior. Standing in the dirt, Reed gave a heavy-footed jump to which the ground beneath her gave way, bending like boards of wood. She wiped away the dirt to reveal the handle of a concealed door. Pulling it open unearthed a flight of stairs descending into the depths of the underground.

Glancing at Julius with an amused smirk, she said, "See? Resourceful."

As they climbed down the stairs, Reed grabbed a lantern hanging on the wall, lighting it. Julius gazed in awe at the vast tunnel before him, littered with crates and barrels of supplies. He was even more shocked to find the tunnel extended further, branching off into two separate paths.

"What is this?" he asked.

"Tunnels that Durham had constructed upon joining the rebellion," explained Reed, turning right at the fork. "He thought since the Militia headquarters and the royal palace had caverns to hide in, so should we. Turns out he might have been right."

They continued further into the dark tunnel until being stopped by two rebel soldiers standing guard. "Hold it right there," one of them said, flashing a steel blade.

"At ease," said Reed, removing the mask from her face.

The soldiers sheathed their swords, backing away in shock. "Commander Skokna, please forgive us. We—"

"Just tell me where the generals are," she said.

"They're having a meeting in the fourth corridor," said the soldier.

"Then, I shall join them." She strutted past the two soldiers as Julius paused for a quick word.

"You wouldn't happen to have any tobacco down here, would you?" he asked.

"Come on, Julius," Reed called after him before they responded. Sighing a defeated breath, he followed her further into the tunnel. To the left and right, it branched off into separate corridors housing other rebel soldiers who hid from the wrath of the Militia above. Many of their faces were similar to the ones Reed witnessed on her journey to Laminfell, void of hope and filled with worry about what the future held. In the fourth corridor to the left, Reed heard the all-too-familiar bickering of her generals. There were four of them in total: Riggs, Mobius, Hues, and Charla. Most of them seemed to have gone through hell with greasy hair and dark circles around their eyes. Riggs was the only one who appeared unfazed. Upon seeing her, he shot to his feet.

"Commander Skokna," he said. The others clumsily followed suit. Peering over her shoulder, he recognized the man standing behind her. "Julius Yates. You're supposed to be heading the operation in Laminfell."

"Yeah, well, there isn't much of an operation to head anymore," he said, rubbing the back of his neck.

"Courtesy of a bad investment," said Reed. "Although, this place seems to be in a similar state. Julius told me communication had gone silent, so I figured you went into hiding."

"When word reached us of the aircraft's demise at Danforth, we scrambled what remaining forces we could." The general's old face darkened with sorrow. "We expected the kingdom to retaliate, but not like this. Freeman and Ivarson marched across the southern plains with a staggering force and burned everything while killing or capturing anyone linked to the rebellion they could get their hands on. It was absolute chaos."

"But no longer," said General Mobius. In the darkness of the corridor, only the whites of his eyes were clearly seen. "With the commander's return, we can instill hope into our remaining forces. We can work on turning the tide of this war once more."

"Don't be ridiculous," General Charla chided. "Did you forget the number of resources we dumped into that failed attack? Decades of work reduced to ash in a single night. Not to mention, the kingdom has destroyed the fraction of resources we had remaining after the fact. It'll take decades more for us to achieve the stature we once held."

"You're not suggesting we give up, are you?" asked General Hues.

"Maybe we should. Durham is the man who helped build the rebellion to contend with the Militia, but he's dead. Watts was the one to construct that behemoth of a contraption to scale over the capital's wall, and he's dead as well. Not to mention that creep of an assassin, Vargo, was our ace in the hole against any of the Militia captains, but unless he's hiding in the shadows, as usual, I'm going to assume he died too."

"That's enough," said Riggs. "Commander Skokna has returned, and she'll be the one to decide what is to become of the rebellion."

They all looked at her for guidance, but Reed stared at the plain white mask in her hand.

"Commander?" Riggs echoed.

Reed pulled her gaze away from the mask to see his weathered face anxiously staring at her. "Everyone, leave. I'd like to speak with General Riggs alone."

The other generals exchanged glances before making their way out of the corridor. Julius followed them, quietly asking where he could get his hands on some tobacco. Once they all left, Riggs studied her with an intense gaze. She felt vulnerable.

"Quite a bit happened during my travels to get back here," she said, shuffling over and sitting on one of the barrels. "If I am to decide the fate of the rebellion, there's something I'd like to talk to you about."

His brow furrowed in suspicion as he, too, sat on one of the barrels. "What is it?"

"You're one of the longest-serving members of the rebellion," she said. "You even served under my father, is that right?"

"I don't think your father would say anyone served under him. More like I served alongside him."

"Either way," Reed continued, "you're the only one here who knew him personally and could tell me what he was like."

"Where is this coming from?" he asked.

Reed flitted her glowing, emerald eyes at him. "I want you to tell me about my father and how he founded the rebellion. Starting with the creed we recite. Was he the one who created it? And don't lie to me."

The general's lips parted as if he were about to say something, then closed again. He shifted his eyes to the floor. "No. When Richard founded the rebellion, it was made up of a bunch of ruffians wanting to help those struggling and abandoned by the kingdom under Lucius' rule. He wanted to help those who couldn't help themselves and give them the chance to live a free life. He was never about killing the royal family or bringing ruin to the kingdom, as the creed claims. Those became the desires of your uncle after your father's death."

"So, it's true," said Reed, thinking back on the fisherman's story. "My uncle did become consumed with anger when he took over the rebellion."

"He wasn't the only one," said Riggs. "I and many others felt his pain. We thought Richard was the only man on the continent fighting for a good cause in a dark time, and Lucius had him killed for fear of losing his power. He even blamed the riots, which brought many of the great royal houses to ruin, as a result of your father's actions, naming him a danger to the kingdom. When in reality, it was his own damn fault. So, after Richard's death, Boris and the rest of us swore an oath of revenge against Lucius and the kingdom. Even when the king died of sickness and old age, we weren't satisfied. Boris was not satisfied. 'The sins of the father must be rectified despite whose head wears the crown.' I remember the first time he uttered those words. It spurred everyone who heard them into a frenzy."

"What about recruiting Durham, Watts, and the others? What do you think my father would've thought of that?"

The old general pursed his lips. "To be honest, I'm not sure what your father would've thought. All I can say is through their charisma, intellect, and connections, the rebellion grew into the fighting force you came to know by the time you took the mantle of commander. Without them, the Red Rebellion would still be a rag-tag group of freedom fighters, causing as much a nuisance to the kingdom as a flea on a hound's ass."

"That's true," said Reed, "but do you think their intentions corrupted the rebellion as you knew it to be? The one my father instituted."

A frown soured Riggs' face as he leaned forward, staring at her. "After all these years, you never asked me or anyone about your father. Why are you so curious now?"

"Because when my uncle took me from my mother, he intended for me to inherit my father's will and lead the rebellion to victory over the kingdom," said Reed, brimming with quiet anger. "For all these years, I had an idea of who my father was and what he stood for, but now, I'm not sure whether those stories can be trusted."

She stared at Riggs, not with the fierce, emerald glare associated with Reed Skokna, commander of the Red Rebellion, but with the eyes of a young girl who had lost her father and was taken from her mother, never to be rejoined again. A window allowing him to see the sorrow, guilt, grief, anger, and stress she had long kept hidden.

"I just want to know who my father was," she admitted, "and why he chose to abandon my mother and me."

The general's shoulders slouched as he heaved a heavy sigh. "Boris never wanted me to tell you this, but your father left you and your mother because he didn't want to endanger you. He knew the kingdom wanted him dead and would kill you two as well. As far as Richard was concerned, he wanted you two distanced from the rebellion as much as possible. That included distancing himself. If he knew you'd become the rebellion's new commander, it would've made him furious. I think Boris slowly came to realize that, which is why he wanted to take you to see your mother."

Reed rose from her seat and marched toward a dark corner of the chamber, using the shadows to hide the tears streaking down her face. "Why? Why did you let me lead the rebellion then if it would've been against my father's wishes?"

"Because we needed a leader."

"You needed someone to herald your need for revenge," she said with a harsh whip of her tongue. She thought back to the fisherman's tale of his days as a slave. Before being branded and working on the failed railways, he was forced to mine minerals on one of the various islands of the archipelago. A venture still practiced to this day. Wiping the tears from her cheeks, she turned to Riggs, wearing a fierce expression. "You said my father wanted to give those who couldn't help themselves a chance to live a free life. I think it's time the rebellion returns to doing the same."

*

"That's ridiculous," cried General Mobius. "Our war is with Argust and its government, not the nobles of the mining industry."

"Our war is to bring freedom to the people of the continent," said Reed with a firm voice and glaring at him with her infamous emerald gaze. Without a glance in Julius' direction, she addressed him with a question. "Captain Yates, how many slaves would you estimate to be in the 'employ' of those nobles?"

Having scraped together more tobacco, Julius sucked on his pipe before breathing out a cloud of smoke. "Let's see, back when I had a finger on the pulse of the incoming mineral production, I would say about five thousand new slaves per year, give or take."

"What would be the point?" asked General Charla. "Disrupting the supply of minerals affects us just as much as the kingdom. It makes no strategic sense."

Reed turned on her like a ravenous dog. "This isn't about the mineral supply or the kingdom. It's about helping the people of the continent. Fighting for those who can't fight for themselves."

"We need to rally all of our remaining forces throughout the continent," said Mobius. "The Militia thinks they've weakened us to the point where we're no longer a threat. We can use that to deal a legitimate blow in some way and let people know that we can still fight."

General Hues turned to Riggs with a worried expression. "Couldn't you talk some sense into her during that private conversation? There's no way she can be serious."

"I am serious," said Reed, not giving Riggs a chance to speak. "During my journey back from Danforth, I've had a lot of time to reflect on our actions up to this point, and I think the rebellion has strayed from its original path. The one my father set before it. I intend to correct our course."

Mobius shook his head, unleashing a mockingly vicious guffaw. "You really must have hit your head back at Danforth to spout this load of shit. I couldn't give a horse's ass what your father intended for the rebellion. Your uncle was the one to convince me to join the cause, and that cause was to take down the kingdom."

Reed snatched one of the daggers from her hip, holding the

blade against the general's neck. The other generals froze in place like statues. Even Julius held the smoke-filled breath inside his lungs. She pressed the sharp edge hard enough into the general's skin that the smallest trickle of blood slithered its way down the length of the blade. Mobius breathed quickly through his nose as his teeth clenched together in a mixture of fear and anger.

"If my uncle heard you utter those words, I have no doubt he'd turn your neck into a fountain." She tensed her hand, making the man flinch before removing the blade from his neck. In its place, she left a small cut wetting his finger with blood as he touched it. "Luckily for you, I'm not my uncle." Sheathing the dagger, she addressed the other generals still frozen with shock. "My father believed in giving the people the freedom to define themselves. I'm choosing to fight for that same freedom off the shores of Papuri. You can choose to follow me or continue to waste away in these tunnels. Just make up your mind before dawn."

Pushing past the remaining generals, Reed marched out of the tunnels. While not going the way she intended, a sense of relief swept over her. For the first time, she didn't follow the steps of some grand plan her uncle had set before her. Instead, she acted on her own desires.

*

As the first light of dawn broke over the horizon behind her, Reed stood alone on the hillside overlooking the endless sea. The wind tossed her hair and caressed her face as it had many times before when she sought comfort with her own thoughts, as would be a common occurrence since not a single person came to join her north. Taking in the expansive sight of the sea and sky becoming one, Reed turned around, ready to embark on her travels. She soon stopped in her tracks, spotting Riggs and Julius climbing halfway up the hillside.

"Good thing we didn't miss you," said the general. "Sorry for cutting it so close, but I tried my best to convince some of the others to come along. Unfortunately, this is all that seems to be coming with you, commander."

"With only two of you, I don't really think I can be considered a commander of anything. Reed will do just fine. Although, I am interested in knowing why you're choosing to come along."

Riggs chuckled. "After our little talk and hearing that fool Mobius spout his nonsense, I realized you might be right. The rebellion may have lost its way. Richard fought for freedom, and I want to continue that fight."

Reed nodded before turning to Julius. "And what about you? Not much profit to be made in what I seek to be doing. Besides, you'd probably be better off casting your red stripe aside and going back to living the life of a businessman."

"You're probably right," said Julius, puffing on his pipe. "However, I did join the rebellion for a reason, and you'll need someone who understands the mining industry's trade and transportation of slaves if you want to take it down. Lucky for you, I know the names worth knowing. Maybe if we succeed, we might be able to settle the score with some low-life pirates down the road."

"Perhaps," she said. "Well, gentlemen, grab your things. First order of business is to hitch a ride on a ship headed to Papuri."

With little cargo to take, the three of them loaded up into the mangy cart. With a flick of his wrist, Julius sent the stubborn mule gaiting down the worn dirt pathway, leaving the remains of the rebellion camp behind them.

31

A knock at Blackwood's chamber door withdrew him from his bed. With no desire to be seen in his undergarments, he tossed a loose-fitting nightshirt over his body and smoothed out his hair with a brush of his hand. Opening the door, he expected to see a servant or guard needing to share urgent information, but found Mary Katherine instead. Her oak-colored hair poured over one side of her face in a casual, messy way. The shawl draped over her shoulders covered much of her torso, but below her waist, he could see the thin, transparent cloth of a nightgown faintly showing the skin of her legs.

"Mary, what are you doing?" he said in a hushed whisper.

She dashed past the door and into the room. "With all the madness of the conclave, we haven't had much chance to just lie with each other and talk." She tossed the shawl onto a nearby chair and crawled into the bed, leaving room for him to join. The white of her nightgown softly glowed in the light from the window behind her. He couldn't help tracing the outline of her figure with his eyes. The curves of her feminine frame subtly shifting like dunes of sand.

He journeyed toward her, but the better part of him stopped to rebuke her. "And we still can't. We shouldn't. Not when all the other ambassadors and curious nobles are present each morning. Someone could catch us."

"No one's going to catch us having a private chat," she said. "All I want to do is talk. Not as ambassador and chancellor, but as Mary and Strom."

Blackwood sighed. Weeks of stress weakened him from rejecting her further. It had been some time since they could be together as lovers and not colleagues. Removing his nightshirt, he climbed into the bed beside her as she threw a sheet over them. She rested her head on his chest, and he wrapped an arm around her, fiddling with strands of her hair between his fingers. Holding her in such a warm embrace, the softness of her skin grazing against his coarse hands, he realized how long it had been since they shared an intimate moment together. The anxiety of the conclave vote distracted him from the hunger in his heart to be with her. Now that he had tasted it again, he never wanted to let it go.

"So," he said, "what's eating at you?"

"I'm still worried about Gwen," said Mary Katherine. "I feel like I'm always worrying about her. Hardee has assembled the best trackers he could find, but we're no closer to finding her than we were before the conclave started."

"We are closer. Hardee sent word to Lawson that one of the hired hunters had two encounters with a woman matching Guinevere's description. Once in Lundur, matching Captain Green's claim, and another in Nabal."

"The Core headquarters," said Mary Katherine. "Why would she be there?"

"I'm not sure," he said. That was a lie. According to Hardee, the hunter indicated the men she was traveling with took her to Kelveux to search for the Burnt Coat, but that information didn't need to be shared. It would only cause Mary Katherine to worry further, and he didn't want to spoil the moment. "The takeaway should be that we have more information on her whereabouts than we did before, and I have no doubt, given enough time, they'll be sure to find her."

"I hope so." She nuzzled closer to him. "How did it all come to this? Months ago, we were talking about leaving Parliament to build our life together."

"Now everything is on the brink of chaos," said Blackwood. "The kingdom might as well be a house of cards about to collapse right into the palm of Rahm's hand."

"Has he made a move to sway Weyman in any way?"

"Not yet." Blackwood turned on his side, sliding Mary

Katherine's head off his chest. "But he's planning something. While we're concerned with holding him at bay with the stalemate, he's looking beyond that. Planning a series of contingencies for everything we could possibly throw at him. Not to mention he has Natalie on his side, and she knows how to drive me mad."

Mary Katherine held his head between her hands. "You're smart enough not to let her trap you like before. Besides, Rahm might have her on his side, but you have me on yours." She leaned in and kissed him. "We can do this. Together."

He caressed her cheek with a finger. "You're too good for me, Mary. If only we had met years before I lost my way."

She smiled. "It's only because you lost your way that we met. There's no sense in wanting to change the past. All we can do is focus on the future."

"You always know what to say. No wonder you were able to convince Noreen to side with us."

"To be honest, I was just as shocked as everyone else. When speaking with her, I didn't threaten or barter in any way. I just talked as I'm doing now with you and left her to decide how to vote. You should do the same. You might find you're more alike than you think."

"Why is that?"

She slid a hand from his face down to his chest, feeling the soft thump of his heart. "You both care deeply about those close to you, even if others think it foolish. You care for the king just as she cares for Gwen."

Blackwood placed a hand on hers, staring at the high ceiling above. Perhaps that was why he judged the young ambassador so harshly. When he looked at her, in some way, he saw a mirrored version of his younger self. The one with ambitions to break the mold set before him before ultimately failing due to his negligence. He foresaw Noreen falling into the same trap, but such naïveté could be avoided. She was an intelligent woman. All she needed was a proper guide to avoid those pitfalls he and many others had succumbed to. A twinkle lightened his dark gaze as he looked at Mary Katherine.

"You're right," he said, "all we can do is look to the future. However, that philosophy can wait until the morning. For now, I just want to focus on the present and being here with you."

32

Two days had passed since the Carnival, and Gwen sat in the field still wearing the white dress and picking flowers while humming the tune to the song of the dance she shared with Mushi. It invoked a sense of joy as it was a night she would not soon forget as Mushi busied himself with feeding and tending to the horses. Her training regimen grew laxer, consisting mostly of sparring and efficiently utilizing nin-nir without tiring, thus allowing more free time throughout the day. Gwen spent much of it wandering the open fields, lying on the beach, and swimming in the sea. Mushi would occasionally join her but spent most of his time sharpening his blade and staring off into the distance with the flower she gave him still tucked into his red sash. She found it difficult to casually speak with him outside of training, mostly because her mind was still fixated on the moment they shared at the end of their dance. Unsure of how he felt about it, she tried to forget it ever happened, which was easier said than done.

"Gwen," Mushi called out to her. "Pack your things. We need to leave. Now."

Due to the urgency in his voice, she dropped the bundle of flowers and hurried into the hut to gather her belongings. She gathered what little provisions remained and packed them into a rucksack with her sleeping pouch. Strapping her sword around her waist, she headed back outside.

"Why the sudden rush?" she asked.

Mushi didn't respond. He stood near the front entrance, wielding his sheathed blade, staring off into the horizon. Gwen followed his gaze to see five figures gliding along the rolling plains and heading straight toward them. Four Militia soldiers, led by a captain wearing a leather-strapped padded jacket, closed fast on horseback. The galloping hooves came to a halt as five horses reared before them, blocking their path. The Militia captain leading the charge had dark skin and black hair pulled back into a series of dreadlocks. The sleeves of his jacket were torn off, revealing the scarred, muscular tissue of his arms. Gwen recognized him to be the captain of the eighth division, Darryl Freeman.

"Well, well," he said in a cocky tone. "Seems our little tip-off from the Carnival was true after all. Smart to hide yourselves here. It was the last place I thought to look."

"What are you doing here?" Mushi asked. "Takata is outside your jurisdiction."

"Normally, you'd be right, but Hardee is busy elsewhere. So, I see nothing wrong with it. Especially if the matter concerns you." His gaze flickered over to Gwen clutching her rucksack and hand ready to draw her sword. "Take the girl. I'll handle the Hand of Death."

Two soldiers dismounted and rushed over to Gwen, restraining her. Mushi didn't move to stop them, keeping his eyes trained on Darryl. The Militia captain stepped down from his horse as well, slipping on a pair of metal gauntlets.

Gwen fought to free herself from the soldiers' grasp. "I am Princess Guinevere Clougher, heir to the throne. I command you to let this man go and return me to the capital."

"I don't take orders from you, woman." Darryl smirked at her. "Green will be the one taking you back to the capital." Turning to Mushi, he pointed a metal finger. "Your head, on the other hand, may get me promoted to surpassing Gunnway as first-division captain. Now that's a look on Green's face I'd love to see."

"If you can take it," Mushi said coldly.

Darryl cracked his neck as a vile sneer crept across his lips. He raised his fists into a fighting position while Mushi remained relaxed, his sword still sheathed in his hand. Taking a step forward, the Militia captain disappeared into thin air. Mushi's shoulder jerked back. Then, his head twisted hard, blood flying out of his mouth, causing him to stagger a bit. Darryl reappeared, pacing around him with a swagger in his step. Gwen blinked and shook her head in a double take, unable to fully comprehend what had just unfolded before her.

"Unbelievable, right?" said Darryl. "Amazing what an extra REV implant can do for you. Don't think I forgot how you made me look like a fool over these past five years. After you helped your old pal Damian escape from Danforth, I hated myself for being so slow. So, I juiced myself up, hoping to get another shot at taking you down. Looks like today is my lucky day because not only am I going to defeat you, but I'm going to do it in the ruins of your own village."

Gwen now understood what had happened. With the assistance of REV implants, Darryl moved at such high speeds, he practically melted into the air itself. So fast, he became invisible to the naked eye. She fought harder to break free from the men restraining her. Mushi didn't stand a chance against an opponent he couldn't see, and she had no intention of watching him die. Kicking one of the soldiers in the groin, she freed an arm and punched the other square in the face. She drew her sword and dashed to reach Mushi's side, but a powerful force struck her in the gut and forced her to collapse to her knees in pain. Darryl stood over the princess, having punched her with his metal gauntlet.

"You two should be ashamed of yourselves," he said to the two soldiers. Composing themselves, they pulled Gwen to her feet. "Can't even handle one princess."

"Leave her alone," Mushi demanded.

The captain vanished again as Mushi was struck with a barrage of invisible blows, nearly bringing him to his knees. Leaning on his sword, he kept himself up as Darryl continued to strut around with pride.

"I'm disappointed," he said. "I thought you'd at least put up more of a fight. All those stories I heard about the infamous Hand of Death over the years, the one bounty no man wished to cash. They said the strokes of your blade struck down hundreds of mercenaries looking to take your head. Where you walked, death was certain to follow. Nothing but silly fables. Tall tales spun together by useless sellswords."

"Are you done talking?" Mushi spat out a mouthful of blood. "Or do you want to get serious?"

Darryl snickered. "If that's what you want."

Raising his fists, the gauntlets rang as blades shot out from each hand. Mushi widened his stance, hovering a hand over the hilt of his sword. Gwen wanted to do something, anything, to help, but this fight was beyond her. After all that training, she was still helpless. The Militia captain danced around, strafing side to side like a predator preparing to strike. Mushi remained as still as a statue. Darryl dashed forward in a gust of wind, blades primed to slash him in half. In that instant, Mushi drew his blade from its sheath. An arc of blood trailed behind the steel of his sword, following the path of his slash. Darryl landed face-first into the grass, cursing in pain as crimson poured out of two deep lacerations on his heels. He tried to stand but fell, as his feet could not support his weight. With a flick of his sword, Mushi cleansed the blade of any blood and carefully sheathed it.

"What are you idiots doing?" cried Darryl. "Shoot him!"

One of the soldiers mounted on his horse drew his rifle and aimed down the sights at Mushi. He didn't fire, however. The gun trembled in his grasp as he was paralyzed by the blood-lusted glare from the Hand of Death. That part of him Gwen sensed hidden deep within, behind his smile, now stood at the forefront. A dark aura seeped out from his very being that drowned the entire field. The other soldiers felt it as well, unable to move. They were gripped by the same fear Gwen felt in Nabal when encountering the mysterious cloaked figure.

"Gwen," said Mushi, "grab your things. We're going."

Gwen picked up her rucksack and hoisted herself onto her horse. Mushi took his time covering himself with his poncho and placing his cone-shaped hat over his head. None of the Militia soldiers moved to stop them. Darryl continued flailing on the ground.

"How dare you let them get away!" he said. "You'll be punished severely for this if you don't stop them this instant."

"I suggest getting your captain immediate medical attention," Mushi said to the soldiers while mounting his horse. "That is, if he wants to continue boasting about that speed he's procured." With a whip of the reins, they trotted off back east.

Once Takata was no longer in sight, Gwen rode up beside Mushi. "You really are incredible. I didn't think you could see him."

"I couldn't," he admitted. "Not completely, at least."

"Then how did you land such a precise strike?"

"Remember how I told you we are all gifted with the power of nin-nir?"

"Yeah."

"After you master the ability to use it efficiently in combat and achieve a perfect balance with what your body can handle, you can take it a step further. With absolute precision and focus, one can harmonize their nin-nir with another's. This heightens their sensory abilities, allowing them to read a person's intentions and movements before they even act on them."

Gwen's eyes widened with astonishment. "You were reading his mind."

"More like I was reading his spirit. Although, this technique is difficult to manifest in battle because achieving perfect harmony takes time. Thankfully, Darryl was arrogant and allowed me the time to accomplish it."

"If he hadn't given you a chance to complete this harmony, would he have killed you?"

Mushi smiled. "If I fought seriously, I'd still beat him. I just thought it was a good opportunity to show you there are still greater heights to climb, even after you master regulating the flow of power within you. In essence, I guess my final lesson is not to get complacent about where you are. Always seek to be stronger."

Gwen felt relieved. Both her mind and heart were put at ease, knowing Mushi, her mentor, was not a man who would die so easily. What continued to trouble her was Captain Freeman's response. Not only did he ignore a direct order, but he said Green would be the one to take her back to the capital. Knowing it was his men back in Lundur that gagged her and almost put her in chains, the notion did not sit well with Gwen. Something strange was going on within the Militia, and she hoped it did not extend to her sister and father at the capital.

33

The echo of Visconti's lengthy exposition droned in Anden's ears, nearly putting him to sleep as he leaned on the far back wall of the sanctum. Between them, hundreds of people gathered with their heads covered by a veil, hood, or other wrappings. He failed to understand how they remained attentive for so long, grasping at every word the old man spoke.

"These may be hard times in which we currently endure," he said, "but the First Emperor blessed us with the strength to overcome it. His strength." His crimson and white robes billowed as he paced the raised platform beneath the towering statue. One could say he fancied himself a king by the way he strutted about above a sea of mesmerized faces. "The war with the rebellion will ultimately come to an end while the Lucius Ambulate alongside the kingdom will endure as they have many centuries before. Beyond a raging storm are calmer waters, and that is where we are headed. Much destruction has taken place in these past months, but we will rebuild. The phoenix serves as Argust's symbol because of its nature to rise from the ashes after basking in the flames of its destruction. So, do not fret. The winds do bring good tidings. Emperor be praised."

The crowd bowed their heads in collective unison, echoing his final words. Anden shook his head, ashamed of the gullible sheep. If only they knew the truth. The faith they followed was nothing more than a curtain for slave trafficking and possibly more insidious labors. Rage pulsed through Anden's veins as he watched the old man pontificate. He wanted nothing more than to march down the aisle and reveal the man's true, horrific nature to the masses. With a single conviction, he would demolish the lies of the Lucius Ambulate and crush it in the process; however, such a hefty conviction required evidence of equal weight. Something they had yet to possess—or did— until Damian handed it over to the heretic roaming the streets. A decision Anden would not have made, but if the exiled pundit could roughly decipher the sigils, it could lead them closer to uncovering the cloaked figures and their goals.

The set of double doors burst open, silencing the sanctum. A wave of refugees from the lower city flooded down the main aisle, led by the wiry hermit hobbling with his staff. All the bowed heads in the gallery turned to face them while Visconti's face hardened with contempt.

"Arios," he spat, "what is the meaning of this? You are excommunicated from the Lucius Ambulate and forbidden from setting foot within the basilica. As for the others, they're a little late for attending the day's service and will need to be escorted out as well."

He nodded to a few pundits sitting in the front row, who stood from their seats and marched up the aisle. As they neared the heretic, a handful of the refugees stepped forward to protect him.

"You've shared your homily," he said. "Now, it's time I shared mine. For years, the Lucius Ambulate closed its doors to many of the refugees seeking some sort of solace. Only the children were taken in on the claim that they were most in need. Many of the parents here accepted this, as would any who sought the safety of their child. However, it has come to light that the Lucius Ambulate under your leadership has been selling them like livestock to slavers and mine owners in the archipelago." He reached into his cloak and pulled out a piece of parchment, holding it up for all to see. "This here is but a single page listing such transactions, and there exists a book with many more."

Anden glanced from the exiled pundit to Visconti, frozen in place. His lips quivered, unable to find words of defense. The crowd remained still as well, unable to comprehend the old man's conviction, but he did not relent.

"And when you're not selling these children to be slaves," he continued, "you're using them as subjects of rituals and dark magic.

The same dark magic which you accused me of to have me exiled and no longer be a threat to your campaign for becoming loren."

"Lies!" said Visconti.

"That so?" The heretic waved a hand jingling with chains, and one of the refugees emerged from the crowd carrying the limp body of a deceased boy. Holding it by the arms, he raised the corpse to display a series of strange symbols embedded in the flesh of his torso. Gasps followed by hushed murmuring filled the sanctum. "This is the most recent victim of the murders you tried to cover up and hide." He pulled out another piece of parchment, this one marked with a copy of the symbols on the boy's skin. "These sigils originate from the ancient text studied by the Lucius Ambulate. Any and all access to such documents must be approved by the loren himself, which means you, Visconti, are ultimately responsible for the demise of these children."

"Don't listen to this man," said Visconti pointing a jagged finger. "He defied the practices of the Lucius Ambulate and the will of the First Emperor."

"Because I tampered in the relics of a dawning age? While you've been keeping secrets and abandoning those who sought your help, I've healed their ailments and cured their illnesses. I did what you failed to do." The heretic thrust his staff toward Visconti. "The First Emperor sought to unite all people across the continent. The one who defies his will is you, and judgment has now come."

The refugees turned rabid as they charged down the aisle

toward the raised platform, mauling Visconti like a horde of fleshlings. As much as the old man pleaded, it didn't help. The pundits were powerless in dispersing the crowd. Even those who, moments ago, were captivated by his words joined the mob. Anden remained on the outskirts of the chaos, witnessing it all unfold as they carried him out of the sanctum. Curious, he followed to see what twisted fate awaited the old man.

*

The line between justice and vengeance was thin, but Anden ultimately figured the old man deserved the punishment decided by the people. Tied to a stake, he hung above the mob, stripped of his luxurious garments. The only thing keeping him decent was a strip of cloth wrapped around his waist. Visconti's predicament should serve as an example of humility, but the mob no longer cared for moralistic lessons. They were bloodthirsty, chanting for the man's death. The exiled pundit hobbled forward, approaching the stake with a torch in hand. Visconti cowered from the flame, flailing violently to free himself from his bindings.

"Arios, don't do this," he said in desperation. "I'm sorry for exiling you. You were right. I did it to guarantee my victory in the election, and I may have sold off some of the children, but it was to finance the Lucius Ambulate. My actions were misguided, but you know I'm no practitioner of dark magic. Please, let me down and cast me away. Exile me."

"It's too late, old friend," said Arios. "Do not fret, though. We will reunite in paradise." He turned toward the mob, hoisting the torch into the air. "As the loren said, Argust takes the symbol of the phoenix, a bird rebirthed in flame. It's time for the Lucius Ambulate to share a similar rebirth basking in the divine flames of the First Emperor." Spinning back around, he tossed the torch onto the pile of wood stacked at the stake's base.

The tinder caught fire, setting the rest of the structure ablaze. The cheers of the mob drowned out Visconti's screams of pain as the flaming tongues whipped against the flesh of his legs. It was a dismal event for those living in the upper city and the refugees cast into the gutters to unite around, but united they were all the same. A stark contrast to when Anden first arrived. Taking a swig from his flask, the light of the fire shimmered against the metal as the flames wrapped around Visconti, engulfing him completely.

34

The pile of petals Victoria plucked scattered into the wind as a slight breeze drifted through the small alcove in the gardens. She stared at the bare stem of the once beautiful flower before tossing it aside like the others. Kaylin was to meet her for further training an eternity ago. It was rare for her mentor to be late, but to dismiss their meeting without a word or warning was unprecedented. Tired of waiting, Victoria pushed through the bushes and out of the alcove, marching into the palace. She climbed up the stairs and proceeded down the halls toward Blackwood's office. The door was closed as it often was since the start of the conclave, meaning he did not wish to be disturbed, but Victoria didn't much care. If anyone knew where Kaylin was, it would be him. Knocking on the door, she heard his stern voice call out from within the room.

"Come in."

Victoria opened the door to find him at his desk, brooding over different pieces of parchment. His dark gaze glanced up at her, his expression remaining stoic. He rarely seemed to smile. The only time Victoria ever witnessed one crack in his demeanor was once when speaking with Mary Katherine. "Victoria," he said, "is something the matter?"

"Hello, Uncle Blackwood." She shuffled into the room, standing behind the chair opposite his desk. "I was wondering if you knew where Kaylin was."

He returned his attention to the papers strewn across his desk. "Captain Gunnway is currently busy escorting some of the ambassadors about the city. Why?"

"No reason," said Victoria. "Just curious."

He looked up at her once more, eyebrows raised. "Curious as to why she didn't show up for your little meetings in the garden?"

A boulder sank into the pit of Victoria's stomach, causing her posture to stiffen. She tried to think of an excuse, but only one question escaped her lips. "How do you know about us meeting in the garden?"

Standing, he guided her over to a nearby window. Looking out, she felt her skin turn pale. The view of Blackwood's office window overlooked the gardens below. She glanced over to the location of the alcove, and thankfully, the foliage of the surrounding bushes masked it from his view. "I've noticed, here and there, that you two gather in the gardens, tucking yourselves away beyond that wall of bushes. What is it that you two do back there?"

Victoria swallowed the panic she felt. If Blackwood learned of her endeavors to use a sword and the ways of the old traditions, then he would certainly tell her father, ending her training with Kaylin.

"We talk about Gwen," she said. "Comforting each other as we hope for her to be found."

Blackwood sighed. "As do we all." Victoria wondered if that was true, given that Parliament was voting to get rid of her father and place her on the throne in his stead. "Forgive me for souring the moment, but I am expecting someone. If that is all, then you should go."

"Right," said Victoria. "Sorry for disturbing you." She exited Blackwood's office. Closing the door, she leaned against it and took a deep breath of relief. Her secret was still safe, it seemed. With Kaylin busy and nothing else to do, the princess aimlessly wandered the halls. She looked at the portraits of the royal lineage ruling over Argust since King Edward, her family's lineage. Eventually, she stumbled upon the portrait of her father in his youth when the hair on his head was gold, and his stature was strong with determination. To the left was a portrait of her grandfather, Lucius II, a man who seemed forged by harsh environments, both social and physical, with a scowl permanently set on his face. Her father spoke few words about him, mostly stating his tenure as king was controversial, to say the least. It was his decisions that indirectly ignited the war with the Red Rebellion, lasting decades. To the right was an empty space on the wall where the portrait of her father's successor would hang. The question still remained, would it be Gwen or herself?

"Strange, isn't it?" Victoria glanced over to see Mary Katherine approaching. "Hard to imagine your father being so young once."

"Makes it harder to believe that he's practically on his deathbed," she said.

"Your father will pull through." Mary Katherine placed her hands on Victoria's shoulders. "He may not look it from the outside, but he still possesses a strong spirit."

Victoria pulled away from the ambassador's grasp. "You should tell the other ambassadors that rather than try to usurp his rule." She glared at Mary Katherine, who looked stunned, unable to find any appropriate words. "He told me about the vote. How Parliament wants to replace him with me in Gwen's absence."

Mary Katherine thinned her lips. "Then, he should have also told you that some of us are stalemating the vote to allow ample time to find your sister."

"And how much longer is that?" snapped Victoria. "It's been nearly four months since Gwen was seen in Lundur, and all we've had since then are rumors of her being at Danforth during the rebel attack."

"Captain Hardee has enlisted some of the best trackers on the continent to aid in finding her. I'm sure with enough time, they'll turn up something."

Anger coiled in Victoria's gut. "A few trackers? With the resources of the entire Militia across the continent, all we can afford to find my sister are a few trackers? The last time we used a few trackers, they let Gwen slip through their grasps, never to be seen again."

"We cannot afford to use every soldier to solely find your sister," said Mary Katherine. "Rebuilding Danforth, helping refugees relocate, and launching a counterattack against the rebels require Militia resources as well. I want Gwen found just as much as you, but we cannot completely ignore the needs of the kingdom and its people."

"As I remember, attacking the rebels was left to a Parliament vote, and it came out being unanimous. All of you decided to expend Militia resources on burning the southern plains to ash instead of searching for my sister. Now, you debate whether or not my father should still be king with Gwen missing. You all have given up on her. Parliament, father, and even you. The only ones who haven't given up on Gwen are Kaylin and me, but you all won't let her go. Instead, she's stuck escorting these pompous ambassadors. If it comes to it, I'll search for Gwen myself before sitting on that throne."

A hot sting of pain burned Victoria's cheek, silencing her. The few wrinkles Mary Katherine possessed deepened with rage as her hand remained raised from slapping the princess. "Don't you dare speak such foolishness. I've been fighting for Gwen ever since the night your father dragged me into the throne room to tell me of her disappearance. You don't think I share your frustrations? Every day, I want nothing more than to leave this city and search for Gwen myself, but I, like Captain Gunnway and you, have a duty to uphold. You are the remaining heir to the royal bloodline. Yours is a life that cannot be squandered, and if it comes to it, you will become Queen of Argust."

"Fuck duty," said Victoria. "I won't take the throne even if the vote passes. It's meant for Gwen."

"Stop acting like an imprudent little girl. We both may hate it, but the reality of the situation must be faced."

"There's that phrase again. Everyone keeps saying that. Well, fine. Let's face reality. You're not my mother, so stop lecturing me as if you were."

She could see in the ambassador's narrow eyes that Mary Katherine wanted to slap her again but refrained. "If that's how you feel, then I shall do as you wish, princess." Turning sharply on her heels, Mary Katherine marched down the hall, leaving Victoria alone.

The princess pulled at her noodle strings of hair, and anguish filled her heart as she let out a silent scream. She took off running back to the tranquility of the gardens. She didn't care what anyone said. She wouldn't wear the crown or sit on the throne. She wouldn't give up on Gwen. As soon as her foot touched the grass, she fell to her knees and tore the blades from the ground in anger.

"It's unbecoming of royalty to throw a fit like a child," said a voice. Victoria turned around to see the bulbous figure of Rahm Krawczyk standing behind her.

"What do you want?" she spat, trying to compose herself.

The ambassador pursed his lips. "Hard to ignore a spectacle such as that. Especially seeing Ambassador Brown strut off in a rare, fiery mood. I would be lying if I said my interest was not piqued."

"It's nothing, and even if it weren't, I'd have no words for you."

"Quite a bit of nothing to stir such a ruckus," he said, "but I understand the sentiment." With ill contempt, he picked a flower from its stem and crumpled it in his grasp, unraveling the petals. "The only one you can confide your problems in is yourself, for you are the only one able to solve them. A lesson I learned when I was about your age."

Victoria averted her gaze from the ambassador, as if he wasn't there. Perhaps if she ignored him, he would go away.

"I can't imagine the stress you must be going through. The declining health of your father, the disappearance of your sister, and now the sudden possibility of burdening the charge to rule the entire kingdom. Such a series of events could drive anyone mad, especially when they're thrust upon you against your will."

"Says a member of Parliament," said Victoria. "The ones trying to thrust that responsibility onto me and abandoning my sister."

"Your sister is not abandoned. In fact, I have it on good authority from Captain Freeman that she was recently spotted at the remains of Takata."

Victoria perked up, snapping her head around to look at the ambassador with glassy eyes. "My sister is alive? Truly?"

He nodded. "Unfortunately, the Hand of Death prevented her rescue." He slammed a fist into his beefy palm. "That's twice now we've allowed her to slip from our grasp. It's unacceptable. If it weren't for the Militia's incompetence, I'm sure your sister would be here with us, and this whole political debacle could be avoided. It's a shame."

"Kaylin could bring her back," she said, "but Blackwood won't let her."

"Captain Gunnway has always been a woman of duty. She does what she's told, even if she may not like it. Admirable for a member of the Militia, but sometimes the rules need to be bent, if not broken, to garner results. 'Fuck duty' is what I believe I heard echoed through the halls. A perfect sentiment."

"And what about facing the reality of the situation?"

The husky man bent down slightly with a smirk creasing his jowl. "Reality is set through the actions we take, not the circumstances. It's based on what we choose to do or not do." With a bow, the ambassador lumbered out of the gardens.

Victoria remained on the ground. She was overjoyed to know that Gwen was still alive; however, fear quickly took its place as she processed the rest of Rahm's news. Gwen might be alive, but she was sighted with the Hand of Death, a traitor to the kingdom. Wondering if

Mary Katherine was aware of the news, Victoria sprang to her feet, anxious to share it. She soon stopped herself, not even leaving the gardens. If Rahm knew, then certainly Mary Katherine did as well. Not to mention, the Militia had already failed twice to save Gwen, and everyone seemed content with Victoria taking the mantle as queen, foregoing her sister. She wouldn't stand for it. That was not the reality she wanted to face. All those years of training with Kaylin weren't meant as a hobby. She learned the art of wielding a sword and the ways of the old traditions in order to protect her family. Unlike the time when she lost her mother, Victoria was not a helpless child. This time she could take action and bring her sister home.

35

Noreen sharpened her wit as she strode through the unusual vacant halls toward the chancellor's study, wondering what it was he desired from her this time. She already sided with him in the vote. What more could he want? Perhaps a stalemate was only the first step in his plans, and he required further assistance. A matter she had no interest in pursuing. She acted on behalf of Gwen's benefit, not his or the king's. Approaching the door, she smoothed the creases in her uniform and made sure the braids in her hair were taut and neat. The one seeming more put together usually carried the advantage, and Blackwood was a stickler for detail. Knocking on the door, she heard a muffled shout from the other side, urging her to enter. Blackwood sat behind his desk, glowing in his elegant white suit. His cape folded open from his shoulders and cascaded down the length of the chair to the floor. His hair was neatly slicked back, and he stroked his groomed goatee as his dark gaze rose from the parchment before him.

"Ambassador Archer," he said, gesturing to the nearby chair. "Please, take a seat." Evidently, they shared the same philosophy when it came to physical appearances in negotiations. His pristine appearance gave Ambassador Fletcher a run for his money.

Noreen sat down, making sure to maintain a proper posture. She glanced around the room, taking note of the bookshelf in the far corner, opulent pieces of furniture, and a self-portrait from his younger years, when a dash of gray didn't pepper his raven hair hanging behind his head. "A fine study you have to work in. It's almost a shame that this is my first time seeing it."

"Some would consider that a blessing," he said. "A summons from the chancellor into his private study is something many wish never to receive."

"Many, but not all," said Noreen. "Based on the vote, I'm sure Ambassador Weyman walked out carrying a decent amount of coin in his pocket."

"Not as much as he liked."

"Is that why you summoned me? Should I expect another failed attempt at a bribe to keep me in line against Rahm?"

Blackwood relaxed, leaning deep into his chair. "Actually, I wanted to offer my gratitude. Despite the hardships you've faced that could be blamed on the king, you still voted to keep him in power."

Out of all the scenarios Noreen imagined, this was not one of them. Issuing a summons for a simple thank you was inconceivable. The gratitude had to be a ploy, a battering ram to tear down her defenses before getting to the core of his reason for summoning her. "I didn't do it for the king. I did it for Gwen. Ambassador Brown clarified that stalemating the vote would allow more time for her to be found."

"Quite right," he said with a nod. "Tell me, do you consider Guinevere a friend?"

"Why does that matter?"

The chancellor rose from his seat, turning his back toward her to stare at his portrait. "You know what I see when I look at this depiction of my younger self recently inducted as chancellor? A man filled with ambition to change the world and raise Argust to the prominence it once held in years gone by. The king believed in achieving much of the same. Unfortunately, that ambition caused us to stumble down the righteous path we set before ourselves. The good we did achieve seems outweighed by the regrets of our wrongdoings."

"A somber tale," said Noreen, "but you still haven't answered my question."

Blackwood turned to face her, his head hanging from his shoulders in a vulnerable state. One she never thought to see him in. "For more than two decades, Peter and I have worked together to rule the kingdom. To me, he's nearly a brother. From the things I've heard about you and Gwen in your younger years, I see the potential for a similar future for the two of you. If that does become a possibility, then I feel it's beneficial for you to take a look at this." Opening a drawer in his desk, the chancellor pulled out a small, leather-bound book with a strap holding it closed.

Noreen tilted her head, curious. "What is it?"

"A journal," he said. "My journal, to be more specific. You see, Chancellor Valcrum kept one, and I learned a great deal from it. So, I decided to follow in his footsteps. From what I understand, you're an avid reader. You might find some useful information, or so I hope. The more we understand the mistakes of our past, the less likely we are to repeat them."

Noreen found herself at a loss for words. This could not be real. She had to be dreaming. Blackwood never talked to her like this. He never was this open, but the fading of his pristine demeanor confirmed it. The mournful look in his eyes filled with regret, the slouch in his shoulders from bearing the weight of his position's responsibilities, and the tender care with which he handled the small book sold the sincerity. It was all real. For the first time, she struggled to retort with a sharp remark. "I don't know what to say."

"You don't need to say anything. Take it as a token of my gratitude and the sign of a promise to see Gwen become queen." Handing her the journal, she could feel the words and knowledge within weigh heavy in her hand.

Tucking it underneath her arm, she looked at him with

newfound respect. "Is that all, Chancellor?"

"It is, Ambassador."

With that, Noreen rose from the chair and left Blackwood's study. Pacing the hall back to her own chambers, she took out the journal and unwrapped the strap to unveil its contents. Across the first page, in bold, cursive strokes of ink, it read:

Following in the footsteps of my predecessor, I, Chancellor Strom Blackwood, have decided to record the account of my tenure from a personal perspective. This is to serve as an unofficial document meant to provide insight and guidance to any and all successors following my departure. May it serve those persons well and provide context to the decisions made regardless of how history chooses to judge their outcome.

36

With the celebration of the Carnival concluded, Bushgrove returned to being the major port town of the west. The massive crowds of tourists were replaced by the bustling locals going about their daily lives. The fleet of ships faded into a handful dealing mainly in cargo, fishing, and transport. While the roads were open enough for Julius to maneuver their cart through the town, the docks flooded with people seeking transport away from the devastated land left in the Militia's wake. Everything seemed barren and plain without the lanterns dangling overhead or the banners draped over the building walls. With no glamor or spectacle offering a distraction, reality regained a foothold, and people grew fearful.

"Seems to be a long line for getting on a ship," said Julius, staring at the crowded docks.

"We'll secure our own vessel if we need to," said Reed.

"We should stop at the Leaky Canteen," added Riggs. "I have a few favors I can pull with Lieutenant Locke to grant us access to a ship."

Julius glanced over his shoulder. "Locke abandoned his post. So, unless you can curry favors with ghosts, it'll be a waste of time."

"We should lie low there for the time being," said Reed. "Gather our wits and figure out a plan."

Julius guided the mule along the streets until they reached an asymmetrical building, with one side having a single floor and the other having two with an angled roof. "Here we are," said the businessman. "The Leaky Canteen."

At first glance, the place seemed abandoned, with glasses scattered across the bar, stools and tables turned over, and papers littered across the floor. Whenever Locke and his men left, they did so in a hurry. Riggs glanced around the room with a disappointed shake of his head while sucking at his lips.

"I thought a man of Locke's stature had more fortitude than this," he said. "The spineless worm."

"Coming from a man who hid in a tunnel for weeks while the Militia paraded around the southern plains," said Julius, striking a match to light his pipe. Riggs glared at him from the corners of his eyes as the glow from the burning tobacco lit up Julius' face and shined off the bent metal of his broken pince-nez. "You want an example of what would've become of Locke? Just look at me. I didn't abandon my post after the days of silence from base camp and paid a hefty price for it. Trust me, if I had the option again, I'd follow in Locke's footsteps."

"I'd expect nothing less from a man without principle such as yourself. Locke, however, was a true military man. He was loyal, dedicated, and meant to keep you and that swine Perrotti in line."

Julius exhaled a cloud of smoke drifting past the general's face. "That turned out well, didn't it?"

"Stop it, both of you," said Reed. Even though she no longer commanded the rebellion, she still found herself dealing with worthless bickering. "None of that matters now. We must focus on figuring out the fastest way to get to Papuri."

"Unless you have a boarding pass of some kind, you'd have better luck going around the Blade's Trench and crossing the bridge at the Western Gate," called down a voice from above. Creaking footsteps drew the group's attention to the stairs on the other side of the room, where Piper descended, wearing the same ratty clothing and oily dark hair. She rested her arms along the railing, staring at them with a mocking gaze. "To be honest, I didn't think I'd see you here again. Well, at least not in chains."

Reed retorted with an equally contemptuous glare. "Sorry to disappoint."

Rapid footsteps clamored across the floorboards above as her brother hurried down the stairs as well. Upon seeing Reed, his face went pale and his jaw slack. "Commander Skokna," he stuttered.

"Stop calling her commander," said his sister. "She doesn't deserve the respect of a formal address. Not after the failure she's sowed throughout the entire rebellion."

Riggs stepped forward, the hairs of his mustache ruffling as he cleared his throat. "Now, miss, may I advise—"

"Shut it, old man," she snapped. "I don't want to hear any advice from you."

The young man pulled his sister close, whispering in her ear. "Piper, that's General Riggs. One of the longest-serving members of the rebellion. You should show at least a modicum of respect."

"To hell with respect," she said, pulling away from him. "Because of their decisions, there's hardly a rebellion left. Stop trying to be the good little soldier and stand up for yourself every once in a while." She rounded on them with fury in her eyes. "As for the lot of you, hurry up in figuring out your travels and leave us alone. We don't want anything to do with the rebellion anymore." Storming up the stairs, she left her brother standing there with a nervous expression on his face.

"Please excuse my sister," he said, climbing down the stairs and addressing Reed and Riggs with a salute. "We've lost a lot of comrades and friends just to reach a bit of safety, and she's taking it pretty hard."

"That's alright, son," said Riggs. "Why don't you tell us your name?"

"Spencer, sir. My sister's name is Piper."

"You can drop the formalities." Julius planted himself on one of the stools near the bar. "We're all in the same boat here."

"Right," he said with a stiff nod. "Sorry."

Riggs gave a friendly pat on the shoulder. "Tell me, where were you and your sister deployed?"

"We served with the platoon just north of Hirane Village."

"You've traveled a long way to make it here," the general said. "I can understand your sister's hostility. Where is it you hail from?"

"From White Horn originally," said Spencer. "If you don't mind me asking, did the commander bring you from base camp to help get things sorted out?"

"You should listen to your sister and stop calling me commander," said Reed. "As of now, none of us are part of the rebellion."

The man beamed a look of intense shock. "What? Why?"

"Didn't see eye to eye on things going forward," she said with a casual shrug. "The other generals and I had a different vision for the rebellion following this tumultuous fallout."

"So, what is it you plan on doing?" he asked.

"Going back to the rebellion's roots," said Riggs. "We're heading to Papuri to disrupt the slave shipments into the archipelago for mining. Make a stand for freedom, just like Richard used to."

Spencer scanned all three of them with stars of wonder twinkling in his eyes. "Would it be too much to ask if my sister and I could join you? She's the one who originally convinced me to join the rebellion, believing in the fight for freedom. She might be a bit brash, but I'm sure she would be willing to help in your mission. Besides, it'll help us get away from here."

Riggs looked to Reed, whose face remained still as stone. "I'm sure we could use a few more abled bodies. What skills do you two possess?"

"Both of us are decent ranged fighters," he explained. "You won't find anyone more accurate at throwing daggers or hatchets than my sister. As for me, I'm a pretty decent shot with a rifle. In fact, I've actually been working on some modifications if you want to see them."

"Sure," said Riggs with a wide grin. "Show me what you've concocted."

Excited, Spencer raced up the stairs and hurried back, carrying a strange-looking rifle. The barrel was extended with a cylindrical attachment, and in place of the iron sight was a fixture in the shape of a miniature telescope. Holding it out for the general to examine, Riggs studied the weapon with mild curiosity. The young man proceeded to detail that the attachment over the barrel suppressed the sound of the gun blast when fired, and the attachment replacing the original sight allowed him to aim more accurately at further distances. Meanwhile, Reed strutted over to Julius at the bar, who continued puffing away at his pipe.

"You really plan on letting the boy scout and his charming personality of a sister join us?" Julius asked.

"If Riggs thinks they can be useful, I'll trust his judgment."

The businessman peeked over her shoulder at the old general fawning over Spencer's modifications. "He seems pretty impressed so far. Although, I'm not so sure the woman shares her brother's enthusiasm."

"Whether they come or not doesn't affect our mission. We need to get to Papuri."

He sighed a breath of smoke. "If only our fisherman friend was still around. We won't get there using that mule, I guarantee you that. We'll need a ship."

Reed tapped the nail of her thumb against her chin. "I would suggest we use the ships on which Locke and his men transported product, but I'm sure they used those same ships to escape."

"Might be a few dinghies left behind, but nothing for extended travel in the western sea."

The front door to the tavern flew open as a wave of blue uniforms stormed in with their rifles raised. "Everyone stay where you are and put your hands up!" one of the soldiers yelled.

They all complied with his demands, raising their hands in the air. Spencer carefully placed his rifle by his feet before lifting his hands above his head.

"We've received reports from various locals and traveling merchants of illicit behavior and extortion," said the soldier, stepping closer toward them. "You'll be brought in for questioning and, if found guilty, sentenced for punishment. Make any moves, and we will fire upon you." With his men keeping their rifles trained on the others, he lowered his weapon and pulled out a pair of handcuffs. Grabbing Reed's arms, he tried to slip them onto her wrists, but she moved too quickly.

Reaching for the dagger at her waist, Reed slit the man's throat and sent him falling to the ground, choking on his own blood. One of the other soldiers aimed his rifle at her, but Julius unveiled the small pistol from his sleeve. A cloud of smoke exploded out of the barrel with a flash as a small hole punctured the soldier's chest, and his body went limp. Lifting his foot, Spencer tossed his rifle into the air and caught it, firing a shot into another soldier's gut. Reed flung her dagger at the last soldier, cutting his arm. It wasn't lethal, but it did create an opening for Riggs to unsheathe his sword and charge at the man, impaling him. With a twist of his blade, the general forced the last breath from the man's body. Four Militia soldiers lay dead on the floor, and more were sure to come.

Reed strutted across the room to retrieve her dagger. When she bent down to pick it up, she heard the click of a hammer. Glancing over, she stared down the barrel of a rifle being held by the soldier Spencer had shot. He writhed on the floor with blood leaking from his stomach, but managed a smirk as his eyes met hers.

"So, you're still alive," he said. "For my brothers at Danforth, I'll make sure you stay dead this time."

His head lurched forward as the smirk faded from his lips, and the rifle fell from his grasp. As his body slumped over, Reed saw a dagger protruding out of the back of his skull. Piper stood atop the stairs with her arm extended.

"Look what you've gone and done!" she shouted. "You let the Militia follow you here and endangered us."

"Us?" said Reed, sheathing her dagger. "They came here because those people you and your brother harassed during the Carnival finally spoke up. This is your own fault. Be grateful we were here to help you clean them up."

The dark-haired woman stomped down the stairs in a fury. "Grateful? If I hadn't sunk a dagger into his head, you'd have a bullet through yours."

"That's enough, ladies," said Riggs, sheathing his own blade. "You can continue arguing after we've made it out of town. It won't take long for more of them to arrive."

"And where do you suppose we go?" asked Julius. "That mule can barely outrun a child, let alone a horse."

Reed turned her emerald gaze to Riggs. "My uncle told me you have some experience sneaking aboard vessels as stowaways."

A smile emerged from beneath the general's mustache. "That

I do, and if it's a passenger ship, then we'll have the added benefit of hiding in plain sight once we're on board."

"The next passenger ship heading to Papuri. When does it depart?" she asked the siblings.

"Less than an hour, probably," said Spencer.

Finally, Reed turned to Julius puffing on his pipe. "If Locke and his men were to leave any boats abandoned, where would they be?"

Removing it from his lips, the businessman tapped the pipe against the bar and dumped out the ash. "Right this way."

*

Bullets pelted into the surface of the water, displacing the mirror image of the twilight sky. Julius and Riggs churned the oars of the dinghy, barreling them across the water and away from the shoreline infested with more Militia soldiers. Spencer peered through the fixture mounted on his rifle as Reed and Piper hunkered down to avoid any stray bullets.

"Stay on this course," said Spencer. "The ship should pass us soon."

Approaching at a fair distance was one of the ships docked at the port, ferrying a number of the frightened people seeking to escape the southern plains. Behind them, the Militia soldiers boarded a small vessel, following them across the estuary. Piper hastily tied a knot around the handle of a hatchet with the other end secured at the front of their dinghy.

"Sure you'll be able to make it hold?" asked Reed.

"Of course I'm sure," she said, pulling the rope taut and tightening the knot.

"Ship's coming up," said Spencer.

Riggs and Julius slowed their rowing, allowing the ship to pass by as it made its way toward the western sea. The Militia vessel closed in on them fast, having four rowers to their two. Gunfire continued raining down on them, splintering the wood of their boat. Standing up, Piper took the rope and twirled it around in her hand and, in a quick, fluid motion, flung it straight as an arrow into the hull of the ship. The blade dug deep into the wood and pulled on the rope connected to their boat. The dinghy lurched forward, causing her to stumble. Piper nearly fell off the side, but Reed grabbed her arm and kept the woman from falling overboard. With their anchor secured, their boat trailed behind the passenger ship at a speed that outpaced the Militia vessel chasing them. The splash of the gunfire in the water diminished as the soldiers became a speck on the sea. Julius rubbed his sore arms while Riggs erupted into a guffaw.

"Now that's what I'm talking about," the old general said. "That really got the blood pumping. I felt at least twenty years younger."

Spencer took one last look through the fixture atop his rifle. "Looks like we're in the clear. Militia seems to have given up completely."

"Told you I could get it to stick," said Piper, giving Reed a condescending side-eye.

Reed couldn't stop the smile stretching across her ruby lips as the spray of the water wetted her face and the wind swept through her raven locks. "That you did." She took out the plain white mask left behind by the merchant.

Piper stared at it curiously. "Why do you have that?"

"I'm supposed to be dead, aren't I?" she responded. "This will help make sure it stays that way."

Riggs shot to his feet, making the boat wobble. "Don't get too relaxed now. We still need to board the ship. Won't last the entire trip on this old thing."

He was right. Reed stepped forward, placing a gentle hand on his shoulder. "You've done your part. Take a rest."

The old man sat down as the siblings joined her at the head of the dinghy. They grabbed hold of the rope connecting them to the passenger ship and pulled with all their strength, reeling their boat closer so they could board.

37

The Holy City was nothing like Gwen remembered from her faint memories as a young girl. It seemed tainted and dirty. The glorious basilica didn't stand atop Illios as a beacon of hope, but loomed overhead as if the statues of the Seven Saints judged all beneath their stony gaze. Her stomach turned over at the sight of a charred corpse dangling from a scorched stake in a bed of ashes. The people were in hysteria, crowding the streets and desecrating any semblance of the Lucius Ambulate they could find. Various statues were vandalized, tipped over, or shattered into ruin. The Militia fought to hold the masses at bay, but there were too many people and not enough soldiers. Mushi and Gwen rode through the chaos until they reached the lower levels, where the anarchy was far worse. The manic behavior scared the horses, forcing them to dismount and proceed on foot. Wesley fought his way through the crowd toward them, piecing together an uneasy smile.

"Good to see you've made it back," he said. His yellow eyes studied Gwen with her short hair, tan skin, and sinewy frame. "Almost didn't recognize you, Gwen. You look good."

"Wish I could say the same for the city," she responded. "It seems to have gone to hell."

"What happened?" asked Mushi.

Wesley turned to him with a dejected look on his face. "Come to the inn we're staying at. We can all explain what's happened."

He guided them to a rundown inn whose patrons had seen better days. The entire interior was a bar fight over food, coin, and whatever else could be considered valuable for survival. Wesley warded off anyone looking their way by making them stare down the barrel of his pistol. Upstairs, they entered a compact room, where Anden and Damian waited. The former Militia captain seemed to be in better health than when she last saw him, and Anden no longer wore his bucket-shaped hat, allowing his brown locks to be on full display.

"Look who decided to show up," said Anden.

"Care to explain why the city is tearing itself apart?" asked Mushi.

"We managed to discover who was committing the murders," said Wesley as he squeezed by to sit at the foot of the bed. With all five of them present, there was little room to maneuver.

"Loren Visconti of the Lucius Ambulate used his influence and knowledge of the ancient text to perform dark rituals on refugee children," explained Damian. "Each of the victims' bodies was marked with a pattern of strange symbols that left them looking like hollow shells."

"He was also selling them to slavers off the coasts of Papuri," added Anden, with a hint of disgust in his words.

Hearing this information shocked Gwen. For such an esteemed institution as the Lucius Ambulate to fall into corruption meant nothing was sacred anymore.

Mushi twisted the end of his pointed beard. "Were you able to find any connections between the rituals and the cloaked figures? What their goals might be?"

"Maybe, if the whole city hadn't found out and torched Visconti like a shish kebab," said Anden. He gave a sideways glance to Damian on the floor.

"Arios told me he would try to translate the sigils on the boy's body," he said. "It may have gotten us closer to understanding what the rituals may be for."

"But instead, he used it as evidence to get the man killed. Not that he didn't deserve it, but now, we're left with nothing. I knew we shouldn't have trusted that old hermit."

"Who's this Arios?" Mushi asked.

"A banished pundit," said Damian. "He was a rival to Visconti for becoming loren of the Ambulate, who exiled him for his interests in engineer constructs. He proved a vital asset in unraveling the mystery of the murders, but it seems revenge took hold of him after learning Visconti was the one behind them."

Mushi rubbed a hand over his face, sighing. "At least he'll no longer be a danger to anyone."

"This madness could be a silver lining," said Wesley, staring out the room's singular window. "Protection around the basilica is scarce if we wish to investigate the matter further on our own."

Damian rose to his feet. "Visconti kept copies of the other victims' sigils in his study. I'm sure there must be some sort of translation or at least more information regarding their use there as well."

Mushi nodded. "The basilica it is, then."

As the others marched out of the room, Gwen caught Anden staring at her. "Something catch your eye?"

He cleared his throat. "Your hair. It's shorter."

Gwen pushed a few strands behind her ear. "And you're not wearing your hat."

He smirked. "Guess we both needed a change in style."

"Seems that way," she said, also smiling. Together, they joined the others on their hike to the basilica in the upper city.

*

The basilica's interior was as grand as the throne room at the palace, untouched by the chaos occurring outside its doors. A spacious room with rows of pews surrounded a giant marble depiction of the First Emperor. The light from the stain-glass windows covered the floor in a shattering of various colors. This was the wonder Gwen expected to witness in the Holy City.

"Visconti's private study is on the second floor. This way," said Damian.

"You and Wesley investigate his study," said Mushi. "Anden and I are going to take a peek in the sacred archives for anything that could help decipher those sigils."

"What about Gwen?" Wesley asked.

"She can stay here and serve as our lookout. If anything happens, she can defend herself, and I have a method of keeping tabs on her."

Gwen clutched the hilt of her sword and gave them all a thumbs-up with a wink. "I'm not worthless, like I was back in Nabal. Go find what you need. I've got this area covered."

Wesley gave her a nod of approval, and the four men broke off into separate corridors on opposite sides of the raised platform.

*

Damian led Wesley through the halls to a staircase leading up to the second floor. Reaching the door with the ornament of the flaming sword, he kicked it off its hinges and sent it crashing onto the floor. Not much had changed since his last visit, as mounds of papers were still stacked high on the desk. The hardcover book detailing Visconti's dealings with the miners resided in its previous position, and sheets of various symbols similar to the sigils carved into the victims' flesh covered the walls. Wesley stared at it all with a contortion to his brow that signaled neither curiosity nor wonder. Instead, he seemed perturbed.

"This certainly seems like the room of a deranged madman," he said, scanning the endless pages of symbols and the deceased loren's efforts to decipher their meaning. His gaze fell onto the painting hovering over the desk. "Nice picture, though."

Damian tore through the drawers. Papers scattered through the air and cluttered the study as he ripped them out, desperately searching. "Where are they? Why aren't they here?"

Wesley tried to calm him down. "Where's what? What's going on?"

"I know Visconti kept the other sketches in one of the drawers," said Damian, "but they're not here."

"They have to be around here somewhere." Wesley started shuffling through the various sheets of parchment littering the floor.

Pulling out the last drawer from the desk, Damian sifted

through it, unable to find the other sketches. Throwing it against the wall, the wood shattered into a mess of splinters. "They're not here. Someone must've taken them."

"Who?" asked Wesley. "Visconti's dead. It's not like he could waltz in here and get rid of them."

Damian pondered for a moment, remembering a pundit that had given Visconti the sketch, to begin with, and was trusted enough to oversee the disposal of the body. "Visconti trusted one other man with this information, a pundit named Theo. He might be the one who took the sigil sketches."

"How do you suggest we find him?"

"There's no way he'd risk being out in the streets right now. He has to be hiding here somewhere, and we'll search every nook and cranny until we find him."

The two men darted out of the study and back into the halls. Going from room to room, they kicked in every door, searching for the missing pundit. They eventually worked their way back down to the first floor. One of the rooms served as a place of prayer with a single pew set before a small effigy of the First Emperor. Another was a place of study with rows of tables and chairs and books strewn about, opened to various pages. Not a single pundit could be found. Damian doubted they had fled the city. Following Visconti's trial by burning pyre, the people would seek to take their heads as well. It was too dangerous for them to attempt an escape. They had to be hidden here.

"Damian," Wesley called down the hallway with a horrified expression. "I think I found him."

Damian hurried down the hall to join him. Wesley stood at the threshold of a room with a stone floor and brick walls. A beam stretched across the far side where whips, flogs, and other instruments of torture and punishment hung stained with dried blood. A furnace resided in the corner with an iron resting against it. The head seemed to be interchangeable with other slabs of iron, each with a different number molded onto its surface. The tool Visconti and his pundits most likely used to brand the refugee children they took in. These, however, were not the reason for Wesley's horrified look. Hanging on the beam alongside the instruments of torture was the mutilated body of a man wearing the robes of a pundit. Blood seeped out of deep lesions and gashes in his flesh and dripped onto the floor. The kill was fresh. Damian stepped into the room toward the body and peered under the veil of his hood. He recognized the face as that of the young man he saw in Visconti's study. This, indeed, was the pundit Theo. Digging through the man's robes, he didn't find any of the sketches.

"Think our murderer is still at large?" asked Wesley.

Damian noticed a bit of powder on the man's robes. Rubbing some on his finger, he held it up to his nose, taking a sniff. The scent was not like the one he smelled back in the alley, similar to the musky fragrance of incense. This smell was different, yet still familiar. It contained more of an herbal scent, much more akin to the cream he'd applied to his wound, just more burned.

With wild eyes, he turned to Wesley, realization dawning on him. "Visconti wasn't the one responsible for the murders. We've been fooled."

*

Anden followed Mushi to the lower levels of the basilica, where the sacred archives supposedly resided. The spiral staircase seemed to stretch on forever, making him think it was bottomless. An air of silence lingered between them, and he couldn't stand it anymore.

"So, how was it training the princess?" he asked.

"Unique," said Mushi. "She's caught on to the basics quite fast. Given enough time, she might prove to be a capable warrior."

"She cause you any trouble? I've found she has quite a knack for it."

"That's something you two might have in common, which is why you can't stand her. Instead of having someone get you out of trouble like I used to, she only makes you dive deeper."

Taking out his flask, Anden guzzled down a gulp of liquor. "Maybe, but that trouble brought us all back together." He offered some to Mushi, but he waved it off. "Why are we going to the sacred archives, anyway? We're not pundits of the Ambulate and have no way of deciphering the ancient text."

"All official interpretations, even very rough ones, are kept alongside the original texts," explained Mushi. "Back in Laminfell, I briefly mentioned I was attending to some business here before heading to Danforth. That business concerned something I found during my travels these past few years. Something I didn't quite understand and proved to be quite dangerous. Desperate for answers, I came here hoping to find some semblance of knowledge regarding its origin and purpose. Of course, the Ambulate's interpretations are sparse and incomplete, but I have a feeling it could be connected to these murders in some way."

At long last, they reached the bottom of the endless staircase. Before them was a large metal door with two keyholes on either side. Over one was the image of a flaming sword and the other a book with a star glistening over its open pages.

"Typically, two keys are needed to enter the archives," said Mushi. "One from the active loren and the other from his trusted head pundit. However, there is a workaround."

Stepping forward, Mushi stood in the middle of the two keyholes where the latches held firm. He dug his fingers into the small crevice between the two doors and, with massive strain to his muscles, attempted to pull them apart. The door ached and groaned as Mushi forced it open, turning the small crevice into an opening. A bit of steam leaked out from his mouth as he gritted his teeth, broke through the latches, and tore open the metal doors in one last push. His breaths were heavy as Anden approached, giving him a pat on the shoulder.

"You always do find a way to make it work," he said. Walking through the opening, Anden expected to see a lengthy hall of shelves housing volumes of books, papers, and whatever else the Ambulate deemed appropriate to place inside the sacred archives. Instead, he was greeted by ash and destruction. The endless stretch of shelves was burned black and collapsed into piles of dead embers. The pages they held dissolved into ash and were swept away by the current of air brought on by Mushi opening the door. Everything was gone. The original texts. Their interpretations. It was all burned away.

"Anden," Mushi's shout echoed loudly in the void of the room, "we need to get back to the sanctum! Gwen's in trouble."

*

Gwen paced the aisles of pews, running a delicate hand over their crafted wooden frames. She imagined the seats filled with followers listening to the loren's teachings. Standing alone in the massive room, it did hold a divine ambiance. The First Emperor reached out his hand as if offering to whisk her away, to protect and guide her. Stepping onto the raised platform, she observed the throne constructed in the likeness of a flame before noticing a plaque at the base of the towering statue. Carved into the metal were symbols she recognized as the ancient language of the time before the Great Calamity. The formation of the symbols seemed oddly familiar to her, and without thinking, she uttered the phrase, "May the winds bring good tidings." Her words rang hollow in the void of the empty room, but she pictured her father saying them to her and Victoria as he did when leaving the palace.

"You're familiar with the ancient text," a voice responded. Startled, Gwen spun around to see an elderly man with a long, gray beard, shrouded in the veil of a hood. He hobbled up the platform using his staff. "Out of all the surviving records in the ancient text, that phrase is believed to be the most accurate interpretation as it ubiquitously shows up in nearly every document we've collected."

"Who are you?" Gwen asked, keeping a distance.

"I'm nothing but an old pundit," said the stranger. "A shepherd tasked with guiding the sheep to the eternal plain of paradise." He gazed up at the statue of the First Emperor. "The Lucius Ambulate preached that it was he who forged the continent, giving us the freedom of life. Unfortunately, that interpretation is misguided. It wasn't freedom we were given in this world, but a prison." Swift for his age, the old man wrapped a bony hand around Gwen's wrist. "Although, it is through his blood, the very blood coursing through your veins, that we may be truly set free."

Gwen tried to yank her arm free from the man's firm grip. "Let me go!" she demanded. With her free hand, she grabbed the short sword at her hip and drew it, slashing at the old man. A flash of bright light blinded her mid-swing as her blade struck the air. The man disappeared. Gwen glanced about the room, seeing him at the opposite end of the raised platform.

"I was told you weren't trained in combat," he said. "It seems I was misinformed."

"You got that right." Twirling the blade, she charged at him and reared her sword for a strike, but he disappeared again in another flash of light.

"It doesn't matter." He stood in the aisle of pews at the center of the room. "You're still not skilled enough to fight me."

The crack of a gunshot echoed in the sanctum as splinters of wood splattered across the empty aisle. The man reappeared at the far side of the room, where Damian emerged from the shadows, blade already drawn. He swung at the hooded man, who vanished in another flash of light, and cut one of the pews in half. The old man stood at the center of the room again. Mushi and Anden sprinted in, standing in front of the raised platform where Gwen resided. Wesley and Damian flanked the stranger from the right and left. He was surrounded.

Mushi removed his hat and poncho. "She may not be skilled enough, but we are."

"Give up, Arios," said Damian. "You won't win this fight."

The hooded man's beard shook as he unleashed a chilling cackle. "If you think I came unprepared to fight all of you, you're mistaken."

A humming resonated in the air, reverberating off the chamber walls. From a nearby corridor, three strange contraptions glided into the sanctum. While mechanical, their form almost seemed fluid, constantly shifting and changing shape. At the core of their mechanical shell was a light shining like the sun. With a wave of his staff, the three constructs raced to Mushi, buzzing over him in a circle. The metal shells opened to fully reveal the light within, followed by bolts of lightning whose strikes drove him to his knees. Groaning in agony, Mushi convulsed on the ground.

"Mushi!" gasped Gwen as she hopped off the raised platform to his side. She tried to touch him, but the electrical surge stung her fingers.

"I know better than to challenge the Hand of Death," said the hooded man, "which is why my little birdies will keep you preoccupied. Took a couple of tries to get them just right, but you can't rush perfection."

Anden and Damian lunged at him with vicious swings intended to kill. With a tap of his staff, Arios flashed away in a blink of light, leaving the two men and causing them to nearly strike each other. A glowing chain lashed out, striking Anden in the cheek and flinging him to the ground. Damian turned, bewildered, to see the chain retract into Arios' hand adorned with strange rings.

"I told you these were useful little tools," he said, continuing to cackle. Damian charged at him as they continued to chase the old man teleporting around the sanctum.

Wesley approached the base of the platform, where Gwen watched Mushi suffer. He glared up at the constructs hovering overhead. Raising a pistol, he unloaded a clip into a construct and hit the glowing light in the center. As the light faded, so did the lightning it emitted, and the mechanical shell fell to the ground with a clatter. Wesley raised his other pistol to shoot down another construct, but Arios appeared behind him.

"You're an unexpected nuisance." With a flick of his wrist, the chain shot out of his hand and wrapped around Wesley, binding his arms. Striking his staff into the ground, the two disappeared.

"Wesley!" Gwen cried. She pounded a fist into the floor.

"Gwen," said Damian, "form up with Anden and me."

She hurried over to them in the center of the aisle and drew her sword. The three of them pressed their backs against each other, covering all angles of the room. Gwen tried to control her breathing, imagining the flame in her mind. If she was seriously about to fight, she needed to rely on the power of nin-nir within.

"How the hell is he doing all this?" said Anden. "We can't even touch him."

"His ability seems to be connected to his staff in some way," said Damian. "If we separate him from it, he'll be easier to kill."

"It's when he taps it on the ground," Gwen said. "Keep him from doing that, and he won't be able to teleport." She glanced over at Mushi, still convulsing in pain as the two constructs continued to pump electricity through his body.

"Eyes up, Gwen," said Anden. "We can't help him until we take this guy down."

Gwen focused, scanning the area in front of her and waiting for the pundit to return. "Right."

The room fell into a deadly silence. All three of them stood at the ready for when the old man returned. Gwen could feel the power surging through her body. When he showed his face again, she would be ready to strike. Light flashed before them, and Arios stood at the front of the aisle between them and Mushi.

"Now that he's out of the way, it's time I took the daughter of the royal bloodline." He launched the glowing chain at her, but Gwen deflected it with her sword.

Summoning all the strength into her legs, she exploded toward him and swung at his waist. While moving at blinding speeds, she still wasn't fast enough. He appeared behind her, reaching out a hand to wrap his bony fingers around her arm, but Anden swung his three-section staff, forcing him to teleport away.

"That was a bit too hasty," he said in a harsh tone. "You need to be careful. If he grabs you and flashes away, it's over."

Damian chased after Arios as he flashed wildly around the room. The glowing chain shot toward Gwen again, but Anden batted it away.

"You can't even let the chain touch you," he added.

"I got it," said Gwen. She took a step to help Damian in the fight, but her leg went limp. After throwing everything she had into that last attack, her body gave out. To the clatter of her short sword, Gwen collapsed to the ground in exhaustion.

"You okay?" Anden reached to pick her up but was struck across the face with Arios' staff. Another strike to his chest sent Anden crashing to the ground.

The old man grabbed hold of Gwen's hair as he picked her face off the floor. Damian moved to save her, but with a raise of his staff, Arios brought him to a halt. "I should offer my thanks, Burnt Coat. Not only did you provide me the opportunity to get revenge on Visconti and frame him for the murders, but you also brought me the key to paradise."

He slammed his staff down, but the chain of Anden's weapon wrapped around his arm. Holding it taut, Anden kept the end of the pundit's staff from touching the ground. With the old man caught off guard, Gwen summoned what little strength she had, grabbed her sword, and slashed his hand. Her face struck the tile floor as he released her, cursing in pain. In that moment, Damian lunged at him, arcing his blade through the air with all his might. Still restrained, the banished pundit had no way of escaping. They had him. As the edge of Damian's sword hurtled toward Arios' neck, one of the constructs flew in, unleashing a bolt of electricity that sparked the steel of his blade and shocked Damian.

Arios sent his chain flying and wrapped it around Anden's neck, strangling him. With his restraint loosened, the old man thumped his staff into the ground and teleported onto the raised platform, slamming Anden into the throne.

"Nifty little creations, aren't they?" he said, standing over them. "Troublesome to make given the pathetic sources of fuel offered by this empty shell of a world. That's why I needed his power for their completion." He lifted a hand, gesturing toward the statue of the First Emperor. "It took quite a bit of trial and error to get the ritual just right for extracting his gift of nin-nir from my chosen subjects. In the end, however, I found success. Now, I'm the closest one on the continent to imitating the power of the First Emperor." With his arms outstretched, he entered a fit of hysterical laughter, basking in his superiority.

The laughter was cut short as a spray of blood streaked through the air. Arios' arm, adorned in the strange jewelry of rings and chains, fell to the ground, severed from the rest of his body. Standing before him, sword drawn, was Mushi. Steam poured out from his skin, wrapping around him like the cloak of a wraith. The dark brown color of his eyes was replaced by the glow of a dull green, brimming with an infinite void of rage from deep within his soul. He looked like a demon, a wild creature unleashed with the singular intent to kill. Gwen understood that when people spoke of the Hand of Death, this was what they meant. Mushi swung his sword again, but Arios flashed away just in time. With a single stroke of his blade, the base of the massive statue was severed, toppling over. The effigy of the First Emperor crashed into the walls of the basilica, shaking the building, as a shower of rubble and debris rained down on them. Anden jumped on top of Gwen, shielding her from the falling stones. When everything settled, the sanctum was in ruin. Mushi stood atop the platform surrounded by the statue's remains, steam coiling around his body. The glow of his eyes surveyed the room for his target, but the two constructs appeared from clouds of dust and slammed him into a wall, surging more electricity through his body. Restrained, the glow faded from his eyes, and the steam stopped seeping from his skin.

Arios hobbled toward Mushi, blood spilling out from the stump of his missing limb. "They warned me about you. Said you were a demon not to be taken lightly. I can now see why."

The click of a hammer silenced the old man. Wesley stood behind him, pistol raised. "Flinch, and it's a bullet through your skull." He crossed the room and pressed the barrel into the old man's head.

The pundit cackled. "Death does not scare me. It only brings us a step closer to the light. You all have no clue of the shackles binding you to a fate of eternal suffering." His eyes shifted to Gwen. "Her blood is the only thing that can set us free."

"Enough with the parables and riddles," said Wesley, pressing the barrel harder into the back of his head. "Tell us exactly who your group is and why they want the princess. What's your goal?"

"It doesn't matter what I tell you," he said. "On deaf ears, it will fall as it has over the years. Causing us to fear what lies beyond. You should fear it, what lies beyond this world. Find comfort, as I have, in knowing that we all will eventually be reunited in the light of paradise."

Wesley pulled the trigger, splattering the insides of his skull across the stone. As his body collapsed, so did the remaining constructs. Mushi freed himself from the wall while Wesley picked up the man's staff and snapped it in half. Aiming his pistol, he fired at one of the constructs, mutilating it until it was nothing but a pile of scraps. He aimed at the last construct, but Anden grabbed his wrist.

"What are you doing?" he asked.

"These things are a product of dark rituals and murder," said Wesley. "They should be destroyed." He ripped his hand free from Anden's to point the gun at the construct again, but Anden stepped in front of him.

"I don't support it either, but it's a bit hasty to destroy them."

"Whatever you decide to do, do it quickly," said Damian, sheathing his blade. "We can't stay here for much longer. People and soldiers will no doubt arrive shortly to investigate the commotion."

Mushi tossed Anden the last construct. "I agree with Anden. We should take these back to Laminfell and have Leon study them. He might be able to offer more insight into how they work. It'll also allow us to gather our thoughts and figure out what to do next."

Wesley begrudgingly holstered his pistol as Anden pried the

strange mass of jewelry from the pundit's severed arm.

With her strength returning, Gwen managed to stand on her feet just as Mushi approached, placing his hat on his head. "You alright?"

"Yeah," she said, relieved it was all over.

"Mushi trained you well," commented Damian. "Albeit a bit reckless."

"Where did he teleport you to?" Gwen asked Wesley.

"Some underground catacombs," he said. "Thanks to all the ruckus, I managed to find my way back here just in the nick of time."

"If one of these cloaked freaks is like this, we're going to have our work cut out for us," said Anden.

"Which is why we shouldn't waste any more time," said Mushi.

They left the basilica through a side door Damian showed them. The noise of their battle garnered the attention of various nearby citizens, who were now hurrying to see what had happened. As they made their way back to the lower level of the city to mount their horses, numerous questions rattled around Gwen's head—the most prominent one revolving around what the pundit said about her blood being the key to paradise.

38

"Lady Victoria, where are your sheets?" the servant asked, staring absently at the barren mattress.

"Someone already collected them," Victoria replied.

"Do you know who it might have been? I'd like to have a word."

Victoria bit her thumb, pondering deeply. "Not really. I wasn't paying much attention when they came in."

The servant sighed in annoyance. "I'll bring you fresh sheets. If there are any left, that is." She marched off in quiet frustration.

Victoria continued meditating as the servant returned moments later and spread fresh sheets over the bed. Once she left, Victoria closed the window curtains, dimmed the light in her chambers, locked the door, and climbed under the covers. Although the sun was still shining, she needed rest while she could get it. Closing her eyes, she lay still, waiting for sleep to take her. All the while, she mentally ran through her plan multiple times, never allowing the thought of it going wrong to cross her mind. It had to work. Her sister's life could be on the line. Minutes dragged on for hours, and counting the steps of her plan seemed like counting sheep, finally allowing her to drift off to sleep.

She awoke to the sound of knocking and a servant calling out, "Lady Victoria! Dinner is ready to be served if you wish to eat."

Victoria scrambled out of bed and unlocked the door. "Dinner sounds lovely." The servant presented her with a silver bowl on a plate steaming with a soup pasta loaded with chicken, onions, and potatoes and garnished with fine herbs. Scooping it out with a spoon, she slurped the noodles in a manner considered improper anywhere else outside her own chambers. She couldn't help herself. The chicken was seasoned and tendered to perfection, the potatoes so soft they practically dissolved in her mouth, and the flavors in the broth had her draining the entire bowl dry. With not a morsel left, she leaned back in her chair and patted her stomach as it all settled. A fine meal, one she would miss in the days to come.

When the sun set, followed by the approaching darkness of the night, Victoria stripped her bed of its sheets and tossed them to the floor. Sliding the massive armoire aside from the wall, she unveiled a small hole where a pile of the missing, dirty sheets resided, along with a sheathed cutlass she had procured by sneaking into one of the armories. Grabbing the mess of bedsheets, she began the tedious task of tying one sheet to the other into one massive makeshift rope, adding small knots every so often in between. By the time she was done and her rope coiled around the room like a snake, a crescent moon glowed in the dark sky above, entering the late hours of the night. Tying one end of the rope to the side rail of her heavy wooden bedframe, she hurled the rest outside her chamber window. The cold air bit into her skin as she watched the stream of cloth unravel toward the balcony below. It came up short of reaching the balcony floor, about ten feet by Victoria's estimation. A hefty drop, but more feasible than the original fifty-foot gap. On her dresser, she scooped some of the jewelry gifted to her from past social festivals and birthdays into a small sack. Shoving it into her trouser pocket, she strapped the cutlass around her waist and clutched the sheet in her grasp. Giving a firm tug, the bedframe did not budge. The anchor seemed secure.

A deep inhale. "First step is always the hardest."

She crawled out the window and descended the rope of bedsheets. Climbing down at a steady pace, Victoria used the knots to maintain a firm hold and footing. An unintended drop from such a height could cause severe injury, if not death. She shook the thought from her mind, keeping her focus on the climb itself. The breeze caused her to sway, unsettling her nerves as her heart beat faster and her breathing became sharper. She didn't want to look down. It would make things worse. She continued downward until her legs found no cloth to cling to. Now came the time for her to look and see how far a drop she needed to make onto the balcony. Casting her gaze below, she dangled higher than her estimated ten feet. Closer to fifteen. Her eyes shot back up to the open window above. It wasn't too late to climb back up. No, she couldn't. She had to push forward for Gwen's sake. Looking down, she focused on a single spot before releasing her grip and dropping onto the balcony. Her boots landed hard on the floor and buckled her legs. Luckily, she recovered by entering a roll and catching herself in a three-point stance.

"Step one complete," she said to herself with a hint of pride.

Opening the balcony door, she entered a sizable study with busts of famous Parliament members and other fancy knick-knacks littering the room. Thankfully, no guards or servants were around. From there, she snuck through the torch-lit halls to the daunting staircase to continue her descent to the main floor. For the past few days, she walked the same path over and over, fixing it in her mind. Weaving her way through the corridors and down the stairs, she reached the lower levels of the palace. A few Militia guards were on duty patrolling the halls, but Victoria waited for them to pass before proceeding beyond the large doors of the Great Hall. Butterflies fluttered in the princess' stomach. A little more than a hundred feet, and she wouldn't have to worry about being caught. That was until a soft jingle of metal and the prodding of paws on tile caught her ear. Turning around, Victoria saw two reflective disks glow in the darkness.

As they drew closer, so did the sound of panting.

"Artemis," she said, "what are you doing?"

The hound bounded up to her, tongue hanging from its mouth and dripping with saliva.

"Shouldn't you be with Helmond?"

Artemis rubbed up against Victoria's legs, bumping her hand with his head. Succumbing to his demands, she bent down and patted his head while scratching his side. He gave her cheek an affectionate lick.

"I love you too, buddy," she said, "but I need to go find my sister. I promise to come back, though, okay?" With one final pat, she separated herself from the hound and continued down the hall, but barely two steps in, Artemis unleashed a small bark.

Victoria snapped around. "Shhh! You're going to get me caught."

He barked again. This time, even louder.

The faint mumbling of curious Militia soldiers and hurried footsteps echoed from afar. Victoria bolted down the hall, Artemis hot on her trail. Turning sharply, she reached the metal door marking the entrance to the Tomb and tore it open. Jumping inside, she quickly shut the door before Artemis could join her as the dog scratched its paws against the metal surface. Victoria remained by the door listening as the Militia soldiers approached.

"It's the cook's dog," one of them said. "What's he doing

running around?"

"Who knows?" said another. "Probably just snuck out of his kennel. Come on, big boy. Time to go back to your master."

She heard Artemis whine as the soldiers dragged him away, and then everything went silent. All she could hear was the sound of her own breathing. The room was dark enough to nearly hide the hand in front of her face. Victoria almost fell by missing the first step of the spiral staircase. Using the wall as a guide, she made her way down to the chasm below. Everything was made of stone, from the walls to the stairs, and even the nine chairs circled around a glowing pit of fire. The shadows crept in from the edges of the room, hiding its true size. Keeping a hand on the wall, the princess paced the outskirts of the chamber, searching for the secret entrance Kaylin had mentioned when telling her of the assassin's attack. With every step, her foot only found the cold, hard surface of stone. Until she reached a far corner of the chamber where the subtle vibrations of a metal grate could be felt. Reaching down, her fingers slid between the small gaps. Wrapping them around the thick bars, Victoria gave a sharp jerk, but the grate didn't budge. She tried again, straining her muscles, but still nothing. Glancing about, she didn't notice any sign of a lock or chain. It simply weighed heavy with raw steel. Lifting it would require more strength than her physical body could produce on its own.

Taking a deep, calming breath, Victoria envisioned casting the bucket into the well. Not gathering too much nor too little. The familiar warmth emanated from her chest as she reached down to grab hold of the grate once more. Straining, she straightened her legs and flipped the grate open in one fluid motion. Jumping in, Victoria was swallowed by darkness again. Holding her arms out in front of her, she marched forward, occasionally bumping into the wall. She journeyed through the abyss for what felt like an eternity. Her feet grew numb, and her strength dwindled. Using the potential power within still took its toll on her body, but she persisted. In the distance, she caught a glimpse of the faintest light and soft sound of crashing waves against the cliffside. It eventually led her to an opening of a cave overlooking the eastern sea, with a portion of the capital visible to her left. She could hardly believe it. For most of her life, Victoria witnessed a similar view from various windows in the palace, but none could beat this. The grass beneath her feet, a harsh wind blowing hair into her face, and a rush of fear made it all the more real as she stared over the edge of the cliff at the rocky shore below. It was liberating.

"Gwen," she said, "I think I understand now why you had such a fascination with those books about the wonders of the continent." She glanced up at the treacherous path up the cliffside. "When I find you, maybe we can take the scenic route back and see some of them ourselves. Then you can become queen and make me a wreath of flowers from the garden like you used to."

Digging her fingers and the toes of her boots into the rock, she started to climb.

39

The breeze carried from the eastern sea swept over Blackwood's weary face. The weight of his body leaned on the stone railing separating the edge of the cliff from the rest of the observation deck. The distant sound of the crashing waves climbed up to his ears as the gulls cawed from overhead. A serene escape from the chaos within the palace. Early in the morning, before the sun rose, he awoke to the calls of Militia soldiers claiming Princess Victoria was missing. In her chambers, they found multiple sheets tied together, forming a single length of rope she used to climb down to the lower balcony. A planned escape, and one at the most troubling of times.

*

"It's my fault," said Mary Katherine, face wrinkled with anguish. "If I weren't so harsh, she wouldn't have felt the need to run off."

Blackwood wrapped an arm around her, offering as much comfort as he could. "You can't blame yourself for her actions."

"She thought we'd given up on Gwen," the ambassador continued to sob. "So much so that she thought it necessary to take the matter into her own hands. We failed her, Strom. Both of them."

"We'll find her. Captain Hardee has already been ordered to search nearby cities, and every available soldier is searching within the palace walls. We won't let her get too far. We won't make the same mistakes as we did with Gwen."

Mary Katherine collapsed in a fit of tears onto the lavish furniture decorating his study. Tearing his cape from his shoulders, he placed it over her like a blanket.

"We need to stay strong, Mary," he said. Easier to say than do. He himself felt like vomiting at that very moment. If this was how Mary Katherine reacted, he hardly wished to imagine Peter's condition. The last thing he needed was the king forfeiting his desire to live.

The door barged open, spinning the ambassador around with a violent twirl and shooting Blackwood to his feet. Captain Gunnway marched in with a hard-edged expression. "I'm going after her. Being on her own, she couldn't have gotten far in half a night."

"You can't go," said Blackwood.

A glare as sharp as steel penetrated him. "I wasn't asking for permission."

"You're needed here to protect the king."

The Militia captain banged a fist into Blackwood's desk, shaking it. "I will not sit idle like before. Victoria is right to be angry. Months went by, and we couldn't find a hint of Gwen's location, and when we did find her, she slipped through our grasp. I will not allow the same to happen with her."

Mary Katherine pulled at his sleeve. "She's right, Strom. Let her go."

"No!" shouted Blackwood. His face turned red with rage as the muscles in his neck tensed with each word. "Right now, upon Peter's death, emergency powers are granted to me. That puts the balance of power in a very volatile state, creating a void that any aspiring tyrant could seize. Finding Victoria is paramount, but that responsibility is being left to Captain Hardee and his team of trackers." Kaylin diverted her eyes to the ground in shame as Blackwood darted his toward her. "Your strength is needed here, keeping the king alive. I want you and our best doctor watching over him at all times."

Kaylin's hand balled into a fist as a tear streaked down her cheek. "As you command, Chancellor."

"Good," he said. "Make sure your troops comb through every street and alley of this city in case she's still here."

With a stiff nod, the Militia captain marched out of his study. Blackwood paced the length of the room, pinching the bridge of his nose.

"You should've let her go," said Mary Katherine.

"Why?" he said, rage still seething from his voice. "So things can fall into more chaos? We still have an order to maintain, Mary. With Gunnway gone, that leaves the first division without its captain, and the seventh division's is already absent on an assignment to find a princess. Not to mention the conclave is still taking place, so all the realm's ambassadors are present here as well. Kaylin needs to stay in the capital."

"And what if Victoria isn't found because you wouldn't let her go?"

"Stop saying that," Blackwood snapped. "You think that's what I want? You think I desire all the power offered on Peter's deathbed right now? I don't. I need him to stay alive." The strength of his voice caused the room to go silent. Mary Katherine stared at him, eyes wide with fear. A fear he never thought feasible to invoke in her. He ran a hand over his face while taking a deep breath. "I need to get some air. Clear my head."

*

Blackwood buried his face in his arms. With both heirs missing, rule over Argust potentially rested on his shoulders. He would become the most powerful person in the kingdom, but with that power came immense scrutiny. Nearly every noble and ambassador would search for an excuse to label him a tyrant, if only to usurp him and claim it for themselves. He didn't want that to happen. He couldn't let that happen, which was why Peter's safety needed to be ensured. At least until they found Victoria.

"Come to clear your head?" said a voice. At first, Blackwood thought it to be a whisper from the wind, but glancing over his shoulder, he saw Rahm bounding across the courtyard.

"More like hoping to find answers," said Blackwood.

Rahm stood next to him, pressing a meaty hand onto the railing. He greeted the scenic view with an apathetic stare. "You won't find them written in the clouds."

"What do you want?"

"Just checking up on you. We may not see eye to eye on most things, but one thing we do agree on is the well-being of the kingdom. Victoria's absence puts that at risk."

"People panic now," said Blackwood, "but Hardee will find her in the next few days."

"And what if he doesn't?" countered Rahm. "We thought we'd find Guinevere in a few days, yet it's been months. The emotional toll of losing one daughter turned the king from a strong warrior into a frail old man. Losing another will certainly put him in a casket, and the lack of a royal heir means the kingdom could be on the brink of collapse if not handled delicately."

Blackwood rolled his eyes. "What are you implying?"

Rahm leaned over the rail to penetrate Blackwood's line of sight. "You've served a long and respectable tenure as chancellor, but anyone can see the responsibility weighs heavy on your soul. It's battered and beaten you raw, made you a shadow of the man you once were. Bearing the entire kingdom upon your shoulders would break you, and if that happens, the kingdom will implode upon itself. I know you tire of your position, so step down and free yourself of this burden."

Nothing would please Blackwood more than to walk away from it all. To hang up his suit one last time before moving out to the country and living the remainder of his life with Mary Katherine, putting his past mistakes behind him for good. No worries about overwhelming power or the scrutiny of being called a tyrant for wielding it foolishly. Then he remembered the look in Peter's eyes. The wave of pain emanating from his gaze as he, too, grew weary from the responsibility as king, yet he forged ahead. Even after losing one of his daughters, he still fought for what he believed to be right. Blackwood's knuckles turned white as he squeezed his fingers around the railing. His jaw clenched tight, grinding his teeth.

"I may not look it, but I've got strength to spare," he said. "If I must, I'll bear that weight."

Rahm sighed. "Stubborn as always."

Something hard pressed into Blackwood's back. Ben Green

stood behind him with his mace raised. Blackwood narrowed his eyes at the ambassador. "I thought such tactics were beneath you."

Rahm pushed off the railing, pacing around the courtyard. "It won't be me that killed you. I believe, after succumbing to such despair with losing both daughters of your dearest friend who lies on his deathbed, you flung yourself over the cliffside. A tragic end to such an esteemed figure."

"The possibility of me being granted emergency power frightens you this much?"

Rahm snapped around with a furious glare. "I want to protect the kingdom. You and that fool of a king have done nothing but help lead to its destruction. Because of you, we fell prey to a false treaty that allowed the rebels to smite Danforth atop its mesa, reports are coming in that Illios has fallen into chaos due to Visconti being burned alive for committing heinous murders, and more rumors surface of the Gray Phoenix returning, and both heirs to the crown disappear, leaving our government volatile. If you had not fought against my vote to install Victoria as ruler from the beginning, this whole mess could have been avoided. Now, it's descended into madness. A madness I intend to rectify utilizing a clean slate just as Edward did." He took a deep breath, adjusting his spectacles. "I don't take pleasure in doing this. You were a worthy opponent, and I always enjoyed playing our little games, but it's time for those games to end."

Captain Green stepped forward, forcing Blackwood into the

railing. The distant white foam of the crashing waves was all he could focus on. Their sound filled his ears, and the salty smell of the sea filled his nostrils as he realized these would be his final moments. Rahm turned his back on them as the Militia captain gave a forceful shove. Blackwood's legs tripped over the railing as he careened toward the sea below. Time slowed as the wind rushed through his hair and wrapped the cloth of his suit tight around his body. Moments of his life flashed before his eyes, one lingering longer than the others. The moment he fell in love with Mary Katherine. The beauty of her radiant smile, dazzling gaze, and the shimmer in her light brown hair as she looked at him from across the Great Hall. An ageless beauty he was thankful to have graced his life. She saved him from his own darkness and made him a better man. If only he could have repaid the favor by giving her the life she had always wanted.

"I'm sorry, Mary."

The words were carried off by the fierceness of the wind. No one to hear them. Accepting his fate, Blackwood closed his eyes as a singular tear was ripped from his cheek. Then, a sudden rush of cold turned him numb as his body crashed into the water, followed by darkness.

40

The journey to Laminfell was one of solemn victory. No banter was exchanged during their days of hard riding, only a tense silence. When they arrived at Leon's cottage, the mechanical chariot was on full display. The skeletal frame of metal scraps now had a plated steel body that shone with a mirror-like reflection. New leather was sewn into the seats, giving them a more cushioned appearance. It looked more regal, something owned by a noble or by the royal family. After such somber travel, it was refreshing to see Anden's face brighten as he set his eyes on it.

"That's a sight worth returning to," he said, hopping off his horse. He raced up to the chariot and marveled at it from every angle. "The old girl looks finer than ever."

"The exterior isn't the only thing that got upgraded." Leon

exited the cottage, having heard them arrive. "I tuned up the engine as well. Should run a little faster with less groaning."

"You certainly worked your magic," said Wesley, "but you didn't need to go all out on her."

"Speak for yourself," said Anden.

Damian strode over to the engineer, placing a hand on his shoulder. "How much do we owe you?"

Leon scratched at his beard, the gears in his head churning. "Consider the upgrades a gift from me. I certainly had the time for them. Getting her back in fair working order, I'd say fifty gold and fifteen silver pieces will cover it."

Damian looked at Anden, who then turned to Wesley with raised eyebrows. Pulling out a coin purse, Wesley sifted through their current funds before responding.

"We can afford to pay the fifteen silvers but only ten of the gold at the current moment," he said.

Leon waved a dismissive hand. "That's enough for now. I know you're good for the rest. Just pay me next time you roll through town."

Mushi approached the engineer with a friendly smirk. "I don't mean to keep relying on your hospitality, but would you mind hosting us for a bit? We've had a long ride and need time to figure some things out."

"Of course. I'll make some tea to help y'all relax." He stepped to head inside, but was stopped by Anden.

"Before you go in, I have some things that may interest you." He took out the strange flying construct and jewelry from their fight in Illios and tossed them into Leon's rough hands.

The engineer studied the contraptions with a curious yet suspicious gaze. "You really dug something up at the Holy City, eh? I'll see what I can do."

The warmth from the fire inside Leon's cottage, coupled with the tea, melted Gwen into the chairs. After camping out in the ruins of Takata and traveling on the road, being able to rest under a closed roof felt like a luxury she'd long forgotten. The tea not only quenched her thirst but eased her stress from past events. The battle in Illios was hard fought, requiring all five of them to defeat one of the cloaked figures. It was troubling to think more roamed the continent. A stillness lingered between the others like the steam from their untouched cups of tea.

"So," said Wesley, "are we going to talk about what happened in Illios?"

"I can tell you what happened," said Anden, opting to drink from his flask. "We got our asses kicked by an old man with toys."

"It's my fault." Damian's head weighed heavy on his shoulders. "I should have been able to catch on to Arios' true intentions. I let him fool me."

"Don't blame yourself," said Mushi.

"Yeah," added Wesley. "We all got played."

The former Militia captain lifted his head toward Mushi. "We couldn't find the sketches of the sigil patterns left on the other victims. Arios must have disposed of them before we got there."

"He burned the entire sacred archives as well," said Mushi. "Whatever it is he was up to, he didn't want anyone finding out."

Anden threw his head back in frustration. "After all that, we're no closer to figuring out what they're after and why they need the princess."

"My blood," said Gwen. The four men turned their attention to her. "He said my blood, the blood of the First Emperor, was the key to opening paradise." Fear crept under Gwen's skin, giving her chills. "What do you think he meant by that?"

Wesley shook his head. "Who knows? The man was a raving lunatic and a murderer, constantly talking about paradise, the truth falling on deaf ears, and fearing what lies beyond. Nothing but a bunch of nonsense."

Mushi perked up as Wesley finished speaking. "What exactly did he say? About deaf ears and whatnot?"

Wesley rubbed a hand over his forehead and scrunched his nose in deep contemplation, trying to remember the exact words. "On deaf ears, it will fall. Something about years of darkness and fearing what lies beyond. Something like that."

"Those words sound familiar," said Gwen. Trying to

remember where she'd heard them before, the melodic hum of Mary Katherine's voice resonated within her mind. A tune she'd not heard for many years, but the memory of it remained like a print in the snow. While far removed from the creature that left it, it still served as evidence of its existence. "They're lyrics from a song. Mary Katherine would sing it to my sister and me when we were younger."

"Beyond the Frosty Peaks," said Mushi. "It's a lullaby stating, 'Beyond the Frosty Peaks so far, lies the truth of who we are. And how the icy winds recall the lost tale forgotten by all. On deaf ears, they do fall. Fall into darkness over the years, causing us to fear what lies beyond. Beyond the Frosty Peaks so far.' Could it be that's what he was referring to?"

"You're basing a clue on a fable from a song sung to children to help them sleep," said Anden with contention. "Seems like quite the stretch."

"All fables have a hint of truth to them," said Gwen, looking at Mushi with a knowing glance.

He nodded back. "Right now, it's about all we got. If the fable does have some truth to it, we might find some answers regarding the royal family's heritage to the First Emperor and its relevance to these cloaked figures' need for their blood."

"Even if you're right," said Anden, "and may I remind you, that's a long stretch, you expect us to travel to the edge of the world from where no one who's dared journey there has ever returned?"

"I agree with Anden," said Wesley. "It's completely ridiculous. Surely, we can find a more concrete lead."

Damian stayed quiet, observing the conversation with his cold, gray eyes as Mushi pursed his lips in thought. "In that case," he said, "maybe Papuri might hold some significance. It was the first place I encountered one of those cloaked figures."

Anden took a long pull from his flask.

Wesley sighed. "Papuri, huh? That's better than nothing, I guess."

"Good," said Mushi, shooting out of his seat. "You go to Papuri while I head south to the edge of the world."

Anden spat out his liquor as Gwen's face froze in shock. "You're seriously considering investigating the validity of a lullaby?"

"If you all don't want to go south, so be it. I, however, am not going to ignore a possible lead that could yield answers, no matter the odds."

Anden shot out of his chair, standing off with his friend. "Don't think we're going to let you go off on your own."

"He won't be going alone," said Damian. He stood as well, towering over everyone. "I'll accompany Mushi south. You and Wesley can investigate Papuri." He turned to Gwen. "As for Lady Gwen, she seems capable of defending herself against most dangers, so I'm sure Leon could escort her back to the capital. I think we're all aware that if these cloaked figures are hunting her, she's better off protected behind the walls."

Mushi looked at her with a measuring gaze, similar to the one at the conclusion of their night at the Carnival together. "I think that's up to her to decide. Whatever she thinks is the right thing for her to do."

Gwen averted her eyes, not wanting to be lost in his gaze like she was that night. A pain in her gut told her she should head back to the capital, but her heart yearned to remain by their side. These cloaked figures were a terror that could not be ignored. Having witnessed the power one could wield, and the atrocities he committed to do so, predicated an evil needing to be stopped. If they hunted her as a descendant of the First Emperor, then it meant her sister and father could also be targets. If she remained outside the walls, their gaze would be fixated on her rather than turn to the rest of her family. Mushi told her the Gray Phoenix served as protectors fighting in the kingdom's shadow. Her kingdom. Before inheriting the throne, she needed to protect it.

"I'm not going back to the capital," she said, determination strengthening her voice. "If these people are going after my family, I want to help you stop them."

"I must object," interrupted Damian. "As the eldest daughter, it's imperative that you return to the capital to inherit the throne. It's too dangerous for you to be outside its walls now."

"And if I do return, they'll probably find a way to take me

anyway," said Gwen, "or my sister or father. Like with Vargo. I'm aware of the danger just as much as you are, and I want to help you fight it. I may be the eldest, but I'm not my father's only daughter. If it comes to it, my sister can still inherit the throne."

Damian opened his mouth to contest her further, but Mushi cut him off. "If that is where your conviction lies, then so be it. You'll join Anden and Wesley in Papuri."

"But I want to go with you to the edge of the world." Gwen wasn't entirely sure why, but she blurted the words out.

Mushi shook his head. "The journey will be much different and far more treacherous than the trek to Takata. While you may be aware of the dangers you currently face, what lies beyond the Frostbitten Peaks is uncertain."

She clenched her hands into fists and bit her lower lip in reluctant acceptance.

"Fine," said Wesley, "but on one condition. We have three months to gather information. After that, whether successful or not, we reconvene at my estate in Sandur."

Anden flew around the room, gathering their cups of tea and pouring them out into the fire, causing it to hiss. Grabbing the bottle of whiskey he'd brought along from Danforth, he filled their cups and handed one out to each of them. "Let's make it official. With this toast, we each promise to return to the Sparrow estate in three months' time." Emptying his flask, he poured the rest of the auburn liquid into it.

"When we reunite, we'll all share another drink just like this. Sound good?"

Gwen rose to her feet, taking her cup. "Sounds good to me."

They all raised their drinks into the air.

"To the edge of the world," said Damian.

"And back," finished Anden.

Their cups clinked together as they each downed their share of the whiskey. While it burned going down her throat, liquor never tasted so sweet on Gwen's lips. The somber mood looming over them during their days of travel lifted as they celebrated their toast. One they hoped to share again in three months' time

ABOUT THE AUTHOR

MITCHELL MOUNTAIN works as a full-time video editor and enjoys storytelling of all kinds. Raised in Indiana, he studied at Belmont University and graduated with a degree in Motion Pictures.